I0692981

LOVE HAS NO LIMITS

Author: Claudia Sultan

ABN: 82385819307

Website: www.BerminghamBooks.com

Facebook: BerminghamBooks
Instagram: BerminghamBooks

ISBN: 978-0-9873156-4-9

LOVE HAS NO LIMITS

Claudia Sultan

To Mum, with love.

PROLOGUE

"...Perched anxiously on the edge of her seat, she looked as though she were teetering on the delicate boundary between disbelief and the harsh sting of her new reality. Her fingers gripped the armrests so tightly that her knuckles turned white, as if they were the only things anchoring her to the moment. Her whole body visibly trembled, a testament to the storm of fear and sadness raging within her. Her eyes, swollen from an endless cascade of tears, told a silent story of overwhelming distress and emotional chaos. Every breath felt tenuous, each one a struggle against the tidal wave of uncertainty crashing down around her. The room seemed to close in on her, amplifying her sense of isolation and the depth of her sorrow."

In 1990, Adriano Di Manos found himself enveloped in the vibrant atmosphere of Queens, New York City, as he emerged from the solemn confines of the church. The weekly ritual of attending Sunday mass was not merely a religious obligation but a cherished tradition that held deep personal significance. However, it was the transition from the solemnity of the church interior to the lively streets outside that truly stirred his soul. The cacophony of smells and sounds that greeted him as he stepped into the throng of fellow parishioners provided a sense of cleansing and absolution he found both comforting and revitalising.

Adriano and his wife Gabriela had left their native Sicily during the turbulent 1980s in search of better opportunities for education and employment in the United States. Just like the 230,000 compatriots who also sought a new life on American shores during that period of political oppression and economic turmoil, they sold all their possessions to fund their relocation. Once settled stateside, they worked menial jobs for meagre wages while learning English, until Adriano finally landed a coveted position as an assistant chef at a prestigious restaurant in Manhattan. But their commitment to the church remained, and they attended mass every Sunday, rain or shine.

As familiar faces hurried past him on their way to fulfil their daily routines, Adriano felt a sense of purification wash over him, relieving him of his worries and burdens. Observing his fellow worshippers dispersing into the cityscape with purposeful strides brought him an inexplicable sense of solace and connection.

As he rubbed his hands together in a futile attempt to ward off the biting cold, Adriano silently cursed himself for disregarding his wife's advice to wear gloves.

A gentle tap on his shoulder diverted his attention towards a figure whose countenance exuded familiarity despite the passage of time—Frank Giovanni. Clad in a dapper brown suit accented by suspenders and an elegant coat, Frank radiated sophistication and charm that set him apart from the congregation. To an outsider, it might have seemed as though Adriano and Frank were brothers, sharing not only a physical resemblance but also a profound camaraderie.

"Let me guess," said Frank with a wry smile, "Gabby suggested you wear gloves, but true to form, you refused. Your stubbornness knows no bounds."

Adriano chuckled softly before replying, "It is a matter of principle. A man must be free to make his own choices, even if they lead to frostbite. But enough talk—let's get out of this cold."

"Absolutely," concurred Frank. "I happen to have some Cuban cigars courtesy of a client that would pair excellently with a bottle of your finest. There is also unresolved business concerning young Abagail and my son that needs addressing."

With another hot breath into his freezing cupped hands, Adriano regarded Frank wearily. "Perhaps we can deliberate over this while engaging in a game of poker. I often find clarity through triumph in such contests."

Frank smirked playfully. "You haven't had much luck winning lately, my dear friend. Still, I am eager to engage in this endeavour with you—perhaps it will bring us closer to resolving our longstanding dilemma."

Entering Frank's home and settling at the card table with cigars dangling from their lips and glasses of whisky within reach, they remained fixed on their game as if immune to the exasperation from their wives. Ignoring the pleas for relief from the smoky environment and concerns for their loved one's health, they casually continued their game without so much as a glance in the direction of their beleaguered partners.

"Your go," Frank nonchalantly stated, signalling their detachment from the current situation unfolding around them. With a collective and synchronised motion, the wives shook their heads disapprovingly as they made their way back to the kitchen. Frank savoured the last drop of his whisky, relishing the warmth that spread through him as he set the glass down on the table. A triumphant smile slowly crept across his face, growing wider with each passing moment as if he had just won a fortune.

Adriano eyed Frank warily as determination flickered in his gaze while observing Frank's evolving expression. With a final exhale of cigar smoke, he couldn't help but raise a quizzical brow. "Why do you wear such a satisfied grin?" Adriano asked.

A mischievous twinkle danced in Frank's eyes as he leaned back in his chair. His smile widened as he revealed his cards on the table. "Full house, my friend."

Adriano shook his head slowly in a display of defeat.

"Don't take it personally," he said, adding salt to the wound.

After a long pause, Adriano looked up at Frank and smiled. He lowered his hand onto the table, revealing a rare and unbeatable royal flush that promptly wiped the grin off his dear friend's face. A stunned silence filled the room as Frank stared incredulously at the winning hand.

A mischievous glint danced in Adriano's eyes as he leaned back in his chair, a triumphant chuckle escaping his lips while he basked in the glory of his victory. "It appears that fortune favours me this time, my friend," he said smugly.

Despite his loss, Frank smiled and graciously accepted the outcome with a slow, measured shake of his head, unable to suppress a chuckle.

With a shared sense of jubilation and mutual respect for each other's skills at play, the old friends knocked their glasses in unison, creating a clinking sound that reverberated throughout the room like a joyous celebration of friendship and familial bonds that cast aside any competitive rivalry.

"Your Abagail shall wed my Joseph," Frank said, looking over at his son sitting next to Abby.

Adriano's gaze shifted from the cards laid out before him to his daughter. Abby and Joey were completely absorbed in a cartoon on the old television set, oblivious to the high-stakes game between their fathers, lost in their own innocent world.

With her emerald eyes flecked with hints of honey and tumbling waves of luscious brown locks cascading gracefully down to rest upon her shoulders, Abby was truly a sight to behold. Her cheeks, tinged rose-pink, added an extra layer of allurement whenever she entered a room, effortlessly melting hearts with nothing more than her warm, captivating smile.

Glancing back at Frank with a sense of unwavering confidence, Adriano flashed a smile that seemed to exude assurance. "My daughter is not obligated to marry anyone," he declared. "She will find her own partner."

"We'll see."

Adriano nodded. Deep down, he, too, believed they were meant to be together. But neither of them could have imagined just how tangled and chaotic their futures would become.

CHAPTER 1

By sixteen, Abby had blossomed into a confident and stunning young woman, brimming with spirit and strong convictions that set her apart from her peers. Her unwavering courage and determination garnered admiration from many, as she fearlessly challenged authority and paid little heed to others' opinions.

From a tender age, Abby's mother Gabriela recognised her daughter's musical talents and encouraged her to sing and learn to play the piano, believing God had bestowed upon her a magical singing voice. Gabriela was a firm believer in allowing her children to follow their dreams and passions. She had not been afforded the same opportunities.

For years, she was a victim of her father's cruel and relentless physical and emotional abuse. With antiquated views on gender roles and societal norms, he held steadfast to archaic beliefs regarding women's inferiority in strength and virtue and opposed Gabriela's aspirations beyond domestic servitude.

But Gabriela was determined to break free from the shackles he placed on her. She had always yearned for independence from her domineering and authoritarian father, who showed little regard for his children's well-being while seeking affection outside his marriage, a huge taboo in the Catholic community. Which was why Gabriela's own mother had turned a blind eye to his indiscretions. In their society, remaining unmarried or becoming a divorcee carried a heavy stigma, prompting her mother to maintain appearances by staying with him rather than risk the label of an old maid. At that time, societal expectations placed immense pressure on women to excel in domestic duties such as housekeeping, cooking, and child-rearing while also prioritising their husband's needs above all else. This allowed him to continue his multiple affairs unchallenged for the sake of upholding appearances.

While times had barely changed regarding the values placed on fidelity and marriage, Abby enjoyed a lot more freedoms than her mother ever did, and her love for music soon became an obsession, leading Father Francesco to suggest she join the church choir at the age of six. However, her parents deemed her too young for such endeavours at the time.

While Abby's vocal abilities had not rivalled those of renowned singers like Mariah Carey, she found joy in performing despite her discomfort with being in the spotlight. Even with this aversion to attention, she embraced every experience with excitement and occasionally found herself caught up in melodrama or engaging in confrontations. With an unquenchable thirst for adventure and knowledge, Abby possessed a kind heart that was both gentle and enduring. Her brave nature allowed her to shine on stage, captivating audiences with her beautiful voice that showcased an impressive vocal range cultivated through hours of practice before school, during music classes, and even in the shower. Recording herself singing for later review, Abby fearlessly experimented with different techniques while honing her craft.

In addition to pursuing music solo, Abby joined forces with her best friends Nick Cavino and Vani Patel to form a rock band named "The Shining Star" in her father's garage. Although facing strict curfews imposed by her father, they obtained permission to practise there and eventually earned a key role in their school festival thanks to their collective talent. While Nick conquered his stage fright by learning drums and Vani managed guitar duties despite lacking vocal prowess, Abby took on the lead singer role with ease, and they delivered stellar performances infused with fun onstage chemistry. Also academically gifted, Abby excelled in high school thanks to an early love for learning instilled by her father who engaged her in discussions about books from second grade onwards. Emphasising friendly competition and underscoring the value of education and sharing knowledge shaped Abby into a well-rounded individual capable of conquering any challenge that came her way.

Micky, Abby's brother, was a twenty-year-old prodigy who possessed an innate talent that set him apart from his peers. From a tender age, he exhibited an extraordinary affinity for numbers and shapes, showcasing exceptional mathematical abilities that left many in awe. His mind was like a well-oiled machine, effortlessly solving even the most intricate math problems with remarkable mental calculations.

What truly distinguished Micky was his utilisation of various scientific methods to tackle these challenges head-on. Through the application of complex algorithms that befuddled those around him, he navigated through the sea of numbers with precision and finesse. His approach to mathematical conundrums was not merely mechanical but rather marked by innovation and critical thinking, rendering him a formidable force in the world of numbers.

It was at St Francis Lewis High School where Micky's passion for mathematics flourished under the guidance of an inspiring teacher. This mentor sparked a newfound perspective within him, driving him to explore more advanced and complex mathematical equations with zeal. His rapid progress in high school culminated in stellar SAT scores that opened doors to a scholarship for undergraduate and PhD studies at Brown University's esteemed School of Mathematics and Statistics. Although Abby was close to Micky, she often felt overshadowed by his exceptional talent for math in their family. While he tackled equations and algorithms as a genius mathematician, she followed her own path as a talented singer. Nevertheless, Adriano and Gabriella, their loving parents, prioritised both children's well-being above all else.

Though Abby looked up to Micky as a mentor figure whose approval she sought earnestly, she never failed to appreciate his unique qualities and admire his myriad accomplishments in the mathematics field. They shared an incredibly deep bond that brought comfort and support, enabling them to navigate many experiences together. Even as their lives took different paths, they remained a source of strength and encouragement for each other.

And soon, she would rely on him more than ever, as her life was about to be turned upside down forever.

CHAPTER 2

Abby's inaugural trip to Sicily, set against the joyous backdrop of her cousin's wedding, awakened an irresistible urge to delve deeply into her Italian roots. This was more than a journey; it was a pilgrimage into a rich tapestry of family history, values, and heritage. Ever since childhood, Abby had been captivated by the allure of Italy—its ancient ruins nestled among sunlit beaches, its lush vineyards, and the vibrant architecture that tells stories of artistry and life. The warmth of the locals and the tantalizing flavours of Italian cuisine, underscored by the musicality of the Italian language, never ceased to fascinate her.

Raised by her proud Italian parents, Abby spoke fluent Italian, a skill honed with loving discipline. This linguistic gift opened doors to meaningful connections with relatives she'd only heard about in stories. Back home, Sundays were sacred; they revered their heritage with lasagna feasts following mass, a delectable tradition that celebrated their Italian roots.

Gathering around the long, ornate dining table, Abby's extended family indulged in a sumptuous spread, complemented by robust wines and fragrant coffee. Each bite transported Abby back to the cherished flavours of her grandmother's secret sauce, simmering gently during festive seasons like Easter and Christmas. September was a time of bustling activity, as the family convened to peel, boil, and preserve tomatoes to the tune of nostalgic Neapolitan melodies.

The magic of hand-crafted pasta, drizzled in premium olive oil, was a staple in every meal. It represented not only culinary excellence but also the harmonious collaboration of the women in her family. These dishes were the tangible representation of love, to be savoured and passed down to future generations.

As Abby savoured every memory, she cherished the moments when her parents recounted tales of their adventures in Italy. These were not just stories; they were vibrant narratives brimming with humour and emotion, filling their home with laughter and sentiments that enveloped Abby like a warm embrace.

Growing up amidst a sea of cousins, Abby often found herself overwhelmed by the intricate family connections. However, her journey to Sicily unveiled the existence of over thirty new cousins. News of their arrival spread like wildfire through Gangi, with Grandma Di Manos sharing the exciting update with her sister, who passed it on, weaving the news into the close-knit fabric of the community.

The family trip to Sicily was also beautiful blend of sunlit memories and cherished companionship, made even more special by the presence of the beloved Giovanni family. Frank and Angela Giovanni had moved to America with dreams of a brighter future, and their unwavering dedication led to the success of their bustling deli. Adriano had first met Frank in 1990, thanks to a mutual friend, the ever-jovial Vincent Salbo. From that moment, their friendship blossomed, nurtured by shared passions like fishing trips under clear skies, golf games on lazy afternoons, lively poker nights, and countless engaging conversations about anything and everything over a strong drink.

A serendipitous picnic arranged at a park brought both families together; instant chemistry filled the air as they discovered common ground among themselves. The wives found solace in one another's company and forged a deep bond founded on shared interests and genuine affection. Their relationship blossomed into a profound friendship marked by unwavering support during times of adversity, sharing advice and deep secrets.

Despite living in close proximity in the same neighbourhood, these women cherished their hour-long conversations and eagerly anticipated weekend getaways planned together as opportunities for fostering stronger ties between families steeped in love and camaraderie.

Frank and Angela, the proud parents of two children named Anthony, affectionately known as Tony, and Joseph, fondly referred to as Joey, were astounded by their children's exceptional talents that shone brightly from a tender age. At the ripe age of nineteen, Tony had already made a significant impact in the world of soccer by securing a spot in the national team while simultaneously pursuing his education at NYU. Not only that, but he had also earned the prestigious position of team captain, showcasing not only his exceptional athletic abilities but also his natural leadership skills.

On the other hand, sixteen-year-old Joey possessed an irresistible charm that made him immensely popular among the girls at St Francis Lewis High School. With his towering stature, captivating green eyes, and beautifully curly brown locks framing his face perfectly, Joey never failed to garner attention wherever he went. His confident demeanour and high intelligence shone through in all aspects of his school life, from dominating as the star player on the Varsity basketball team to holding the esteemed title of student body president. Despite receiving numerous flirtatious gestures from admirers leaving romantic notes in his locker or bag, Joey remained disinterested in such advances.

Joey had been Abby's childhood best friend since they were ten years old. She harboured deep feelings for him that she struggled to express. Completely enamoured by Joey's kindness and genuine nature towards her amidst their school peers' judgmental attitudes, Abby cherished every moment they spent together. While Joey remained oblivious to her affections for him, Abby treasured their friendly banter during science and math classes as well as their competitive matches in tennis, chess, and academic assessments.

One day during art class presented Abby with a golden opportunity to reveal her secret crush on Joey through an innovative game called the dark room. As students scribbled messages on a black screen within a sixty-second timeframe under dim lighting conditions before sharing them once the lights came back on, Abby took a bold leap by confessing her admiration for Joey with the words "I like Joey Giovanni."

The ensuing reactions from their classmates ranged from amusement to curiosity as whispers filled the air, speculating about each message displayed on the black wall.

Now, in Italy together, it was a day of particular exhilaration and anticipation for Abby as she eagerly awaited the chance to spend quality time with Joey in a foreign land that held a special place in her heart. The romanticised allure of this exotic destination only served to heighten Abby's sense of excitement and connection to both the location and her crush. Spending time with Joey in that idyllic, almost magical setting felt like a dream she had always longed for. It was a chance to create memories she believed would last forever, warming her heart with the sweet innocence of teenage love.

Yet, reality did not unfold as she had imagined. Returning to America, she carried with her the bittersweet taste of a holiday that revived her soul but left her yearning for a deeper connection with Joey. Despite the cherished moments, disappointment lingered over the missed opportunities to enhance the bond she had so deeply desired.

CHAPTER 3

The familiarity of her weekly community church events awaited her—a ritual she accepted out of love for her family, even if she wasn't particularly drawn to it. Every Wednesday evening, Abby found herself at the local community hall, where the air seemed thick with whispers and gossip, stories entangled like thorns in a rose bush. The teenage girls bickered over fleeting affections, their antics splashed across the digital universe, inviting both laughter and judgment from distant onlookers. Embarrassed by such chaos, Abby often drifted to a quiet corner, seeking the comforting presence of Joey, who always appeared effortlessly charming, a calming horizon amidst the storm.

Her heart ached with regret over the unspoken words she wished she had shared with Joey under the Sicilian sun. As she entered the gathering, she drew in a deep breath, a gentle reminder that she endured these evenings out of love and respect for her parents, and for the tender chance it occasionally offered to be near

21

Joey. Raised in a devout Catholic household, the glow of faith was ever-present in Abby's life. Each room in their home was graced with crucifixes, silent guardians of their devotion to Christ.

From her early years, Abby's parents sowed seeds of faith within her, nurturing a journey that began with her baptism and continued through confession, communion, and confirmation. Yet, despite her diligent participation in Mass services, often led by the kindly Father Francesco, she sometimes felt a quiet struggle within, a whisper of disconnect wrestling with her spirituality.

Her father's insistence on attending church as a declaration of their devotion weighed heavily on Abby. Missing these gatherings could invite gossip and judgment, something her family strived to avoid. Torn between her responsibilities to her family and her emotions for Joey, Abby found herself balancing these inner conflicts—a dance between duty and love that clouded her spirit.

CHAPTER 4

In the gentle embrace of her close-knit Catholic community, Abby grew up being taught that premarital intimacy was strictly forbidden. The very notion of engaging in such actions before marriage was unimaginable and fraught with the risk of severe consequences for those who dared defy long-held traditions. Abby's upbringing was guided by a deep-seated moral compass, instilled by her parents with the belief that waiting until after marriage was not merely important, but essential.

In the warmth of this community, adherence to these values was expected, and any deviation was met with stern disapproval. Abby's mother, in her tender yet firm manner, often stressed the seriousness of avoiding premarital sex. She spoke of how such actions could tarnish a young woman's social position and reputation. In their town, families would go to great lengths to hide any missteps, fearful of losing the respect they so carefully maintained.

Unfortunately, Abby's cousin Romana had failed to keep her transgressions hidden well enough. When Abby returned home from school one day, she was greeted by a sombre scene at the dining table where her mother and aunt sat with sad expressions etched on their faces. Her aunt's red eyes and smudged mascara betrayed recent tears shed over distressing news about Romana— Abby's twenty-five-year-old unmarried cousin had been caught engaging in sexual activity with her long-term boyfriend.

Romana had spent her entire life dutifully striving to meet the expectations of her mother and conforming to the stringent beliefs and cultural standards dictating her behaviour. Grappling with internal conflicts and sexual whims, she had always made a concerted effort to uphold honesty and obedience towards her parents' desires. Little did she anticipate that falling in love with the man of her dreams would result in the utter destruction of her world.

Upon discovering she was now labelled a repugnant and dishonourable daughter who had brought great anguish and shame upon her family and siblings, Romana was left utterly shattered. Even though she was an adult well past the age of consent for intimate relationships, their devout adherence to Catholic values demanded chastity until marriage, viewing virginity as something pure and sacred within their societal framework.

Overwhelmed by her thoughts, Abby found herself compelled to express her stance on the subject of premarital abstinence. She deemed their traditional viewpoint as unacceptable and believed it failed to reflect the changing times. Abby held onto an idealised view of love, envisioning it as akin to a fairy tale with magical qualities. In light of this, she felt an inherent need to defend both her cousin and their love since Romana struggled to defend herself against the unrelenting onslaught of insults and anticipated ostracism from their community for life.

"For the love of God, leave her alone!" she exclaimed passionately, her voice quivering with emotion as she forcefully stamped her foot. Her mother and aunt stood by, aghast at the intensity of her words. "Romana is not a child; she's twenty-five and a fully grown woman. She has the independence to make decisions for herself, regardless of how unconventional they may seem to you and others. The treatment she has endured at the hands of those around her is nothing short of abhorrent. She deserves happiness just like anyone. What if she has chosen to be intimate before marriage? No one has died. Life goes on, the world is still spinning, you know. Just leave her alone!"

Abby's heartfelt plea only served to heighten the distress felt by her aunt, whose tears flowed freely in response. In a state of frustration caused by what she perceived as Abby's lack of understanding and insensitivity towards their cultural norms, values, and traditions, Abby's mother stood up with a stern expression and pointed decisively towards the door. "Leave this room immediately!" Her command was delivered with an air of authority that made it clear she could not hide her disappointment in her daughter's behaviour.

Abby's sincere apologies for causing embarrassment to her mother with her outburst fell on deaf ears, and she couldn't help but overhear as she left the room her mother's murmurs filled with anger and foreboding, predicting Abby would ultimately bring about her own downfall.

Abby had always believed her mother devoted herself to moulding her into the person she desired her to be simply because

Abby was her flesh and blood. However, Abby often found herself grappling with internal conflict due to strongly believing in asserting her own unique qualities and characteristics to her parents, which caused her great anxiety. Raised in an environment where obedience reigned supreme, Abby was keenly aware that dating was strictly prohibited within the confines of her family. Her main focus was meant to be on academics and maintaining the family's revered reputation and honour, which was why she harboured deep fears about revealing her secret romantic involvement with Joey Giovanni.

Her mind inevitably drifted back to the night of the school dance, a significant event marking the end of their junior year, where Abby and Joey celebrated together. "Hurry up, Abby!" her mother bellowed, calling from downstairs in their grand two-story home, reminding Abby that Frank would soon arrive.

Abby stood in front of the ornate mirror in her bedroom, captivated by the reflection staring back at her. The knee-length dress she wore, adorned with delicate ivory embroidery, had been chosen by her mother for the school dance. However, Abby was not content to simply conform to tradition—she added a touch of her own flair by pairing it with black lace-up boots reminiscent of ballet shoes.

As she heard her mother's voice echoing down the hallway, Abby quickly reached for her hair straightener, determined to tame her thick, unruly waves into submission. With skilled fingers, she smoothed out any rebellious strands and neatly tucked a few behind her ear before applying a coat of cherry lipstick from her mother's extensive collection.

Glancing over at the clock radio on her nightstand, Abby's eyes widened in alarm when she realised it was already 5:25 pm. Mr.

Giovanni would be arriving soon to escort her to the dance, and she had yet to make her grand entrance. The sound of the front door opening and cheerful greetings drifted up the stairs, prompting Abby to hastily switch off the hair straightener. Grabbing her denim jacket and clutch purse with a shoulder strap, she descended the staircase, ready for an evening filled with music and memories waiting to be made.

At the foot of the grand staircase stood Joey, his eyes eagerly scanning the room as he awaited Abby's descent. Consumed by a whirlwind of emotions crashing over her like tidal waves, Abby found herself speechless and at a loss for words as she made her way down the steps. A mixture of embarrassment and nervousness gripped her heart, causing it to beat erratically with uncertainty.

But then something shifted between them as their eyes met in a moment of connection. Laughter bubbled up from deep within Joey and Abby, breaking through the tension that hung heavily in the air. Their shared amusement acted as a beacon of light on what had felt like a cloudy day, instantly forging a bond that transcended any awkwardness or doubt.

Abby couldn't help but be struck by Joey's stunning appearance in his impeccably tailored suit. A wide grin spread across her face as she finally found her voice and complimented him on his choice of wardrobe.

"Hey, Joey, nice suit," she exclaimed with genuine enthusiasm, a sparkle of admiration shining in her eyes for his impeccable sense of style and fashion.

In response, Joey flashed a warm and appreciative smile before casting his gaze upon Abby's elegant dress. "I like your dress," he replied, genuinely impressed by the effort she had put into looking radiant for the special occasion. They exchanged compliments, their playful banter adding an extra layer of charm to their interaction as they sauntered towards the car where their friends awaited their arrival.

Upon reaching the grand entrance of the school hall, they were greeted by a sight that took their breath away. The meticulously decorated space was adorned with black and pink balloons, intricately hung streamers swaying gently in the air, and twinkling lights illuminating every corner. The DJ stationed in one corner spun lively tunes that filled the room with infectious energy and encouraged teens already on their feet to dance with wild abandon.

Amidst the sea of moving bodies on the dance floor, they managed to spot their friends and eagerly made their way over to join them. It was there that Joey mesmerised everyone with his awe-inspiring dance moves, gliding across the floor with precision and grace that left onlookers in admiration. In an impulsive moment, he took Abby by the hand and twirled her around during a slow song, causing her heart to skip a beat as she struggled to maintain her balance amidst the raucous laughter and applause.

As they savoured refreshing fruit punch and piping hot slices of pizza during animated conversations and fits of laughter, they eventually found themselves back on the dance floor as the night progressed. Moments before the festivities drew to a close, Joey and Abby conversed in their shared experiences during junior year, tinged with unspoken tension hinting at something deeper simmering between them.

Their time at the dance came to an end as they headed towards their lockers to gather their belongings. Walking past the illustrious wall adorned with photos of past achievements elicited nostalgia mingled with sweet air freshener lingering in the corridor. Outside, crickets hummed softly, providing a soothing background melody that enhanced the bittersweet ambiance surrounding this final farewell.

Just as they returned to the school hall for one last glimpse before leaving, Joey suddenly halted in his tracks. "Abby! Wait!" he called out with barely contained excitement evident in his voice.

Intrigued by this sudden interruption, Abby turned around curiously, asking, "What's up?"

Struggling to gather his thoughts, Joey hesitated and looked down, pausing to gather his composure by taking a deep breath. Abby instinctively reached out, delicately cupping his face with her palm.

"Joey, just tell me!" she urged, locking eyes with him in a display of unwavering support that seemed to grant him permission.

Seemingly encouraged by her words, Joey tentatively touched her hand before leaning in to kiss her, so gentle it mirrored the delicate fluttering of butterfly wings.

Their lips met in a graceful dance of affection, momentarily eclipsing the world around them as they basked in the warmth of intimacy and the promise of new beginnings. Emboldened by this newfound connection, Joey drew closer to Abby and pressed his lips against hers before tracing his tongue along her bottom lip.

The suddenness of this unexpected gesture left Abby momentarily stunned, unsure how to react as a group of giggling girls approached them before disappearing around the corner. Breathless from their impromptu affection and locked within each other's gaze, Joey seized the fleeting opportunity before they were once again subject to prying eyes by pulling Abby close for a second kiss while securing his arms around her waist. Inspired by scenes witnessed in movies, Abby stood on tiptoes and wrapped her arms around Joey's neck as they kissed again.

Separating from their embrace, Joey could no longer contain his emotions. "I like you," he said with a bashful smile. "Will you be my girlfriend?"

Filled with elation at this unforeseen turn of events, Abby couldn't help but emit a shy yet grateful smile. "Yes," she replied softly. "I will be your girlfriend."

CHAPTER 5

Abby soon found herself constantly restless each night, unable to drift off to sleep as her thoughts were consumed by the recent kiss with Joey, now her boyfriend. Fidgeting nervously with the delicate fabric of her nightgown, Abby struggled to focus on anything else, incredulous that this exciting new relationship was actually happening. The fluttery sensation in her stomach was overpowering, prompting her to place a trembling hand over it and repeat in disbelief, "Joey is my boyfriend." Never in her wildest dreams did Abby imagine her crush would reciprocate with the same feelings. The mere thought of seeing him again filled her with a mixture of excitement and nerves, emotions she had never experienced with such intensity before. Each time she closed her eyes, she was transported back to their perfect kiss, sending waves of blissful euphoria through her.

But these fond memories were tinged with fear as she couldn't shake the nagging feeling she was treading the forbidden path Mama had warned her about. Apprehension aside, the thrill of exploring this newfound relationship excited Abby, propelling her towards the unknown. Her mind wandered back to the moment she locked eyes with Joey and felt the warmth of his lips against hers, igniting a desire for more kisses so wonderful in their own unique way. Aware of the societal norms imposed upon her by conservative and religious family values, Abby harboured a deep-seated guilt for pursuing a romantic involvement against their strict rules.

Abby knew she had to keep the relationship hidden from her parents to uphold the family's honour and respect. She was conscious her parents would not approve of their relationship. Moreover, dealing with the attention from other boys at school made her anxious and uneasy. She often found herself having to justify why she could not date them by mentioning certain aspects of her identity. The fear of losing any semblance of freedom prevented Abby from engaging in romantic relationships, and she did not want to disgrace her family name. Trying to comprehend her parents' strict rule against dating proved challenging for Abby as she strongly believed nothing was wrong with it.

Dating seemed normal, something everyone around was doing, so it was difficult to understand and accept why she was prohibited from it—a stark contrast to American customs that held more liberal views regarding dating.

Growing up in a culture where young girls were expected to remain pure until marriage, Abby felt the weight of her family's expectations. Her father, with his heart full of love and protectiveness, watched over her with a vigilant eye, while her mother anxiously ensured that Abby understood the significance of keeping her purity intact. To Abby's mother, this aspect of her daughter's identity was not just a personal virtue but a precious link to salvation, an ideal cherished deeply. The thought of straying from these expectations—of engaging in premarital intimacy—was suffused with fear of not just personal disappointment but also the potential shame it could cast upon their family, sparking harsh whispers and scornful glances from the townsfolk. Joey, who cared deeply for Abby, understood the pressures she faced, and in his gentle, understanding way, he chose not to rush her but to respect her boundaries, always hoping that one day she might share his affections. For Abby, though her own emotions rumbled with the natural desires of youth, she resolved to honour her family by preserving her chastity as long as she could, feeling a sense of duty that ran deeper than personal desire.

As time passed, Joey and Abby found themselves becoming increasingly at ease with the discreet nature of their relationship. Their desire for each other only intensified, but they managed to keep their affections hidden from prying eyes, especially their families. The mere notion of being romantically involved was uncharted territory for them, adding an exhilarating sense of danger to their affair. But Abby couldn't shake off the unease she felt about deceiving her parents and constantly having to be on guard around them.

Their covert rendezvous became a regular occurrence, marked by secret outings, affectionate notes exchanged between them, and subtle gestures of intimacy shared in the school hallways. Behind the school cathedral walls during lunch breaks, stolen kisses were exchanged in secrecy. At every turn within the school grounds, they remained inseparable, offering unwavering support to each other as they navigated the complexities of their forbidden love.

Whenever they met, a palpable tension filled the air between them—a silent acknowledgment that something extraordinary was unfolding before their eyes. Abby's upbringing as a devout Christian girl had instilled values against dishonesty, but she found herself adapting to this deception to protect what meant most to her—her relationship with Joey.

Against all odds, their bond quickly grew deeper and transformed into profound love. They flirted and kissed and even explored the initial steps of physical intimacy, discovering the sweet harmony that resides in shared, tender moments.

The warmth radiating between them didn't go unnoticed by their closest friends who had figured out their secret romance. This newfound hope kindled within them visions of shared dreams; a tale of first kisses and a blooming romance intertwined with magic and wonder, all born from the discovery of true love beneath the twinkling stars.

CHAPTER 6

One splendid summer's day, Joey and Abby made the bold decision to play hooky from school to celebrate their one-year anniversary. Venturing out to Riverside Park in New York City, they eventually stumbled upon a quaint spot nestled beneath the shade of a towering tree. There, Abby found herself comfortably leaning back against Joey's chest, their fingers intertwined as she gently caressed his hand with her thumb. Engaging in loving conversation, they debated spending their day at the beach or revelling in the thrills of an amusement park.

In a tender moment that followed, Joey uttered the words, "I have something for you," prompting Abby to sit up and fix him with an eager gaze. Her eyes widened with anticipation.

"For me?" she asked, blinking excitedly.

He nodded. "Yes."

A radiant smile graced Abby's lips as Joey extended his arms around her shoulders and leaned in for a kiss.

Abby winced, shook her head, and held up her geography textbook, shielding their faces. "No, we can't. Not here, what if someone sees us?"

He chuckled. "Abby, look around, do you see anyone here?"

She quickly scanned the park. They were completely isolated; even the people walking their dogs were nowhere to be seen.

Taking advantage of this rare moment alone together, Abby closed her eyes and began to sing with angelic beauty. Her melodic voice floated through the air like a gentle breeze rustling the leaves above. Mesmerised by her enchanting serenade, Joey watched on with rapt attention as the serene sound enveloped them both with its spellbinding embrace.

As Abby's song filled the tranquil space around them, Joey reached out to tenderly caress her face before leaning in for another kiss. The sweet gesture made Abby's cheeks bloom red as she returned his affectionate gesture with equal fervour, embracing him warmly within her arms. In that fleeting moment of shared intimacy and musical magic, time seemed to stand still for Joey and Abby amidst the idyllic setting of Riverside Park.

In a matter of moments, they slowly moved apart, causing Abby to emit a joyful giggle, which prompted Joey to affectionately plant a kiss on her nose. "You are truly adorable," he whispered. Glancing towards his school bag momentarily, Joey unzipped it and retrieved a luxurious velvet pouch. Taking hold of Abby's hand, he gently placed the pouch into her open palm. "I hope you like it babe," he said with a warm smile.

"Oh, I'm sure I will love it, you goofball!" she replied with a mischievous grin, graciously accepting the gift and eagerly unwrapping the small bag to reveal a stunning gold ring adorned with a sparkling ruby. Her lips curled into an appreciative smile as she gasped softly. "Oh my goodness, Joey!" she murmured in awe, covering her mouth with her hands before revealing her delighted expression once more. "It is absolutely beautiful, I adore it." Sliding the ring onto her middle finger, she gazed at it lovingly before straightening and discreetly scanning their surroundings for prying eyes. She then leaned in to tenderly press her lips against his, eliciting a smile from Joey.

Moments later, she drew back slightly and whispered gratefully, "Thank you, babe, I will treasure it forever." She pressed the ring against her heart protectively before Joey suddenly realised something was amiss.

"Oh no!" he muttered under his breath.

"What's wrong?" asked Abby.

"I forgot to give you the card," Joey said as he retrieved it from between the pages of his science textbook.

Taking the card from him, Abby opened it and read its contents with a soft smile spreading across her face.

> *Hey there, beautiful,*
>
> *Happy one-year anniversary, babe! Each day with you is special, and I just want to celebrate how awesome you make my life. When I look into your eyes, all I see is a future full of love and happiness together. You are the brightest, most caring, and loving person I know. You complete my world. I love you so much!* 🖤

Joey's feelings were evident as he met Abby's tearful gaze and pressed his lips together in a tender smile. There was no room for pretence or frivolity; only raw, unfiltered emotions poured forth from his soul.

"Joey," she whispered, biting her bottom lip, "I love you, too." The simple declaration sent tremors of joy through Abby, compelling her to pull Joey close in a warm embrace. Their kisses were sweet and tender, igniting sparks of passion within them.

As Abby inched close to Joey's neck, tracing the contours of his face with adoring eyes, a flicker of worry crossed her mind. "What if someone sees us?" Her inner anxiety urged caution and restraint, urging her to disentangle herself from this intimate embrace. But Joey was reluctant to let go. "Come on, babe, no one knows we are here."

A tentative smile graced her features as she relented. "Ok, fine," just for a few minutes though."

Sitting on Joey's lap in his loving embrace, Abby traced his jawline with gentle fingers while he whispered loving words in her ear. His hands roamed from her shoulders to her hips as she tangled her fingers in his hair, revelling in the sensation of being so intimately connected. Time seemed to stand still in their secluded corner of nature, lost in each other's embrace. Despite the inevitable return to reality growing ever closer, Abby couldn't bring herself to break free from Joey's firm hold.

As Joey's lips slowly traversed along Abby's neck, eliciting a soft moan from her, she abruptly pulled away. "Stop Joey!" she exclaimed, disentangling herself from his embrace. Her eyes scanned the park, wary of any prying eyes. "We can't do this, not here!"

"I'm sorry, babe," Joey responded, releasing her waist as she stepped back with her hands on her hips, staring down at him intently. "Oh, come on, don't be like that," he said with a charming smile.

Abby shrugged.

"Babe, please come back and sit down, I promise I'll behave," he said.

"Promise me you won't do that again!" Abby demanded.

Joey put his hand on his heart. "I promise I won't kiss you on the neck in public."

Reluctantly, she sat beside him, and they held an animated conversation about their aspirations of relocating to New York City and embarking on carefree adventures together.

Over the next three and a half hours, they shared jokes, played games, and engaged in light-hearted water fights under the blazing sun. Hand in hand, they strolled along idyllic pathways by the riverbank, envisioning their future home in the neighbouring suburbs. Breaking out in impromptu dances, they let go of their inhibitions and cherished these joyful moments as a couple.

Their connection was so profound that conversations flowed effortlessly between them, punctuated by shared laughter and knowing glances. In these quiet interludes between banter and camaraderie, Abby and Joey grew even closer. Their love was a symphony of stolen kisses, whispered promises, and the comfort of intertwined fingers. Still, Abby harboured apprehensions about their secret romance after reading an article in Cosmopolitan predicting eventual heartbreak from hidden relationships. This trepidation lingered within her, but she remained resolute in preventing such an outcome from ruining their love story.

Abby returned home from school that day with a heart overflowing with joy and elation, her spirits soaring as she arrived home. Greeting her parents with warmth and affection, she bestowed kisses upon their cheeks before swiftly ascending the stairs to retreat to the sanctuary of her bedroom. After a rejuvenating shower, Abby found herself back in her room, ready to unwind and relax.

Abby's mother came into her room with a basket of impeccably ironed clothes perched elegantly on her left hip. Startled by her sudden intrusion, Abby turned towards her mother with a gentle expression filled with concern, inquiring softly, "What's the matter, Mama?"

Her mother hesitated briefly before finally saying, "Your papa wishes to speak with you downstairs."

A wave of apprehension washed over her. Her thoughts raced, fearing that he knew about her secret relationship with Joey. Her pulse quickened as she nervously descended the staircase, each step feeling heavier than the last. Apart from Vani and Nick, who had sworn secrecy about Abby's relationship with Joey, no one else knew.

Standing outside her father's study, Abby contemplated knocking when she caught snippets of his conversation on the phone.

"I will speak to Abby and call you back soon."

When he hung up the phone, Abby's stomach dropped.

Summoning all her courage, Abby tentatively knocked on the door before gingerly turning the knob and entering the dimly lit room. Heat rose to her cheeks and beads of sweat formed on her palms as she observed her father's piercing gaze. Gesturing for Abby to take a seat in the plush rose-pink armchair opposite him, he took a puff off his cigar and stared at her.

The tension in the room was palpable as Abby sensed something in the air. The dramatic atmosphere caused a tightness to constrict around Abby's chest while anxiety coursed through her.

Abby's father slowly rose, his eyes boring into her with intensity as he spoke. "Abby," he began, his voice calm but tinged with a hint of menace. "Do you have a boyfriend?"

In that moment, Abby realised her high school romance was on the verge of unravelling.

Abby instinctively shook her head and replied, "No, Dad, I don't have a boyfriend." Her voice quivered slightly, hands trembling beneath her crossed legs. An anxious glance darted back and forth between her mother who had just entered the room with an unwavering stare fixed upon her.

Concealing her shaky hands under her thighs, Abby nervously shifted her gaze between her parents.

Taking a deep breath, he continued, "Mrs. Bianchi spotted you leaving Kew Gardens Cinema this past Sunday afternoon in the company of a young man wearing a Yankees baseball cap."

A dilemma arose within Abby; should she reveal her relationship with Joey to her father? The way he looked at her rendered her almost mute. Realising she needed to confer with Joey about their situation, always cautious about being seen together publicly, Abby struggled with conflicting desires for transparency and deception towards her parents. The burden of hiding the truth weighed heavily on her conscience, but the pressure to conform as a dutiful daughter tempted her to rebel.

Abby's mother fixed her with a penetrating gaze, her eyes filled with intensity as she raised her index finger in a commanding gesture, insisting Abby come clean and tell the truth. This caused

Abby to become flustered, prompting her to avert her eyes and lower her gaze in an attempt to avoid direct confrontation with her mother. "Well... it's a bit complicated," Abby said. Before she could explain further, her mother cut her off.

The fire in her mother's eyes only intensified, prompting Abby to turn towards her father for support. Filled with apprehension, fear, and guilt as she met his brown eyes, Abby began recounting the events that had led them to this moment. "Dad, you know Nick? He's a friend from school who often lends us a hand at the restaurant when he stops by. Vani invited him along without my knowledge." Realising that maintaining her secret was crucial to preserving her relationship with Joey, Abby made the tough decision to continue deceiving her parents, for now at least.

In the meantime, she apologised for withholding information about Nick and admitting fault in keeping secrets from them. She acknowledged the seriousness of the situation wholeheartedly and vowed to heed their warnings moving forward. Spinning such a lie left her feeling a sense of deep shame.

"Abby," said her father with a sense of authority and seriousness, "I just want to make sure that no one speaks about you in a way that makes me feels uncomfortable, so if you're thinking about making plans with Vani, just remember it's important to focus on your friendship with her. Let's keep our circle for now, leave the boys out of it.

Abby internalised his message completely, understanding her parents' motives were rooted in love and concern. However, their unwavering stance on this matter struck a chord within her. Silently nodding in agreement, she responded with tightly pressed lips. "Yes, Papa, I understand. It won't happen again."

Her mother's sharp tone pierced the air as she exclaimed, "It better not happen again!" With finality in her voice, she rose from her seat signalling the end of the conversation.

Quietly unlatching the door, Abby left the room. Standing just outside, she listened attentively as her parents continued to discuss Mrs. Bianchi. "I had higher expectations of Abby," said her mother.

Struggling to contain the emotions swirling within her, Abby leaned against the hallway wall in contemplation. Fear gripped her heart as thoughts of a normal and healthy relationship with Joey seemed increasingly distant. Frustration gnawed at her insides as she made her way towards her room, each step heavy with uncertainty. It was then that Micky appeared before her, blocking her path with an air of curiosity tinged with mischief.

Ignoring his presence, Abby brushed past him and opened the second door leading to her bedroom. From behind, Micky's voice rang out with a taunting question. "Are you secretly dating Joey?"

Slowly turning to face Micky's smug expression, she met his gaze with a mixture of disbelief and apprehension. His knowing smile held a hint of arrogance that sent a chill down Abby's spine, leaving her questioning how much he truly knew about what was transpiring behind closed doors.

Shocked and unsettled by her brother's question, Abby couldn't help but release a disbelieving laugh. "Be serious, Micky!" Her voice, tinged with disbelief, was barely audible. As she awaited his response, her throbbing headache intensified. Despite their close bond and unwavering support for each other, Abby couldn't help but harbour a sense of trepidation about how Micky would react to the news she had just shared with him. However, something different appeared in his gaze this time around. Instead of

43

reprimanding or scolding her for her actions, he leaned in closer and whispered, "Be careful not to get caught."

Pausing momentarily before posing the inevitable question that loomed large in her mind, Abby finally mustered up the courage to ask. "How did you find out?"

"At dinner, when Joey was here, I accidentally dropped my fork and reached down to retrieve it I noticed how swiftly you withdrew your hands from each other."

With fear bubbling within her like molten lava threatening to erupt, Abby couldn't help but ponder whether anyone else had borne witness to such an intimate moment between them. Trusting Micky with her deepest secret and relying on him for support during trying times, she found solace in his assurance that he would guard her secret with utmost care. Before bidding farewell and making his exit from the house, Micky turned to Abby and said, "If you ever need someone to talk to, I'm just a phone call away."

In that moment, it dawned on Abby that Micky was her only ally. The realisation he now stood with her in support of her relationship didn't seem entirely devastating; perhaps he could cover them in times of need. With a newfound quiet confidence settling within her, Abby retreated to her bedroom and settled at her desk to work on an impending English assessment.

As she powered up the computer and cast a fleeting glance out of the window, a whirlwind of thoughts swirled through her mind like leaves caught in a gusty wind. Suddenly relieved, Abby remembered all photos and letters exchanged between her and Joey were securely tucked away inside her school locker, a reassuring reminder no tangible evidence linked back to Joey existed in the house.

Planning for tomorrow's conversation with Joey about the importance of discretion over their relationship, Abby couldn't shake off the nagging worry they might inadvertently be discovered by some curious family friend or nosy relative.

CHAPTER 7

As the months passed by, the bond between Abby and Joey only grew stronger. What had begun as innocent kisses during their final year of high school had blossomed into something far more meaningful and intimate. With each passing day, their love deepened, uncovering hidden layers of vulnerability and strength. Their friends marvelled at how they managed to maintain such a deep and enduring bond.

On a scorching summer's day, they made a spontaneous decision to skip school and escape to Rockaway Beach, seeking each other's company without prying eyes.

Arriving early in the morning, they were met with relentless heat. The sky was painted in a brilliant shade of blue, illuminated by the radiant sun, while the ocean below sparkled like a vast expanse of diamonds under its warm embrace. The harbour bustled with activity as boats crossed the waters, ferrying both locals and tourists alike to various destinations.

As they kicked off their shoes and socks, stowing them in their bags, Joey couldn't help but admire Abby's perfectly painted red toenails with an affectionate smile. Taking her hand in his own, he led her across the scorching sand towards the water's edge.

"Wow, this sand is really hot!" said Abby as they gingerly tiptoed across the shifting dunes towards the shoreline.

With a rush of nerves, Abby slowly unzipped her school tunic, revealing a striking, red one-piece swimsuit with delicate spaghetti straps that gracefully accentuated her curves and featured a daringly low-cut neckline. Her heart raced as she nervously bit her lip and blushed, ridden with guilt for skipping class and praying they wouldn't be caught.

Joey watched in silence as she unveiled her fair skin, his intense gaze lingering on every inch of her body, from her petite breasts to her slender waistline. With a warm smile, he said, "Wow, babe, you're absolutely stunning."

Blushing from his compliments, Abby felt herself drawn closer as Joey placed his hands gently on her hips, further deepening the blush that he found so charming and endearing. As he reached behind her head and released her ponytail, allowing her hair to cascade freely around her shoulders, Abby's cheeks burned even brighter.

Taking a beach towel from her bag, Abby wrapped it around herself before stealing a glance at Joey, noting the snug fit of his black pants and white shirt against his chiselled chest. Shifting uncomfortably in search of a better position, she let out an involuntary gasp as Joey discarded his shirt, unveiling a physique that left her breathless. Standing before him, Abby roamed her eyes over his sculpted form admiringly. She found him undeniably attractive with perfect muscle definition hinting at hours spent working out.

Her attention was momentarily diverted when Joey unzipped his pants and allowed them to fall to the sand, revealing sleek black swimming trunks beneath.

"Are you ready?" he asked.

Abby's luxurious lashes fluttered delicately like the wings of a butterfly as she fixed her gaze upon him, her eyes alight with eagerness and anticipation. With a resolute nod, she responded "Yes."

In a display of strength and agility, he bent down with effortless grace, hoisting her up in his powerful arms. The sudden movement elicited a surprised squeal from Abby, prompting her to instinctively wrap her arms tightly around his broad shoulders for support.

As he carried her towards the shoreline, a surge of excitement and joy surged through Abby's veins, invigorating her senses. Drawing closer to the water's edge, he turned to face her with a gentle smile. Without hesitation, he leaned in to give her a passionate kiss. The intensity of the moment ignited a yearning within Abby for more as she found herself lost in the blissful connection they shared.

Setting her back down on the soft sand, he held her hand as they braved the refreshing sea together. Joey's muscular physique glistened in the water as he drew Abby close against his chest, their bodies melding together in an intimate embrace.

In that tender moment, with the soothing ocean sounds and the comforting warmth of the sun, their love was set free. It was a deep and profound love that transcended language barriers and resonated through their intertwined hearts.

Joey was not just Abby's first love; he was also her steadfast anchor in turbulent seas, a soothing presence synchronising the rhythms of their lives. As he briefly withdrew from their kiss to lavish soft kisses upon her neck, Abby emitted soft gasps with every tender touch.

His exploration of her mouth with his tongue sent pleasurable shivers coursing down her spine, kindling an intense passion between them that was almost magnetically irresistible. Trailing teasing strokes with his fingers over one of her breasts, Joey elicited soft moans from Abby as she struggled to catch her breath within their fervent embrace. Before long, they found themselves seeking out a more secluded spot along the beach where they could revel in each other's company away from prying eyes.

Still damp from their playful frolic in the sea, Joey laid out a towel on the sand and beckoned for Abby to recline beside him. With her head nestled comfortably in the cradle of his arm, she knew what lay ahead but welcomed it eagerly nonetheless, as long as they remained shielded from potential onlookers.

Abby harboured a fervent desire for more fulfillment in life. She yearned to prioritise her own happiness over conforming to societal expectations.

As she and Joey explored their most intimate desires for the first time, her mind became a battleground of conflicting thoughts. Though reason urged her to retreat and avoid making a mistake, neither she nor Joey made such a move.

In a moment of vulnerability, Joey gazed at Abby with tenderness and softly inquired if he could touch her.

Without hesitation, she replied, "Yes," feeling a flutter of butterflies dancing in her stomach. Following his lead, Joey directed her to close her eyes and relax. With uncertainty gnawing at her, Abby complied, pondering whether Joey had ever engaged in sexual acts before.

As he leaned in and planted gentle kisses on her neck with his soft lips, it became evident that Joey possessed a certain expertise. Abby found herself taken aback as his hands roamed across her body, tracing delicate circles on her thigh with fingers quivering with desire and passion.

When he paused momentarily, Abby's eyes flickered open. "Is something wrong?"

He chuckled and replied honestly, "Oh... nothing, I'm just a little nervous."

Upon noticing his slight nervousness, Abby reached out and stroked his face. "We don't have to continue if you're not comfortable."

Joey shook his head. "Abby, I want to continue, but only if you do."

Despite her lingering doubts, Abby nodded. "Yes, I want to go ahead." She made it clear they use protection and forbade Joey from ejaculating inside her.

Understanding the gravity of the situation, Joey nodded in agreement before taking a deep breath and continuing.

"I won't hurt you," he reassured as he cautiously explored beneath her swimsuit with one finger followed by another.

A whimper escaped Abby's lips as he continued, causing her muscles to tense and quiver in response to his touch. Time seemed to stand still as they became lost in each other's presence.

Their movements were synchronised in a passionate dance fuelled by unspoken understanding and longing for one another.

Helpless against his touch, Abby gasped for air and let out cries of pleasure as they shared intimate moments together.

When he withdrew his fingers from her skin, she gazed up at him with anticipation as he uttered the words, "I want you, okay?"

Her breath came out in a short rush, "Yes... yes."

The fiery passion burned with an insatiable desire as she longed for him to penetrate her. Their gazes locked in a heated exchange as he positioned himself on top of her and she willingly opened her legs.

"Are you sure?" he asked once more. With unwavering confidence, she boldly affirmed, "Yes, I am. I want you inside me."

A faint smile appeared as he lowered his head to bestow tender kisses upon the delicate skin of her neck, his favourite move. In that fleeting moment, the heat from their intertwined bodies and the fervent passion that painted the canvas of their shared desires were all she knew.

With gentle precision, he removed the strap of her swimsuit from her shoulder, revealing the soft curves of her exposed breast. He lovingly caressed and sucked each nipple until they throbbed with pleasure. With an indescribable ecstasy coursing through her veins, she yearned for his member to penetrate her.

Locking eyes with him once more, Abby knew it was too late to turn back now; she found herself unable to escape or resist as his hand glided down her thigh, tracing the contours of her body in a tender prelude to the main act.

As he positioned himself between her open legs, driven by primal urges beyond control, he swiftly discarded his trunks and entered her wet and heated core while she eagerly wrapped her legs around his waist.

Anxiety tinged with apprehension flickered across Abby's widened eyes; this unexpected turn of events caught her off guard. "Oh, Joey!" she moaned loudly as a searing pain shot through her vulva, causing discomfort but with no desire to halt or resist him. Clinging tightly to him with his warm chest pressed against her hardened breasts, she stuttered breathlessly at the electrifying sensations flooding through her.

As he lifted his head to meet her gaze once more, his soothing green eyes sought reassurance in the whirlwind of emotions engulfing them both. "Are you alright?" he whispered.

"Umm, I think so," she replied unconvincingly through clenched teeth, inhaling deeply as if trying to dispel the mounting discomfort that threatened to end their intimacy.

He leaned in closely, their warm breaths colliding as he delicately pressed his lips against hers, simultaneously caressing her sensitive vulva with a tenderness that fuelled the desire within her. Pleasure rinsed through them as she enveloped his hot and thick erection within her tightness.

Gasping for air and moaning in ecstasy, she felt herself on the precipice of her first sexual climax, teetering on the edge as the charged atmosphere pulled them together like magnets. With soft moans and happy tears, she whispered, "Oh, Joey."

As their passion intensified, he quickened his pace until they both reached a mutual climax that shattered any remaining innocence. With a whimper of her name, he released inside her, holding onto her tightly as warm fluid cascaded down her inner thighs.

"I love you, too," she replied before leaning in for another kiss. Their eyes locked for what seemed like an eternity.

Fifteen minutes later saw them seated at a restaurant table, eagerly anticipating their meal after their physical exertion had left them ravenous. "I can't believe we forgot to use protection," Abby said with crossed arms, casting a questioning glance at Joey.

"I know," said Joey. "It never even crossed my mind."

"Why'd you finish inside?" Abby asked.

"I'm sorry," he said, so softly and quietly she barely heard him. "I got caught up in the moment."

Abby slouched in her seat, staring out at the ocean with a glass of water in hand as she contemplated what had just happened, closing her eyes to collect herself.

In a gentle tone, Joey reached out to hold her hand and asked, "Do you regret what happened between us?"

Abby opened her eyes, and locked gazes with him before squeezing his hand and replying, "No, I have no regrets."

This profound moment marked their transition from innocence to a deeper understanding of themselves and each other—a chapter in their shared story filled with newfound complexities and intimacy.

Later that night, Abby found herself unable to sleep. Every inch of her body seemed to throb with the remnants of their heated intimacy, leaving behind a trail of tender bruises and a pelvis that felt as though it had been shattered into a thousand pieces. Yet these physical discomforts paled in comparison to the crushing guilt.

It was as if she had committed an unforgivable sin by giving in to the seductive allure of temptation. As she ran her fingers over her sore and swollen lips, each touch serving as a stark reminder of their passionate tryst, her heart pounded furiously against her ribcage, threatening to burst forth from its confines.

In that one moment of sexual bliss, her entire world had been upended and irrevocably altered. The mere thought of her mother stumbling upon the truth filled her with an acute sense of shame, and she envisioned the disappointment, disapproval, and outright disrespect she would surely bring upon her family name.

CHAPTER 8

On Sunday morning, Abby found herself seated in the back of a crowded room filled with thirty other young adults, her attention fully captured by Father Francesco as he emphasised the significance of preserving one's purity until marriage. Clutching tightly onto the promise ring gifted to her by Joey, a tangible representation of their deep love and unwavering commitment to each other, Abby couldn't help but feel an intense connection between them as they exchanged furtive glances during the sermon. Recollections of their perfect days spent together at the beach inundated her thoughts, stirring up a fervent desire that had long been dormant within her, yet conflicted with her devout aspiration to lead a chaste life in accordance with her religious beliefs.

Within Abby's heart, a gentle storm was unfolding, leaving her feeling a bit out of sync. She was caught between feelings of confusion and curiosity. Even though she appeared to be a devout member of her church community, Abby was exploring a side of herself that didn't quite match her moral beliefs. This internal exploration, while risky, was a journey toward understanding herself more deeply. Determined to keep her private thoughts hidden from those around her, Abby chose to bravely walk this delicate path, seeking personal growth and insight.

As senior year rolled around, the focal point shifted towards preparing for the looming SAT exams. Pressured by both sides of their families to excel academically, Abby and Joey were compelled to dedicate themselves wholeheartedly to their studies at the expense of indulging in leisurely pastimes or spending quality time with friends. Hours upon hours were devoted to arduous sessions at the library, their singular focus honed on mastering test material crucial for securing admission into prestigious university programs. To eliminate any potential distractions that might impede their academic progress, they consciously limited expressions of affection towards one another and adopted a pragmatic stance in navigating the course of their courtship.

Fighting against an ardent longing to be reunited with each other, they made the difficult decision to temporarily place their relationship on hold while fulfilling obligations during the final months of high school. With the SATs looming ominously, they poured every ounce of effort into acing these pivotal exams and submitting college applications to their preferred institutions, NYU ranking highest on their list closely followed by Yale. Joey set his sights on MIT and Berkeley as potential options for pursuing advanced studies in business management and commerce while Abby patiently awaited her chance to study law.

Exam day came about quicker than Abby imagined possible, and she strode confidently into the examination hall, her eyes scanning the room for her designated seat with a calm and collected demeanour. Her extensive preparation for the SATs had instilled in her a sense of assurance she was ready to conquer whatever challenges lay ahead.

Taking her place at an unoccupied table, she eagerly surveyed the room in search of Joey, who sat on the opposite side. The exchange of glances between them conveyed a mutual longing for the day's end so they could finally enjoy some quality time together. As Joey met Abby's gaze, his expression seemed tense, yet he managed to muster a smile as he silently mouthed, "Good luck."

Both Abby and Joey had devoted countless hours to studying for this exam, sacrificing precious sleep and leisure activities in their relentless pursuit of knowledge up until the very last minute. This day symbolised a pivotal moment in their lives, as success on this test held the promise of liberation from academic pressures and the prospect of embracing a more enriched lifestyle in America.

An announcement echoed through the hall from the front, informing the students the exam would start in five minutes. They were reminded to write their names and student numbers on each page of their examination booklet before tackling the questions without any communication. A stern warning against cheating was issued with instant disqualification and forfeit of retaking the exam.

Abby diligently scanned the questions within her booklet during the allotted five minutes before writing her name and student number at the top left corner of each page.

"Time is up," announced the headmistress. Abby closed her eyes briefly to silently pray before dragging her calculator closer to her paper, needed to tackle various mathematical problems presented across the fifteen sections.

At the end of the first exam, the headmistress called out, "Pens down, please! Take this time to use the restroom and grab a bite to eat. The exam will resume promptly at 11:10 am."

A group of students hurriedly left the exam room.

Abby caught up with Joey outside and warmly greeted him with a hug.

"How did you go?" she asked.

"I think I did alright," Joey replied wearily. "And you?"

"I grasped the concepts in the mathematics analysis, although it was quite challenging. I'm confident I did well in the English section."

"Don't worry, everything will be fine," he said, rubbing the back of her neck. "Let's grab some lunch before the next exam."

During the examination that followed, Abby once again clung tightly to her rosary beads, as if they possessed some magical ability to stimulate the neurons in her brain and enhance her cognitive abilities. She found herself grappling with the challenging science and history questions, feeling the weight of the test bearing down on her.

As 3:00 pm rolled around, the headmistress announced the conclusion of the exam and instructed all students to cease writing, lower their pens, and close their booklets. Abby glanced up at the clock, only to find her vision blurred from hours of intense focus. She sat upright in her chair, grounding herself by firmly planting her feet on the floor and briefly rubbing her fatigued eyes for momentary relief. The exhaustion that had been building throughout the day peaked, leaving her yearning for sleep.

Filled with relief and joy at finally being released from the exam hall, Abby linked arms with her friend Vani and eagerly scanned the room for Joey. Upon spotting him in the crowd, a semblance of comfort came over her weary face.

A smile instantly brightened Joey's features as he watched Abby approach him with excited steps. Without hesitation, she leapt into his awaiting arms, wrapping her legs around his waist in a display of sheer elation.

In a tender gesture, Joey ran his fingers through Abby's tousled hair before sharing a long kiss filled with passion and affection as their classmates erupted into cheers around them. Following this intimate moment, they joined their peers in spirited water balloon fights that served as a finale to high school.

The festive atmosphere persisted as they gathered at Wendy's Burgers for fries and shakes. Here, they let go of inhibitions and revelled in each other's presence with laughter and camaraderie as the exam tension faded into insignificance.

CHAPTER 9

Abby had grown accustomed to keeping her private life secret to navigate the suffocating protectiveness of her parents, which seemed to have reached new heights as they now closely monitored her every move. The lies had become second nature to her, seamlessly slipping from her lips with increasing complexity each day. Frequently, she would concoct elaborate tales for her mother about spending time with Vani and other schoolmates, faking outings to the local shopping mall or beach. There had been opportunities to come clean about her romance with Joey, but Abby found herself shackled by fear of losing him if she dared to reveal it.

One morning, she roused herself from bed, her stomach rumbled with hunger and the tantalising coffee aroma alerted her to the need for caffeine. Alas, time was not on her side; she was meeting Joey soon and needed to get a move on.

Fifteen minutes later, she emerged from the bathroom filled with nervous energy when Micky asked, "Where are you going?"

"I am spending the day with Vani and Joey at Deno's Wonderland in Brooklyn," she whispered.

He stayed silent for a moment, then leaned in and murmured, "Don't do anything stupid."

Annoyed by his lack of trust in her judgment, she sighed and rolled her eyes. "I won't, relax!" She rushed off saying, "Gotta go!"

As she sprinted down the hallway into her room, she caught her mother's startled gaze as she emerged from her own bedroom.

Abby rushed into her room and closed the door. In a hurried frenzy, she flung open her dresser doors and retrieved a crimson thong and bra ensemble that didn't quite match. Disregarding all sense of tidiness, she carelessly discarded her towel on the floor before changing.

Joey had booked a motel two hours away from New York City where they could be themselves, far removed from prying eyes. Contrary to what she had told her brother, they were not going to any theme park.

The motel was situated amidst narrow alleyways and sparsely populated streets. It was basic in design and barely clean, but it was all Joey could afford. That and one shared meal between them. Casting a fleeting glance at her reflection in the mirror, she smoothed out the floral embroidery on her garden dress in an attempt to assuage her frayed nerves.

Feeling anxious about leaving the house, Abby sped downstairs and snatched her purse by the door. "Mama, I'm heading out now. I'll be back around 5.00 pm." She rushed out of the door to avoid her mother's questions and a potential curfew.

As soon as their bus left Queens, a sense of relief came over them. Joey affectionately wrapped his arm around Abby's waist as they journeyed towards their destination. Several hours later, they arrived at a dubious motel in Lukeman's Bay. Abby couldn't help but wonder if any of these people were acquainted with her parents or relatives but knew it was just her paranoia going into overdrive, as it so often did when she snuck around with Joey. However, when she inadvertently caught sight of herself in a mirror behind the front desk, shame overcame her.

"Abby, let's go!" said Joey, gently laying his hand on her shoulder.

Abby's body tensed up involuntarily, a reaction that did not go unnoticed by Joey. Concern was etched on his face. "You know, we don't have to do this, we can leave now if you want?" But Abby, determined to push away the doubts swirling in her mind, shook her head resolutely. "No, I want to," she asserted.

Taking hold of her hand in a show of solidarity, Joey led Abby towards the waiting elevator. As they walked side by side, Abby gazed at a striking watercolour painting hanging on the wall. The piece, entitled "The Zoo" by Winogrand, depicted a powerful lion surrounded by six tigers within a cage set against an African backdrop, a visual representation of family ties that resonated deeply with Abby.

Though inwardly conflicted about their urban escape, Abby maintained a composed facade as they entered the elevator car swiftly and ascended to room 4110.

Once inside the room, Abby took stock of their surroundings with quiet contemplation. The room itself was cosy, boasting fairly modern furnishings like a sleek television and a plush queen-sized bed adorned with crisp white linens. A private bathroom completed the ensemble, providing all the necessary amenities for their brief stay.

As she peered out through the window at the serene waters of the Hudson River meandering through Tappanzee below, Joey placed his hands on her shoulders. "Babe, we are safe here," he murmured softly into her ear, enveloping her in a comforting embrace and placing a tender kiss on her cheek.

Abby closed her eyes briefly and drew in deep breaths to steady herself against the rising tide of anxiety threatening to consume her fragile composure. Turning back towards Joey, she replied, "I know, I know." Joey's touch grew bolder as he gently cupped Abby's chin and drew her closer to him before kissing her. Feeling emboldened by his loving attention and gentle guidance, Abby reciprocated tentatively by tugging lightly at his shirt, an unspoken invitation that did not go unheeded.

With tenderness and passion, desire and trust, Joey nuzzled against Abby's neck affectionately. "Let's move this to the bedroom," he said.

With deliberate slowness, he lowered the zipper of her delicate floral dress, unveiling the lacy fabric of her bra and the tantalising red thong that hugged her curves. His hand moved with a feather-light touch down the curve of her spine, tracing each vertebra before cupping her firm buttocks in a possessive grip. She stood as if transfixed, a statue awaiting his next move. As his fingers expertly unhooked her bra, it slipped from her shoulders to her feet, leaving her bare chest exposed to his hungry gaze. The contrast between his soft caresses and the intensity of his touch caused her to bite down on her lip, a barely audible gasp escaping as she closed her eyes to savour the sensations coursing through her body. His hands found their way to her breasts, teasing and coaxing her nipples to stiff peaks. She struggled to catch her breath as he lowered his head, taking one taut bud into his mouth and lacing it with wet kisses and firm suction that elicited moans of pleasure from deep within her throat.

Sinking to his knees before her, he deftly removed the last barrier between them, sliding off her red thong with a swift motion that left her feeling exposed and vulnerable in the most exhilarating way. Standing naked before him, she felt a flush of heat rise in response to the dark curls that framed her mound but did little to conceal the lush contours of her vulva and inner folds.

Joey's eyes widened with admiration as they lingered on the intimate sight before him, an unspoken connection forming between them that transcended mere physical desire. In a moment of shared vulnerability, he shed his own clothes and stood naked before her, his arousal evident as he pressed against the warmth of her waiting flesh. His hands continued their exploration of her ivory skin, stroking and caressing every inch of exposed flesh as he drew closer until their mouths met in a fiery kiss that spoke volumes without words. But just as quickly as they had come together, she broke away abruptly, dropping to her knees beside the bed with a sense of determination in her eyes. Taking him into her mouth with newfound confidence born from uncertainty, Abby followed an instinctual rhythm guided by half-remembered advice gleaned from glossy magazines like Cosmopolitan. Her left hand cradled his gonads gently while the right gripped his hardness, eliciting groans of pleasure from him as she explored every inch with eager enthusiasm. A subtle smile played on Abby's lips as she wondered if she was indeed performing this act correctly—after all, this was uncharted territory for both of them. Her mind flashed back to snippets of advice read in passing about fellatio techniques;

emboldened by this useful yet limited knowledge, she dove deeper into pleasuring him with unwavering determination.

Joey's words of encouragement provided a powerful source of motivation for Abby, propelling her to exert even more effort as he surrendered himself to the sensations that gripped him. With his eyes tightly shut, he allowed himself to fully experience and relish in this new and exhilarating encounter. The sheer delight on his face was unmistakable, radiating such pleasure in this unforgettable moment.

As she began to take him into her mouth with newfound confidence, Abby skilfully employed techniques learned from Cosmopolitan's sex education, ensuring every movement was executed with precision and finesse. Her adept use of her tongue and hands elicited intense pleasure within Joey, driving him towards the brink of ecstasy with each tantalising stroke.

The growing tension in Joey's body intensified as he found himself unable to resist the urge to hold onto Abby's head firmly, his excitement building as he grew increasingly rigid within her warm embrace. The forceful thrusts at the back of her throat sent waves of pleasure coursing through him, while the sensation of her hands gripping him tightly only heightened his arousal.

With a final sigh of satisfaction, Joey succumbed to the wave of pleasure, unable to contain himself any longer. Despite his attempts to pull away, Abby maintained a firm grasp on his buttocks, eager to savour every last drop of his essence as it spilled onto her waiting tongue and dribbled down her chin.

Though her jaw ached from the intensity of their passion, Abby felt a sense of pride knowing she had rewarded Joey in the best possible way.

"Abby, that was amazing, it felt so good." With a smile, he gently lifted her off the floor and laid her back on the bed. "It's your turn now."

In response, Abby giggled as she stretched her legs a little, then quickly brought them back together, teasing Joey with a friendly smirk. "So, what do you think?" she asked with a wink.

Joey took a quick glance and then looked back at her, a cheeky grin growing on his face. "Yeah, definitely got my attention. I think it's pretty cool."

He bent down with a fluid and graceful movement, pressing his lips tenderly against hers. The sensation of his reawakening erection pressing against her stomach sent a rush of excitement through her. Cupping one of her breasts gently, he sucked it, eliciting gasps of pleasure from her. Her heart pounded with anticipation as he expertly licked and nibbled on each nipple, teasing without causing any discomfort. The building suspense caused her entire body to tense up in eager expectation.

With his deep moan resonating through the room, she widened her eyes as he arched her hips and descended towards her vulva. Using his tongue to flick over and suck her sensitive clit, he made her writhe and moan with delight. He guided her through an experience of unparalleled ecstasy during their first encounter. Matching the rhythm of his mouth with the movement of her hips, she gripped the bed frame for support and tilted her head back, releasing louder moans and gasps as he intensified his efforts. Unable to hold back any longer, she reached peak sexual arousal. Spreading open her wet folds with his fingers, he eagerly drank in her sweet juices as she cried out in long bursts of joy, experiencing powerful orgasms that left her breathless. Each shudder from her vulva captivated her completely, overwhelmed by this mind-blowing experience that left her begging for more.

As they lay together in their intimate cocoon, a whirlwind of emotions swirled between them. The air was filled with the lingering echoes of nervous laughter, flowing juices, and the comforting warmth of skin-on-skin contact that both exhilarated and soothed them. Joey's hand traced every curve of her body before finding its way to her vulva, giving it a gentle squeeze that elicited a soft, "Oh yes!"

Savouring their shared moment, they basked in the gentle afterglow of pleasure and the raw vulnerability of exposing their true selves to one another.

Gathering the condom he had prepared earlier from a nearby table, he casually discarded its packaging on the floor before rolling it onto his throbbing member. Clearing his throat nervously, he asked softly, "Are you ready?"

She nodded with a faint, nervous smile.

The room was permeated with not only the heady scent of passion, but also with the delicate fragrance of trust, vulnerability, and a silent promise of intimacy as Joey pressed his lips against hers. Their kiss lingered for a moment, his hand tenderly caressing her nipples before trailing down her neck to plant a soft kiss between her breasts. With both hands, he explored her exposed chest, moving from one perky nipple to the next. Her body quivered under his touch, yet she made no objection.

As he established a slow and steady rhythm, their amorous liaison transformed into an unforgettable experience brimming with fervent desire. Each deep thrust conveyed his insatiable longing for her. She welcomed him eagerly, emitting a soft cry, enjoying him between her legs, adjusting her hips to allow for further penetration in her most intimate region. Though she felt dwarfed by his size initially, any discomfort swiftly dissipated. His thrusts began leisurely and escalated in intensity and speed. Abby's hips shifted as she encircled his waist with her legs, meeting each forceful movement with equal fervour. He dove deeply inside her, stretching her innermost folds apart and eliciting cries from her with every motion. She felt every inch of him as he plunged deeply within.

With increased pace came louder moans from Abby while their kisses grew more heated. His hands roamed over every curve of her body, showcasing his insatiable desire for her. Their position shifted as she mounted him, relishing the firm pressure of his touch on her breasts. Each powerful thrust evoked moans and gasps from Abby as he relentlessly pounded into her. Grasping onto his waist tightly, she bounced up and down ardently, transforming moans into high-pitched screams while he groaned in unison. The mounting pressure culminated in desperate exclamations of ecstasy as she clung onto him tighter still, experiencing a shuddering climax that left her breathless with immense satisfaction. Her orgasm seemed never-ending as his movements intensified further, supporting her weight as they approached the climactic pinnacle where his member delved deeply in her core, resulting in a prolonged groan of release. The pulsating warmth of his member throbbed within the confines of the condom, delivering indescribable pleasure to them both.

Exhausted beyond measure, Abby could no longer remain upright and collapsed beside Joey on the bed as their breaths gradually returned to a steady cadence. Shortly thereafter, he rose from the bed to dispose of the used condom wrapped in toilet paper before collapsing back onto the mattress beside her.

The room basked in the gentle glow of sunlight streaming through the window, casting a serene ambiance over the rumpled sheets and lingering echoes of their intimate rendezvous—a whispered testament to their second encounter filled with shared passion and uninhibited desire. He wrapped his arms around her shoulders and pulled her closer to him.

"Abby," he whispered.

"Yes?"

"Do you love me?"

Without hesitation, she replied, "Of course, I do silly."

The declaration brought a sense of relief to him. "Good, because I love you, too, and I want you to stay with me forever, understand?"

Abby's smile widened. "I'm okay with that."

With a tender gesture, he lifted her chin and initiated a passionate kiss before they settled into each other's embrace. As the moments passed by in content silence, Joey's stomach grumbled, breaking the tranquillity. Recalling the snacks she had packed earlier, she hesitated to leave behind the comforting warmth of their bed.

Feeling self-conscious about exposing herself by getting up, Abby attempted to cover herself with the blanket, only for Joey to playfully remove it.

"For real Abs, you're beautiful just the way you are!"

He drew her close for a passionate kiss, overpowering her with his hand on her buttocks. Eventually breaking away from their passionate exchange, Joey sat back, admiring Abby's nudity. Taking charge of the situation now, she gathered her belongings and clothes from the floor while urging him to join her.

"Wait a sec before you grab your clothes," he teased, a playful glint in his eye.

Abby raised an eyebrow, smiling. "Oh, are you thinking we should have another go at it?" she giggled.

"Absolutely!" he said with a cheeky grin. "Wanna hop in the shower with me?"

"Sure thing," she giggled. "But remember, just showering! We're out of condoms, and my hair's got to stay dry."

In a swift motion that lasted less than two seconds, she relinquished her grasp on her bag and hastened towards him in a state of undress.

He pressed her firmly against the bathroom door, prompting her to rise on her toes to reach his awaiting lips with hers.

Just as she had settled into this new position, he unexpectedly swept her off her feet, causing laughter to echo throughout the room.

With a skilful hand, he adjusted both the hot and cold taps before pinning her against the shower wall.

She elegantly brushed aside a strand of hair as lukewarm water cascaded between her breasts.

Standing beneath the cascading water alongside him, she felt the warmth of his bare skin against her chest, feeling their erect nipples making contact.

Leaning in closely, he tenderly kissed her parted lips, exploring her mouth with his tongue. The rhythm of his heartbeat pulsed against her as he cupped one of her breasts and sucked greedily on its sensitive nipple. A wave of heat surged through her core, eliciting a soft moan from deep within as pleasure washed over her.

His warm breath teasingly caressed her earlobe as he whispered, "Abby, I want you."

Lost in the moment, she found herself grinding against him instinctively while revelling in his tender kisses along her throat and the tantalising flicks of his tongue across her aroused nipple. Her desire burned fiercely within as she eagerly met his advances without reservation.

Instead, she shifted her position to meet his member, clenching his shoulder.

He held her firmly by the waist and thrust deep into her vulva with force as the water rained down on them.

She moaned into his kiss, her hips entwined with his, making her insides clench with soft howling sounds.

As their bodies pulsated in a rush of pleasure, he took her mouth in his, driving her to sexual oblivion. She gasped and moaned helplessly "Joey, oh wow." Her nails dug into his back. Their connection intensified with each thrust and kiss until they reached an explosive climax that left them both physically spent but emotionally fulfilled.

However, as Abby gazed up at him with a changed expression, a sense of unease crept into her mind.

"Hey, what's up?" Joey asked, trying to keep it chill but really curious.

"It's nothing," she mumbled, playing a game of hide and seek with her bra around the room.

"Come on, spill it," Joey prodded gently, trying to catch her eye.

As Abby continued her quest for her clothes, she blurted out, "I think we messed up".

Joey's eyebrows shot up in surprise. "Really? You think so?" He lightly placed his hands on her waist and gently turned her to face him, their eyes locking.

Abby hesitated, a hint of worry in her voice. "Why did you, um... you know? What if something happens?"

Joey flashed a comforting smile. "Hey, don't stress, you're not going to get pregnant."

Abby stayed quiet, her teeth softly nibbling at her lower lip, as her eyes drifted around the room.

"Trust me, you're not gonna get pregnant," Joey said with a playful grin, glancing at his watch. "But hey, we should really get moving. We gotta get ready and catch the bus if we wanna be home by 5:00 pm, remember?"

With lingering doubts nagging at the back of Abby's mind, she nodded and took a deep breath before getting dressed. Dismissing all negative thoughts threatening to destroy her happiness following what had been an enchanting day with the love of her life proved challenging but necessary for Abby's peace of mind.

CHAPTER 10

The next morning, Abby found herself waking in a bad mood, feeling exhausted. To her surprise, after glancing at the clock, it was only 10 o'clock in the morning and yet the room remained shrouded in darkness due to the closed curtains, with only slivers of sunlight filtering through the gap. The cheerful chirping of birds outside her window served as a stark contrast to the emotions swirling in her mind. Lost in thought, she absentmindedly twirled a strand of her hair around her fingers, thinking about what had transpired with Joey at the hotel yesterday. As she lay buried under the covers, she couldn't help but feel a pang of regret as she reflected on how foolishly she has acted.

With a heavy head, she struggled out of bed and slowly made her way to the bathroom. The warm water from the shower revived her senses, and as she returned to her room, she thought about taking a pregnancy test. In a rush of panic, she hastily grabbed an oversized t-shirt and slacks. Having gossiped about Mrs. Giuseppe's daughter, Maryanna, and her scandalous affair with Roberto, the mechanic from down the street, and now fearing she also might be pregnant, she wondered if karma had played its cruel hand. Descending the stairs, the tempting aroma of freshly brewed coffee greeted her as she entered the kitchen. A sudden spell of nausea turned her complexion pale.

"Are you okay, Abby? You look unwell."

"I'm fine, Mama."

Abby watched her mother busy herself with breakfast preparations, too weak to help.

At the dining table, she tried to eat but was unable to stomach anything. Placing her hands on her belly, she looked up at her mother and said, "I can't eat this, Mama. I feel sick. I think I need to lie down."

"I thought as much," she said, wearing a concerned expression on her face. "What's wrong? Something you ate?"

Abby shrugged. "I think I may be coming down with a cold or something." The fatigue and pain in her stomach made her writhe.

"Okay, let's get you back to bed. I'll run to the pharmacy and grab something for your stomach cramps."

As they climbed the stairs, her mother draped her arm around Abby's shoulders. As she lay there, fear gripped her heart as thoughts she might be pregnant flooded her mind once more. Memories of unprotected sex with Joey on the beach and in the hotel haunted her, fuelling her anxiety.

Later that afternoon, she realised she had a social gathering and wouldn't be able to attend, adding to her frustration. She forced herself out of bed and reached for her computer. Messaging Vani and Joey on MSN, she explained why she wouldn't be coming.

"Mum, are you here?" she called out before checking every room in the house. There was no response. Anxiously, she hurried downstairs and entered the living room. Picking up the landline, she dialled Joey's mobile phone. As he answered, she whispered softly and urgently into the receiver, "Joey, it's Abby. I sent you a message on MSN."

Her initial excitement bubbled into a cauldron of fear as the unmistakable sound of her mother's car revved in the stillness of the driveway. Panic seized her heart, prompting her to hastily end the call and scurry back up the stairs. Upon reaching her room, she swiftly closed the door and snuggled beneath her covers. The only sound breaking the oppressive silence was the muffled thud of a car door shutting, echoing in sync with the frantic rhythm of her own pounding heart.

After what felt like an age, Abby's mother finally entered the room holding a bowl of steaming soup and some medication procured from a nearby pharmacy.

Reluctantly taking an assortment of pills, Abby soon became dizzy and fatigued, eventually drifting off into a fitful sleep. In her dreams, she was transported to a tranquil beach where the gentle waves lapped the shore, painting a serene tableau before her mind's eye.

As evening descended upon the household, voices resonated from downstairs, their tones carrying through the air with unmistakable clarity. Recognising her mother's voice within the cacophony of other sharp voices and laughter, Abby roused herself from bed and made her way to the bathroom for a shower. Emerging revitalised from her ablutions, she settled on the edge of her bed to dress before padding down the stairs barefoot.

Standing poised in the centre of the living room, Abby eavesdropped on the animated conversation unfolding between her mother and the Giovanni family. Steeling herself with forced cheerfulness, she ventured into the kitchen in search of Joey, but he wasn't there.

Seating herself at one end of the table opposite Mr. Giovanni, Abby blushed coyly when he complimented her freshly washed hair before tucking her long fringe behind her ears and eating.

Before the first forkful could meet her lips, Abby glanced up from her plate and caught Mrs. Giovanni's penetrating gaze. "My darling, you look pale; are you okay?" Before Abby could respond, two deep voices called out, "Hello." Micky and Joey were standing in the doorway.

"Are you helping your mother at the store these days?" Mrs. Giovanni asked, causing Abby's stomach to knot tightly beneath the layers of anxiety threatening to spill over.

"No," Abby replied, feeling small under all the watchful eyes. "I'm just enjoying summer break for now."

"She will be," her mother interjected firmly, glancing across at Abby, who wilted without uttering protest or defiance. "From next week onwards, you will work five hours daily at the store without negotiation."

This decree weighed heavily on Abby's fragile heart as it signified less time spent with Joey, whose presence felt more vital than ever.

Feeling utterly drained and exhausted, Abby voiced her frustrations to her mother with a tone of desperation. "Mum, that's just not fair! I deserve to enjoy my summer with my friends. Please, I beg of you, do not force me to do this."

Mrs. Giovanni discreetly observed the interaction from the corner of her eye, listening intently but choosing to remain silent.

In response to Abby's plea for some freedom, her mother calmly asserted, "You can still enjoy your summer after completing your shift at the store."

Leaning forward and resting her elbows on the table, Abby said, "I'll work three hours at the store."

Mr. Giovanni turned to Gabriella. "Let the child enjoy her summer before college," he said with a smile. "Look at that adorable face. How could you say no to her?"

Mr. Giovanni was a short man with long, black hair and a smattering of facial growth. His comforting eyes made it difficult to refuse him. There was something special about him; he had a way with words, and his charming manner helped him get his way. Eventually surrendering to Mr. Giovanni's influence, Abby's mother nodded. "Very well."

Abby expressed her gratitude to Mr. Giovanni through a radiant smile as she felt his support. In return, he winked at her knowingly, conveying his understanding of the struggles faced by youth in such situations.

Later excusing herself from the dining area, Abby hurried up the stairs towards the bathroom where she knelt before the toilet and threw up her lasagna. She stood shakily, leaning against the wash basin for support before splashing cold water on her face and brushing her teeth.

Returning downstairs feeling unsettled yet composed enough to settle onto the sofa in the living room, Abby was taken aback by Joey's presence with concern etched across his features. "Are you okay?" he asked softly.

Meeting his gaze, she replied sombrely, "No, I feel terrible, but I will live."

Joey scanned their surroundings cautiously before kissing Abby's forehead and gently caressing her hair. "I love you, Abby."

She reciprocated with equal affection, saying, "Awe, baby, I love you too" and holding his gaze with a smile. Their intimate moment was abruptly interrupted when Micky barged into the room. "Hey, love birds, the parents are on their way."

Joey's expression shifted momentarily, displaying shock and uncertainty.

"Babe, relax, Micky is on our side, he won't tell a soul," said Abby.

Exchanging glances, he gazed up at Micky, who said, "Your secret is safe with me, but if you hurt my sister, you're dead!"

The evening unfolded with a series of unexpected events that left Abby in a state of constant amazement. It all began when she was given her first mobile phone, a thoughtful gesture to commemorate her achievement of being awarded a scholarship at the prestigious Yale Law School. Overwhelmed with gratitude for this generous gift, Abby's heart swelled with joy, despite feeling under the weather. Unable to contain her elation, she enveloped her parents in a tight embrace, their love and support providing her with an added sense of comfort.

As twilight set in, Abby settled into the cosy confines of her bed and powered up her new phone. With unwavering determination, she quickly composed messages to her boyfriend and closest friends, Vani, and Nick, eager to share her excitement with them.

As the clock struck 11:00 pm, Abby made the decision to initiate a call to Joey. Nestled snugly beneath the warm covers, they engaged in lively conversation for hours, discussing trivial matters that brought them laughter until they were both too exhausted to talk.

CHAPTER 11

The following morning, Abby awoke with dizziness and nausea. It was in this moment she realised her period was two weeks late. Waves of disbelief crashed over her as she hastily made her way to her desk, hands shaking as she fumbled to unlock the first drawer and retrieve her diary.

Frantically flipping through the pages, her heart rate skyrocketed when she stumbled upon her last entry regarding her period, which had occurred precisely five weeks prior. Her breathing grew laboured, and her knees gave out beneath her, causing her to collapse to the floor. Placing a trembling hand against her throat, she swallowed nervously. Eyes shut tightly, she drew in a deep breath as scary thoughts swirled through her mind.

How had she found herself in such a predicament? Running her fingers through her hair, she tentatively rested a hand on her stomach and whispered, "Oh no...." Tears welled up in her eyes as she gazed at herself in the full-length mirror, filled with shame.

Doubts crept into Abby's mind as she questioned whether God was punishing her for engaging in intimate relations with Joey. Now faced with bearing the consequences of those actions alone, she stared at her isolated, ashamed, flawed, vulnerable reflection. Her heart pounded furiously while tears flooded from her eyes.

Abruptly brought back to reality by the sound of voices echoing in the hallway from outside her room, Abby sprang up from the floor and hastily wiped away her tears before composing herself. Summoning all her available strength, Abby opened the bedroom door and descended the stairs towards the commotion. The front door stood slightly ajar as Luciana, a friend of Abby's mother, entered their home unannounced. "Hello beautiful, how are you?" asked Luciana.

Putting on a brave face despite her troubles, Abby returned Luciana's greeting with a kiss. "Hello, Mrs. Rucci. I am well, thank you. How are you?"

"I'm doing well, darling, but it's so hot today," she said, fanning herself with her hand. "The breeze feels like an oven."

"Abby, please go upstairs and turn on the air conditioning," said her mother as they entered the kitchen.

Abby ascended the stairs to activate the cooling system before grabbing her handbag and rejoining her mother in the kitchen, only to have her appearance scrutinised. "What's wrong, Abby?"

"Nothing, Mama, I'm fine. I didn't sleep well last night and woke up with a pounding headache." She nervously adjusted her hair, hoping to divert attention away from any deeper issues she wasn't yet ready to discuss.

"Make sure to take some Panadol. And where are you going today?"

Abby didn't want to answer any more of her mother's questions, fearing she had detected the nervousness in her voice as she picked up her spoon to eat her cereal. "Mama, I'm spending the day with Vani and some other girls from school at Playland Park."

"Okay, make sure you're home by six," her mother said while Mrs Rucci gave a flashing grin that hinted at a deeper understanding than Abby was comfortable with.

Abby hurriedly finished her breakfast and bid farewell to her mother and Mrs Rucci.

Walking towards the bus stop under a cloudless sky, she attempted to call Vani but without success. Left only with a cryptic text message from Vani that suggested meeting at some obscure spot near Wendy's Donuts, Abby caught the next bus.

The slow journey into town was conducive to reflection on her choices and the many uncertainties on her mind. Frustrated by both traffic delays and her overactive mind, she remained silent during the journey as she thought about taking a pregnancy test.

The bus driver announced their next stop: "Queens Mall."

The looming possibility of an unplanned pregnancy had Abby worried as to how such shocking news would impact both her and her family.

Disembarking from the bus with a sense of urgency, Abby made her way down the path towards the shopping centre. Her heart raced as she searched for Vani near Wendy's donut shop. A chuckle escaped her lips upon seeing Vani devouring cream-filled donuts, her face smeared with icing. Despite her messy appearance, Vani greeted Abagail with a bag of donuts and a hug.

"Morning," mumbled Vani with a mouthful of donut, offering the bag to Abby.

"Thanks," said Abby with a half-hearted smile as she accepted them.

"What's up, you sounded really nervous on the phone," asked Vani with furrowed brows. "And why are we meeting here? Joey and Krish are waiting for us at the entrance at eleven, remember?"

Tears welled up in Abby's eyes as she shook her head in response to Vani's question.

"Abby, what's going on, talk to me!"

Abby gazed at Vani but remained silent. The concern on Vani's face only seemed to intensify Abby's emotional fragility.

She released a sharp breath. "I really messed up, I don't know what to do, I am terrified." Her voice quivered, drawing curious glances from passersby.

Vani pressed for more information, but this only caused Abby to cry harder.

Vani pleaded with Abby to stop crying and explain what was going on. After taking a deep breath to calm herself down, Abby glanced up at Vani and quietly muttered " I think I may be pregnant."

"Oh my God, Abby," Vani said, raising her hand to her mouth. "Why didn't you use protection?"

Abby tried to speak, but no words came out. Instead, she rested her head against her friend's shoulder.

Vani gently patted Abby's back while assuring her everything would be alright, silently cursing Joey under her breath for putting Abby in such a difficult situation.

Twenty minutes later, they arrived at the pharmacy, where Abby timidly approached the counter. "I need a pregnancy test please," she said softly.

Vani, clutching Abby's waist tightly for emotional support, exchanged a knowing glance with her as they made their way into the women's restroom inside the department store.

"Abby, I will be right here waiting for you," said Vani. "You can do this."

Abby nodded and proceeded towards one of the bathroom stalls. With a sense of apprehension, Abby closed the door and unzipped her pants. Squatting above the toilet, she held the thick plastic stick and urinated slowly, closing her eyes in silent prayer.

"Lord, please spare me from being pregnant," she whispered as she awaited the results. After five agonising minutes, Abby emerged from the cubicle holding the pregnancy test up to the light. Two distinct pink lines appeared on the test, confirming her biggest fears. She collapsed to the bathroom floor, coming to terms with the fact she was indeed pregnant.

Vani sat beside her.

"Why is this happening to me?" Abby cried out in anguish as tears streamed down her face. "I don't want this." She wasn't ready to be a mother; she had worked so hard at school so she could start her career on the right foot.

She opened her eyes and looked at the pregnancy test again, hoping it wasn't true, that she had misread the lines. They remained, reminding her of her failure to protect her family's honour and reputation. What a nightmare! She looked up at Vani for answers.

Vani just stared back, her eyes filled with sadness. She opened her mouth to speak, but no words came out.

As they sat on the bathroom floor crying, time seemed to slip away unnoticed. Abby's gentle sobs were interrupted by heavy footsteps approaching from inside the bathroom. Their attention turned to an elderly woman with grey hair and a long-pointed nose who stared down at Abby with disdain as she rounded them.

In a hurry, they stood and quickly left the bathroom but were stopped when the old woman grabbed Abby's arm.

"Lady, let go of her!" Vani barked but was ignored as the old woman leaned in close and whispered into Abby's ear, "For everything you gain, you will lose something."

The cryptic words echoed in Abby's ears as they hastily fled the bathroom, leaving the mysterious, old woman, who watched them scuttle off with an eerie smile.

In the hallway outside the restroom, curiosity compelled Abby to steal one last glance back at the enigmatic figure. In those piercing, olive eyes that bore into hers with unwavering intensity lay a chilling prophecy that sent shivers down Abby's spine; she was facing a future fraught with uncertainty and sacrifice.

CHAPTER 12

Abby found herself in a precarious situation, with less than thirty minutes to summon the courage needed to disclose her pregnancy to Joey. Little did she know this pivotal conversation would take place at a bus stop on the infamous 42nd Street. As fate would have it, Joey was sitting under the bus shelter alongside Krish, a trusted friend who shared his many common interests.

When he spotted Abby getting off the bus, he eagerly approached her with a bright smile. "Good morning, beautiful." He gave her a long kiss, but Abby withdrew from his embrace and uttered, "Joey, we need to talk."

"What's wrong, babe?" asked Joey, confusion overriding the big smile that had greeted her.

Tears cascaded down Abby's cheeks before she said, "I'm pregnant."

Joey was left momentarily stunned into silence, staring into Abby's eyes for several seconds. "What? Seriously?"

"Yes."

"You're lying, right?"

"Joey, why would I lie about something as serious as this?"

Vani and Krish stood by helplessly as emotions ran high between Abby and Joey.

"Seriously, what the actual hell, Abby!" he barked. "There's no way this can be happening." He laughed incredulously, shaking his head in disbelief. "You're joking, right? Is this some kind of prank? Krish, are you in on this?"

Krish shook his head. "No, man, I had no clue about this either. I'm sorry, bro."

"Joey, please look at me," Abby said.

Joey glanced up.

"I'm expecting a baby." She took out a pregnancy test from her bag and gave it to him. "See for yourself."

Joey's shoulders sagged when he noticed the two lines on the test, which he tossed into the air in anger and disbelief. "No, this can't be right!" He paced back and forth at the bus stop while Abby and Krish attempted to assuage his distress.

"Just leave me alone!" he yelled, pushing them away.

"I'm sorry, Joey."

Vani tried to comfort Abby, who placed a hand on her stomach and took deep breaths.

Coming face to face with Abby once more, Joey's emotions erupted like a volcano. Rage and confusion danced in his eyes as he turned towards her, the intensity of his gaze piercing through her. A long pause hung between them as Joey's eyes fell upon Abby's stomach. "I don't want to be a dad, Abby," he stated. "I have big plans for my future, and fatherhood does not fit into my plans."

Abby met his gaze with a mixture of sorrow and defiance. "Do you really think I planned for this, Joey? It's not my fault!"

"Then whose fault is it, Abby? Let me guess, mine, right?"

A heavy silence enveloped them as Abby struggled to find the right words.

Joey turned away with a resigned sigh, his disappointment palpable.

Abby took a deep breath, feeling her insides twist into knots. Gasping, she fell to her knees.

"Oh my God, Abby!" Vani shrieked as she hurried to her side. "Are you alright?"

"I'm okay... just not feeling well." She folded her arms over her stomach.

Joey shifted his attention towards Abby and stood, glaring down at her in silence. In that moment, Abby realised he didn't care about her. She opened her mouth to speak, but Joey raised his hand to stop her.

"Abby," he muttered, "I don't want it." He pointed to her belly. "If you decide to have this child, you're only thinking of yourself."

The impact of his words rendered her utterly speechless, leaving her in a state of shock and disbelief. Just when she thought she had unravelled everything to know about him, he revealed a side that was foreign and unrecognisable. A weight that seemed to crush Abby's spirit. Joey's once familiar and comforting presence now felt like a stranger, his words cutting deep into her heart like a sharp knife. She wondered how someone she had known so intimately could become so cold and detached. She felt her heart shatter into a million pieces as the reality of their relationship ending sunk in. His distant demeanour made her feel isolated and abandoned while his anger and coldness towards her terrified her to her core.

"It's over between us," he said, his voice flat and expressionless. "I can't deal with this. It's best for both of us to split up, and I really don't want to have a baby. You need to get an abortion."

His cowardly declaration saddened Abby, who looked at him with pleading eyes, feeling helpless and shaking. Her voice trembled as she spoke. "Please don't do this! You love me, and we love each other! Why are you causing me such pain?"

Acting on pure instinct, she hurried towards him and grasped his shirt as tears streamed down her cheeks. "Don't leave me! Please!"

Her face was drained of colour as she stared at him intently, but he remained silent.

Tears flowed down her cheeks as she kept her eyes fixed on him, yet he uttered no words. "Joey, I need you!" she whispered. "I love you! I cannot do this without you! Why are you hurting me like this?"

But Joey remained stoic, maintaining eye contact with Abby as he delivered the crushing blow. "No, Abby!" he said firmly. "We can no longer be together." His words cut through the air like a sharp knife, leaving Abby feeling utterly devastated.

At that moment, a bus pulled into the station with a loud screech of brakes; however, neither of them boarded it. Vani and Krish also opted to remain and relocated to the now free seats of the bus shelter.

Abby desperately implored Joey to cease causing her pain, shouting for him to step up and take accountability, to embody the ideal man she required him to be, and salvage their relationship rather than cowardly walking away. Despite her pleas, he distanced himself from her, triggering panic within her that caused her to collapse to her knees.

"Get up, Abby!" he shouted.

Vani swiftly approached and calmly encouraged Abby to compose herself and breathe deeply. The constriction in Abby's chest signalled a panic attack, yet she couldn't bear the idea of being abandoned. "No, no, this cannot be happening! How can you cause me so much pain?"

Her heart felt as though it might burst from her chest at any given moment. She turned her sorrowful gaze towards Joey in search of comfort, which he failed to provide. He remained silent, observing her intently with menacing eyes before gathering his belongings and slinging his bag over his shoulder. "Abby, I'm sorry, but I am finished here!"

She couldn't restrain herself and her scream tore through the bus shelter, startling those around her.

Joey attempted to calm her by grasping her wrists but was met with resistance as she cried out in protest: "Don't touch me!" She then begged him not to leave and promised they could overcome their predicament together, opting for an abortion if necessary.

However, Joey remained silent and unyielding despite Abby's pleas.

The more she pleaded, the angrier he became. When Joey refused to speak, she cried out, "Please, don't leave me! I promise we can deal with this problem! I'll have an abortion. Joey, please say something! You can't abandon me; we made a promise."

He maintained eye contact with her for a few more seconds before letting go of her wrists and stepping back.

She had never experienced such intense loneliness, rejection, and abandonment in her entire life. Abby loved Joey more than anything, but now she questioned if she truly understood him at all.

"I'm out of my depth here, Abby. I know you are scared; I am too, but I can't commit to this child or you right now. I am suffering, too. I'm angry with myself, angry at you, and I'm angry at God. I need to get away, clear my thoughts and focus on myself." He pointed at her stomach with a look devoid of emotion or empathy. "I am sorry, but this is not my future. I am not responsible for this child, Abby, you need to get an abortion. So please leave me alone, do not call or message me. Have the abortion, focus on your career, and we will see where things go in the future."

As reality dawned upon Abby in all its harshness and brutality, she watched helplessly as Joey walked away without looking back.

She had no idea how much time she spent on the wet ground, hunched over in the rain. As she struggled to pull herself from the ground, slipping on the pavement in the process, she realised she had no choice but to face the future alone. She had entrusted a nineteen-year-old man who had disregarded their relationship in a heartbeat. From that moment onwards, she swore off love completely.

* * *

Joey came to a profound realisation as he contemplated the daunting challenges that awaited him if he were to remain by Abby's side. The weight of the decisions ahead of him loomed large, from confessing their concealed relationship to his unsuspecting parents to bearing the repercussions of his actions and ultimately finding the courage to embrace impending fatherhood. However, he realised he was incapable of fulfilling these requirements.

As he made the difficult choice to walk away, a sense of peace enveloped him, albeit tinged with an ache in his chest. Though his emotions seemed dulled by detachment, deep within himself he understood that prioritising Abby's well-being necessitated this painful separation. Tears brimmed in his eyes as he murmured a heartfelt apology to her, struggling to contain his sorrow.

With a heavy heart and a mind consumed by confusion and conflicting emotions, Joey headed home.

CHAPTER 13

The room was illuminated by a gentle, soft glow emanating from the bedside lamp, casting a serene ambiance that enveloped Abby as she sat on the edge of her bed. The events of the afternoon lingered in the air like a dense fog. How would she muster the courage to divulge her pregnancy to her parents? How could she have succumbed to such a grave sin, betraying not only her family but also her faith. The guilt and shame bore down on her conscience like an unbearable burden, threatening to suffocate her. In a moment of overwhelming despair, Abby let out a gut-wrenching scream into her pillow. After what seemed like an eternity of anguish, she finally found the strength to compose herself and emerge from her bedroom.

Standing at the precipice of the stairs leading down to the living room where her parents awaited her presence, Abby hesitated, grappling with the decision of whether to come clean about her pregnancy.

Entering the living room with trepidation, she found her mother and father seated solemnly in anticipation. Suppressing her tears and mustering all her courage, she looked at her parents and uttered in a sheepish whisper, "Mum, Dad... there's something I need to tell you."

Her father's brow furrowed. "What is it, Abby?"

At first, words failed to escape Abby's trembling lips as fear held firm grasp over her voice.

"S-something's wrong," she began after a prolonged silence. Finally summoning all her resolve, she said, "I'm pregnant."

The confession hung heavily in the air as silence reigned for a brief moment before being shattered by her mother's piercing voice. "You're what?"

Abby repeated softly once more through quivering lips, "I'm... I'm pregnant."

Abby found herself in a state of distress as her mother loomed over her with an air of panic, her voice raised in a frenzied tone demanding answers. "How did this happen? When did this happen? And who is the father?"

The sheer intensity of her mother's inquiries caused Abby to let out a piercing scream, her emotions getting the best of her as tears streamed down her face uncontrollably.

It took a few moments for her father to fully comprehend the gravity of the situation. He slowly rose from his seat. Approaching Abby, he delivered a resounding slap across her face that sent shockwaves reverberating through every nerve ending and called her every name under the sun. As the pain radiated across her cheekbone, he unleashed a barrage of accusations and reproaches that cut deep into Abby's wounded soul.

Her mother collapsed heavily to the floor clutching her chest while uttering anguished cries that pierced through the heavy atmosphere.

Abby sank to her knees and tried to console her mother, but she pulled away. Consumed by guilt and shame for causing such immense pain to her parents, Abby lacked the courage to meet her father's gaze directly.

"I am sorry, please forgive me, Mama!"

Her mother continued to weep and ignored Abby, muttering, "My daughter is carrying a child out of wedlock." It was heart-wrenching to witness her parents endure such suffering; she felt like an awful daughter for causing them immense pain.

Looking up through her tears at her father, who sat on the couch with his face buried in his hands, silently sobbing, she stumbled away from the sofa and knelt at his feet. He also recoiled from her touch.

After some time, her father looked up, wiping his tears with the handkerchief he kept in his pocket. "Gabby, take her to a gynaecologist to confirm this pregnancy, but don't speak of this to the family."

In a gentle tone, Gabriela nodded and softly replied, "Yes."

Her father locked Abby in his angry stare. "Abagail, who is this boy?"

"It doesn't matter, Papa, he doesn't want anything to do with me and the baby."

His sudden outburst made the girls flinch as he slammed his hand on the table. "Abagail, who is the father?"

"Dad, I beg of you, please stop asking about the father of this child. He is no longer important to me; I will have an abortion."

At this moment, her father became even more furious. His eyes were dark and tired, giving him a worn-out and fierce look. His voice was so loud and deep it would make anyone uncomfortable.

Abby had never witnessed this side of her father before. She watched as he rose from his chair and struck her across the face once again.

Her mother attempted to intervene, but he was much stronger than her and easily brushed her off.

"You have no right to request an abortion! Let me make myself perfectly clear... terminating this pregnancy is not an option under my roof."

His voice resonated with such forceful authority that it left no room for argument or dissent as he vehemently opposed any suggestion of abortion as a viable solution. "Abby, do you understand, abortion is out of the question. I will not allow my daughter to end the life of an innocent child. It contradicts our principles and what God wants, do you understand me?"

Abby nodded ever so slightly, confirming her understanding as her tears streamed down her face unabatedly.

"Having an abortion is morally unacceptable and considered a sin, an act of taking away an innocent life. If you were a practicing Catholic, you would not have brought this disgrace upon yourself and your family, by adopting the views of a non-believer."

Her mother's voice cut through the silence, drenched in judgment. "Because of your disgraceful choices, I will carry this shame with me to my grave."

It became clear to Abby that she had no chance of winning this battle; in fact, she had lost their respect and trust completely. Her father proceeded to lecture her about the importance of respect, honour, and family traditions. He emphasised she had jeopardised their family, culture, and values through her sinful actions. The situation escalated further when Abby's parents decided to involve her brother Micky in the conversation, seeking his support in condemning Abby's actions. His reaction mirrored that of his parents: anger and disappointment towards his sister for deviating from the expectations set by their shared upbringing.

Bearing the heavy burden of her family's disapproval, Abby felt crushed under the weight of their judgment, her spirit shattered. The emotional turmoil left her defenseless, unable to muster any resistance against their relentless criticism. Inside, a storm of anger brewed, not just at her family's harsh words, but at herself for not being able to stand up against them. Resigned and broken, she internalised their accusations, surrendering to the belief that their harsh assessment of her was justified. Her mother twisted the knife deeper, declaring with palpable contempt again "Your disgraceful actions will haunt me with shame for the rest of my life."

Abby's father once again put her under the microscope. "Abagail, this is your last warning," he said in a stern tone. "Who is the father?"

Abby knew she had to be honest with him. Joey was reluctant to involve his own parents in the matter. She had envisioned sharing the news of their pregnancy together, presenting a united front as a couple to their families. However, Joey's sudden abandonment had left her unsure of how to proceed.

With tears welling up and emotion heavy in her voice, Abby took a deep breath, embracing the vulnerability of honesty. "I've been secretly seeing Joey Giovanni for two years now." Her words hung in the air for a moment as she gathered the strength to go on.

"He doesn't want this baby. He's in favour of me having an abortion because he's not ready to be a father and wants to concentrate on his career. He said we should go our separate ways." Her heart felt both bare and weighted, caught in the melancholy of love and loss.

Her mama's expression was a mixture of sadness, tenderness, and shame while her father's countenance was clouded with anger. It was a terrifying sight as he exuded a darkness that could instil fear in anyone.

He kept repeating the name, "Joey Giovanni," and Abby confirmed it by nodding.

In a sudden outburst of rage, her father leapt from his seat and bolted towards the front door, seizing a baseball bat along the way. Gabriella intervened just in time, positioning herself between him and the exit while using her authority to halt his impulsive actions.

"Adriano... STOP!" she said, holding onto his wrist.

Abby begged her father not to harm Joey and promised to comply with whatever course of action they deemed fit.

Together, Abby and her mother managed to steer him back towards the living room. Gabriella refused to release him until he relinquished the baseball bat and returned to his seat.

"Adriano, listen," she said. "I have a plan, and if you don't like it, then we will go and see Angela and Frank together to discuss the matter rationally."

Reluctantly, her father placed the baseball bat back where it belonged before returning to the living room. Abby could see her parents were suffering greatly, but there was little she could do except hope her Mama's plan held the best possible solution.

CHAPTER 14

Abby found herself reeling after all the raised voices, accusatory glances, and harsh words thrown around like daggers. But now, in the aftermath, a heavy silence hung in the air.

Abby's mother sat quietly, her gaze fixed on her coffee cup. Breaking the silence, she said, "Abagail will be sent to the Missionary Sisters of Christ in Roma, where she will remain until the child is born, and will continue her studies at the University of Roma and obtain a bachelor's degree in law."

She paused, then continued. "Abby and the child will reside with my close friend Maria Bianchi."

"Maria?" Adriano uttered, his eyebrows raised.

Maria was in her early sixties and had recently become a childless widow. She had gained fame as an esteemed artist for her mesmerising paintings of enlarged flowers. Even though she never remarried, she took on the role of raising her nephew after her brother's death until he eventually left to study overseas. Maria and

Abby's mother had grown up together in the same village, formed an exceptionally strong connection, and became the closest of friends. Despite living separate lives, they had maintained a strong bond through letters and cherished memories from their childhood together.

Abby's mother reiterated that Maria would be responsible for taking care of the child until she turned five, at which point Abby and the child would return to live with them in the States. They intended to inform the community that the child, who had tragically lost her parents, was a daughter of a distant relative and now under their care as though their own.

"Adriano, I feel it's best if Angela and Frank don't find out about this pregnancy. I know that within our Italian community, some might still see Abagail as a symbol of virtue, but in truth, she has lost her way, both to us and to God. It breaks my heart to think of the judgment she'd face, not just from others, but the one she might feel herself."

Abby was consumed by a deep, confusing storm of emotions, ensnared by a fear that paralysed her and a longing that weighed heavily on her soul. She was lost in a predicament she had never imagined, a haunting realization tearing at her heart—she did not want this child. Yet, warmth lingered within her for Joey, with no resentment or blame towards him for their tangled situation. Instead, she carried the heavy burden of responsibility beside him, feeling the sting of her own naivety. She had believed conception would be a long journey, unprepared for how quickly and profoundly her world had shifted.

Her father, though, demanded justice. "The coward must be held accountable for his mistake."

She sighed, feeling a deep, restless ache in her chest. "I know, darling. I understand your urge for justice, but I'm worried about Angela. She's always eager to gossip, and if this gets out... it could turn into a wildfire. Abby's future and her chances for a decent marriage could be endangered. Our businesses might suffer, too. What kind of parents would that make us in the eyes of the community?"

Sensing her husband's discomfort, she reached for his hand, her voice gentle but edged with despair. "We're trapped, aren't we? No clear path seems safe or right."

Abby's father frowned and shook his head initially but eventually relented under Gabriella's persuasion, slowly nodding his head.

Abby was overwhelmed with a profound sense of sorrow that burdened her already anxious heart. Her parents were making life-altering decisions on her behalf as if she were not present, determining a path forward without her input. Feeling ill-equipped to assume the role of a parent and lacking the means to provide for this unborn child, thoughts of motherhood or marriage had never crossed her mind; they seemed activities reserved solely for adults. The notion of being sent away to some monastery in Italy to carry out this pregnancy while continuing her legal studies felt surreal.

The shame, isolation, guilt, and disappointment that had momentarily subsided now flooded back into Abby's heart like a tidal wave of emotions as she considered the fate awaiting this innocent child who would grow up without knowing its father.

Abby reluctantly succumbed to the intense pressure from her parents. They believed if she had sinned once, she would likely sin again and that she wasn't mature enough to make decisions on her own. Despite legally being an adult, she couldn't argue against their reasoning.

Suddenly nauseous, she rushed to the bathroom, where she collapsed to the floor and vomited. Her mother followed her and held her hair back, comforting her by patting her on the back and assuring her everything would be alright, before handing her a cloth. Shortly after, she returned to the living room.

"Abagail," her father uttered, and she gazed into his sad eyes, unable to hold contact for more than a few seconds. "You will depart for Italy on the upcoming Friday," he announced.

Despite her deep yearning to challenge their values, she understood that further defiance would only deepen her parents' sorrow, marking a breach that felt irreparable. Yet, within her heart lingered a quiet hope to heal her own scars. With a heavy heart and tears tracing her face, she unwillingly surrendered to her parents' wishes, feeling a poignant mix of love, loss, and resignation.

She did not have the choice to end her pregnancy, but she never had any intention of giving up on the life she had imagined for herself. As the first woman in her Italian family to be awarded a scholarship to Yale University, she had navigated the college application process on her own. Her parents believed in her abilities, and she proved them right. It was her responsibility as the first female in her family to pursue higher education and see it through. She was determined to learn, study diligently, and achieve as many goals as possible. She took advantage of every opportunity and hoped her experiences would open doors for her cousins and other girls in their community. This represented the essence of the American dream: working hard, studying hard, and securing well-paying jobs and opportunities. However, everything had been turned on its head. Yale had always been her dream, the beacon of hope guiding her path. Now, that hopeful vision seemed shrouded in darkness, her future appearing grim and lifeless.

CHAPTER 15

A visit to the gynaecologist confirmed Abby's pregnancy. The ultrasound scan revealed she was approximately six weeks pregnant, although the sight of the foetus did not pique her interest in the slightest. She met her mother's gaze, seeing the same trepidation reflected back at her.

As the doppler machine picked up on the faint but steady heartbeat of the tiny life growing inside her, resentment towards this unborn child bubbled inside her. Was it selfish to even consider terminating the pregnancy or secretly wish for a miscarriage? How could she possibly navigate the unforeseen challenges that life had unceremoniously thrown in her path? Feeling utterly helpless, Abby saw no escape.

Her parents remained deeply saddened by the situation, with her father's emotional distance becoming increasingly difficult for Abby to ignore. Blame for bringing pain and sorrow upon their family was rife. Micky, once close to his sister, now barely spoke to her as tension lingered like an unwelcome guest in their home. It became evident over time that Abby's presence only served to amplify everyone's discomfort, casting a gloomy shadow over their once lively household.

She retreated into solitude, seeking solace in her room except when hunger or sickness forced her out. Her parents' worried gazes followed her every move, silently keeping watch over their troubled daughter. Occasionally, her father entered her room before quietly retreating without saying a word.

Meanwhile, Vani and Nick were taken aback upon learning that Abby's parents had made plans to ship their daughter off to a monastery in Italy. Vani called Abby's mother to dissuade them from such drastic measures, but all pleas fell upon deaf ears. The decision was final—it was a private family matter.

In a moment of levity, Nick jokingly suggested staging a rescue mission to whisk Abby away from impending exile. Despite chuckles rippling through their group at his absurd proposal, there was an underlying seriousness lacing his tone that left them all contemplative about what lay ahead for Abby.

The day of her departure finally arrived, signalling the imminent journey to Italy that awaited her in just a few hours. As she descended the stairs to join her father for breakfast, she found him already seated at the table engrossed in the morning paper.

Catching sight of her, he gestured for her to take a seat beside him. "Abagail," he began with a reassuring tone, "I know you're scared, but rest assured the monastery will provide you with excellent care. Your mother and I will visit before the delivery. I'm sorry this has happened to you, but we must trust in God's plan and try to come to terms with it."

At that moment, Abby's mother entered the kitchen and halted in her tracks, causing an interruption in their solemn discussion. After exchanging a brief glance with her husband, she silently exited the room without uttering a single word. While Abby felt a sense of relief her father had finally addressed her concerns, she was also profoundly saddened at the thought of leaving him. The desire to bridge the emotional distance between them had been gnawing at her for some time now.

Longing for her father's embrace, Abby rose from her seat and hugged him tightly, wrapping her arms around his shoulders. "I'll miss you, Papa," she whispered softly as tears gushed from her eyes. There was a poignant pause before he returned the gesture, both of them shedding tears together.

"I know this is unjust and I am sorry. I love you so much, Abby." He gently stroked the back of her head, silently sobbing.

Pulling away slightly from her father's embrace, she locked eyes with him as she reciprocated his sentiments.

"I love you too, Papa," she murmured before leaning back into his warm embrace. Their tender moment was interrupted by Gabriela and Micky entering the room, both wiping away their own tears near the doorway.

Seeing their distress, their father called them over for a heartfelt family hug, which filled Abby's heart with warmth despite the sorrow weighing on them all.

As they separated from the group hug with smiles breaking through their tear-streaked faces, they realised one day they might look back on this moment with laughter instead of pain.

Micky reassured Abby he would make sure to visit after his midterms were over while expressing how much he would miss her.

Nodding in acknowledgment, she replied, "I love you too, Micky."

The ride to John F. Kennedy Airport was shrouded in silence as Abby reflected on the draining ordeal leading up to this moment.

The vain attempts to reason with her parents prior to departing left her feeling utterly defeated. The prospect of potentially returning to her previous life post-childbirth seemed inconceivable as she grappled with accepting her parents' narrow vision for what lay ahead. Resilient by nature and always ready for a fight when necessary, Abby had reached breaking point, her energy reserves depleted entirely.

The situation was beyond her control and reluctantly, she had no choice but to let go of her dreams and desires by taking a step back from the world. Every night she had cried herself to sleep, painfully aware Joey was moving forward with his life while leaving her behind and unfairly burdened by carrying their secret unborn child.

With her eyes closed, she was transported back to the days of her youth, a time filled with an abundance of joyful memories that brought a smile to her face. Despite the slight blurriness that surrounded these recollections, they still managed to evoke within her a sense of immense warmth and happiness that seemed to radiate from deep within her heart.

These cherished memories included moments spent building forts with her beloved family, mastering the art of riding a bike for the first time, and immersing herself in the world of books. They also included flying kites on breezy afternoons, indulging in quality mother-daughter bonding sessions at the mall while shopping for clothes and getting their nails done, and learning how to cook spaghetti and pizza alongside her father. The extravagant birthday parties they hosted or attended, as well as the thrilling family trips they embarked upon together, were also vividly etched in her mind. The music they sang and danced to served as a tangible expression of their shared emotions and experiences. She fondly recalled those unexpected moments when her father would surprise them by picking them up from school and whisking them away to spend leisurely afternoons at the beach, where they discovered the simple pleasure of feeling the sand between their toes, building sandcastles, eating fish and chips followed by ice cream.

Arriving at the airport, Abby watched her father unload their suitcases from the car with a sense of powerlessness. She hated farewells, so to prolong their time together, she clung tightly to him as he poured his weight and sadness into their embrace. Eventually, with eyes filled with sorrow, he released her, causing Abby's heart to shatter into a million pieces. Turning to Gabriela, he kissed and hugged her before making his way back to his pickup truck. As he drove away, Abby caught a glimpse of him looking back at her through the rear-view mirror until he disappeared.

The flight to Rome took eight hours. Looking over at her peacefully sleeping mother clutching her handbag, Abby struggled to find sleep. Every time she closed her eyes, Joey's face appeared in her mind. Placing a protective hand on her belly, she pondered whether time could heal the pain and alleviate her fears. In a barely audible whisper, she uttered, "I do not love you; I will never love you. You are not my miracle but a curse—a constant reminder of my mistakes, misery, and punishment. I resent you." She made a solemn vow to keep herself guarded from any form of affection or attachment towards her unborn child.

The expectation of impending motherhood typically evoked feelings of excitement and sacredness for most women as it symbolised the creation of new life. For Abby, instead of joy and anticipation, she wanted to terminate the pregnancy but was held back by the fear of society's harsh judgement. Seeing herself as unworthy and unfit for motherhood due to the circumstances surrounding the conception of this child only added to her feelings of shame.

Abby could not understand why others found pleasure in being pregnant when all she experienced were bouts of sickness and physical discomfort that left her drained and frustrated. Just as she managed to find some semblance of peace in sleep, a bizarre dream rattled her awake. Perspiration beaded on her forehead as queasiness took hold; this sudden awakening caused Abby to drop the crackers she had been nibbling on earlier, startling her nearby mother seated beside her.

"Are you okay?" she asked.

No, she was not, how could she be? Struggling internally with conflicting emotions and thoughts about her impending motherhood during those final minutes before landing in Rome brought no comfort for Abby. Anxiety continued its grip on her psyche leading up to what awaited them upon arrival in Italy's capital city.

CHAPTER 16

The journey to the Convento de Santa María en Aracoeli was one of the longest journeys Abby had ever embarked upon. Seated in the back of the taxi, her mother reached out and clasped her hand in a gesture of reassurance.

"Abby, don't worry. Papa, Micky, and I will be back soon to see you," she said in a warm tone.

After thirty-five minutes, they pulled up outside the Convento de Santa María, where Sister Mary Rosetta Mancini's waited their arrival.

Abby still resented her mother and felt disheartened by her lack of sorrow. Her mother hugged her, but Abby hesitated, struggling to contain her tears. All she wanted was to convey her frustration at being forced to come there, and to at least have those emotions acknowledged. "I will never forgive you for this," she whispered.

Her mother withdrew from the hug but retained a gentle grip on Abby's shoulders. "I understand what you're going through right now, Abby," she said, clearing her throat before dabbing Abby's wet eyes with a tissue. "But one day you'll appreciate my actions."

Sister Mary Rosetta Mancini appeared and greeted Abby with an excited voice. "Greetings, Mrs. Di Manos and Miss Abagail; welcome to Convento de Santa María en Aracoeli."

Sister Mary Rosetta Mancini was a nun with striking beauty who hailed from Baden-Württemberg in Germany where she was born in 1965 as the eldest daughter among six siblings to Gunter and Ursula Schneider, a doctor and a teacher respectively.

At eighteen years old, Sister Mary Rosetta Mancini enrolled at Akademie der Bildenen Künste, also known as the Fine School of Arts situated in Munich where she studied music and dance. Upon graduating in 1986, she diligently worked two jobs to amass sufficient funds enabling her dream of establishing a music and dance studio in Munich where children were taught various forms of artistic expression, encompassing dancing, singing, and musical instruments.

One morning, while strolling through Munich's streets, Bishop Marco Zollner from Italy chanced upon Sister Mary Rosetta Mancini's studio where he heard the faint melodies intermingled with children's voices earnestly praising God through lyrics such as: "God is great; God is love; God rides a bike." These snippets left an indelible impression upon his heart, evoking a smile. This encounter subsequently proved transformative for both individuals despite their significant forty-year age gap.

Bishop Marco Zollner harboured profound interest in nurturing spiritual growth amongst individuals, which led him to forge a friendship with Sister Mary Rosetta Mancini. As a result of this newfound bond between them, he extended an invitation for her to visit Convento de Santa María en Aracoeli in Rome, where he held pivotal responsibilities within the Roman community.

Sister Mary Rosetta Mancini, with a heart full of compassion and dedication, embarked on a transformative journey when she chose to join the Convento of Aracoeli. Her dream was to share her deep love and knowledge of music with the village children and guide the church choir with elegance and skill.

In 1987, amid the chaos and demands of her professional life, she began to contemplate a monastic life. Though she was not raised in the Christian Roman Catholic faith, nor held any spiritual affiliations, she felt an irresistible call towards the peaceful haven of a monastery. Without having previously set foot in a place of worship, Sister Mary Rosetta Mancini found herself drawn to the enlightening aspects of religious life, embracing Christian teachings with open arms. Despite leading a life that included moments of indulgence, a relentless pursuit of success, and charitable work, she was haunted by feelings of melancholy and a yearning for deeper fulfillment.

The serene presence and unwavering devotion of the women in the monastery had a profound influence on her. Their peaceful spirits, dedication to spiritual reading, and earnest prayer practices spoke eloquently of their faith. Through her profound connection with music, a comforting balm to her soul, Sister Mary Rosetta Mancini discovered her true calling.

After a year of probation, filled with rigorous training and introspection, she took her solemn vows, becoming a nun at the Monastery. Initially, the strict schedules and limited contact with the outside world challenged her, yet she summoned immense courage to face her fears, persisting along her chosen path.

While she occasionally yearned for freedom beyond the monastery's walls, Sister Mary Rosetta Mancini stayed true to her resolve, her heart unwavering. Within her new community, she led a life of spiritual fulfillment and contentment. Her compassion was unwavering, unshaken even when standing before Abby, who hesitated to accept her extended hand.

"Abby don't be rude, please shake Sister Mary Rosetta Mancini's hand," her mother ordered.

Abby disregarded her mother's request.

Surprisingly, Sister Mary Rosetta Mancini was unaffected by this. "It's fine," she said. "Abby just needs time, isn't that right, Abby?"

Abby said nothing.

Her mother remained tight-lipped, then looked at her watch. "Abby, I have to go now."

"Please take me with you, Mama, I don't belong here. Please, I want to go home." She hoped her mother would change her mind and finally understand the anguish she was going through.

"Abby, we will come to see you in a few weeks," she said tearfully, embracing her tightly for one last hug. She released her, thanked Sister Mary Rosetta Mancini, got back into the taxi, and was driven away, leaving Abby to face her troubles alone.

Abby yearned desperately for familiarity, hoping against hope her mother would relent from leaving without her by expressing poignant pleas for reprieve from this awful situation.

Abby had never experienced living independently away from the familiarity of her home. The prospect of leaving behind her cherished friends, beloved family members, and the reassuring comforts of home was a daunting reality to face.

"Life must continue despite the pain and changes surrounding us," said Sister Mary Rosetta Mancini.

As Abby glanced up at the nun, she noticed an intense scrutiny in her gaze, indicating a deep concern for her well-being.

"Now, grab your bags and come with me," she said.

Abby responded with an eye roll, picked up her luggage, and obediently followed her.

CHAPTER 17

The monastery, a magnificent structure built in the Roman architectural style nearly two millennia ago, was perched on the edge of a cliff overlooking the stunning Centina Sea. Its unique design, which deviated from traditional monastic layouts, featured a grand cathedral constructed from brick and was crowned with a bell tower. The monastery interior was a feast for the eyes, adorned with vibrant frescoes painted by local artists and exquisite artwork and sculptures scattered throughout its halls and walls. The sturdy pillars, ceilings, and towers were all meticulously crafted from brick and had withstood the test of time.

Over the years, this monastery had earned a reputation as a must-see attraction in Italy, offering accommodation to visitors seeking solace or spiritual enlightenment. It was divided into distinct sections to cater to both religious pilgrims and secular travellers. As Abby embarked on a tour of the cathedral under the guidance of Sister Mary Rosetta Mancini, she marvelled at the elegant art displays that surrounded her. The monastery grounds served as the dwelling place for a community of sisters and would be Abby's home for the next eight months. Stepping onto the premises felt like stepping into paradise. A breathtaking cloister garden bloomed with an array of flowers including roses, lilies, tulips, orchids, carnations, and freesias bathed in gentle sunlight filtering through lush foliage.

As they strolled along winding pathways lined with engraved tombstones commemorating departed clergy members, they came upon a vast vegetable and fruit garden bursting with aromatic herbs and exotic trees. Another path led them to a serene garden featuring an impressive waterfall embraced by ancient trees; Abby was spellbound by its majestic beauty.

Upon entering the heart of the monastery where forty-five nuns resided, Abby was struck by its opulent architecture marked by slanted windows, intricate sculptures adorning numerous rooms, and majestic columns. Security measures were visibly stringent as emissaries stood watch over various areas to deter any unauthorised individuals.

Sister Mary Rosetta Mancini guided Abby to her room within the monastery's quarters. She stepped into the cramped and underwhelming room, displaying her dissatisfaction with a sour expression. She shook her head. "No, no way! I cannot accept this room; are you kidding me? I absolutely refuse to stay here!"

The room contained necessities such as a bed, bookshelf, small desk with a lamp, and sink, but lacked any windows. "I demand a room that overlooks the ocean."

"I'm afraid this is the room assigned to you and there's no negotiation," she responded firmly.

Abby moved closer to the edge of the bed and sat on the corner.

"The rules of the monastery are not to be taken lightly," Sister Mary Rosetta Mancini declared with a tone that brooked no argument, her countenance grave and authoritative. "It is imperative you familiarise yourself with these regulations and adhere to them without fail, for any deviation will result in disciplinary measures." With an air of solemnity, she proceeded to outline the first rule: the prohibition of cell phones within the premises. "I now request you surrender your phone."

Abby folded her arms. "No, I'm sorry, I need my phone."

Sister Mary Rosetta Mancini remained resolute in her stance. "Rules are rules, Abby. There can be no exceptions."

"What am I supposed to do with my time then?"

"Reflection is vital for personal growth and self-improvement. Take the opportunity to contemplate your life and circumstances. When was the last time where you sought comfort in prayer and absolution from God?"

Abby retrieved her phone and noticed three missed calls and unanswered messages from Vani and Nick. She maintained silence as she looked at her notifications.

"Hand me the phone, Abby!" Sister Mary Rosetta Mancini insisted.

Reluctantly complying with the command, Abby handed her phone over to Sister Mary Rosetta Mancini.

"Rule number two involves rising each morning at 5:00 am for attendance at the morning prayer session before proceeding to your quarters for breakfast at 8:00 am."

"5.00 am, are you kidding me?"

Sister Mary Rosetta Mancini gave her a cold stare.

"Rule three, you will join the sisters for breakfast. Rule four, you will assist Sister Mary Francis and Sister Mary Josephine with cooking and learn to sew and attend the weekly choir with Sister Mary Bernadette. Rule five, you have access to explore the gardens after 1:00 pm before retiring to your chambers for the evening."

"When can I contact my family and friends?" Abby asked.

"You are permitted contact only with your family members," said Sister Mary Rosetta Mancini.

"Is this some kind of joke, you can't actually do this?"

"I assure you, Abagail, this is no joke—these rules are non-negotiable. Moreover, we have the rule of silence; conversation, laughter, and physical contact such as embracing are prohibited here. Our days will be filled with continuous prayer and labour for the monastery."

"Sounds like fun," Abby responded, shifting her gaze towards Sister Mary Rosetta Mancini.

"The bathing facilities can be accessed down the hallway on your right; please go freshen up. Dinner will be served at 6:00 pm under the guidance of Sister Mary Louise Magdalene."

With her final instructions imparted, Sister Mary Rosetta Mancini exited the room.

Alone in this unfamiliar setting, Abby sank to the floor, cradling herself tightly and sobbing uncontrollably. The desire to scream surged within her, fuelled by an intense loathing for Joey and herself alike. Despite her efforts to suppress it all, anguish gripped her heart too fiercely to ignore—tears cascaded freely down her cheeks as a whirlwind of emotions clashed tumultuously within her soul. Her cries were a desperate plea for salvation that resonated deeply and reverberated along the barren monastery corridors, alerting all those living there to her distress.

CHAPTER 18

In the admissions office at Yale University, Joey stood among a sea of eager students, his forced smile masking his conflicting emotions as he prepared to have his Student ID card photo taken. While the prospect of embarking on this exciting new chapter in his life filled him with anticipation, there was also a poignant sadness in his heart.

He took out his phone and scrolled through old photos until he landed on one of Abby. Memories of their shared laughter, whispered secrets, and lazy Sundays spent tangled in each other's arms flooded back to him. The fond reminiscence was shrouded by a sense of loss and regret. The love that once felt invincible had been shattered by an unexpected pregnancy that threw their lives off balance.

He knew, with unsettling clarity, that even if they had accepted the child and gone through with marriage, their bond would eventually crumble under the weight of unspoken truths and unmet expectations. In a moment of painful self-realisation, Joey acknowledged he should have supported Abby when she needed him most, especially during her visit to the abortion clinic.

"Damn it!" Joey whispered in frustration, berating himself for leaving Abby to face such a difficult decision alone. Despite the hurtful words exchanged between them, deep down he knew he still loved her dearly. Their once joyful relationship now seemed like a distant memory, lost in a sea of unresolved emotions and regrets.

The encounter with Mr. Di Manos just days prior remained vivid in Joey's mind. The shock of unexpectedly running into Abby's father at his own father's deli left him speechless. Mr. Di Manos' piercing glare instilled fear in Joey as he scrambled unsuccessfully to find an exit. Visions raced through his mind about what Mr. Di Manos might do, from wielding a knife to delivering punches or even strangling him. And he knew he probably deserved it.

With fury in his eyes, Mr. Di Manos approached Joey with menace, causing Joey's heart rate to skyrocket. Gripping Joey firmly by the shoulder, Mr. Di Manos dragged him into the backroom inside the store, pinching and twisting his arm. All Joey could do was say, "I'm sorry, I'm sorry!"

"You shattered my daughter's heart, you despicable little man. How could you get her pregnant and then abandon her like that? You are a coward who will never be a true man. You are a worthless piece of shit because you choose to be. You have ruined her life; my beautiful daughter is suffering because of your actions. If you were a decent human being, you would have helped her."

He then released his grip and grasped the back of his neck tightly, pinching the flesh like dough.

"I apologise for causing her pain," said Joey. "You're right, I am a coward."

"Listen closely, you worthless and pathetic excuse for a human. Should you have the audacity to reveal the pregnancy to anyone, even your parents, I will personally end your life. It is imperative this stays quiet. Do you understand?"

Joey nodded.

Abby's father released him and delivered a forceful blow to his stomach as a warning to stay away from Abby and left the deli.

Joey anxiously scanned for witnesses, relieved no one had seen the altercation. Although terrified of Abby's father and determined to honour his promise of staying away from her, Joey still yearned for an opportunity to see her again. Was it too late to offer support by accompanying Abby to the abortion clinic?

With remorse as he stood in the queue to have his picture taken, Joey grabbed his phone and composed a message. "Hey, Abby, can we please meet up? I deeply regret everything."

Just as he was about to send it, Vani appeared before him. She conveyed her disappointment through her intense gaze, Joey rose from his seat and met her accusing stare head-on, grappling with such guilt.

"Joey, it's best if you keep your distance," Vani said, waving her finger as if scolding a misbehaving child. Memories of his heated argument with Abby at the bus stop flooded back to Joey's mind as he processed Vani's words.

"How is Abby doing?" he asked.

"Are you kidding me?" Pointing her finger at him, she continued, "You have no right to ask about Abby's well-being after what you put her through. What were you even thinking?"

After a long pause, Joey shrugged. "I know I messed up, but I still love her and want her back. I just don't know what to do."

In response, she frowned, shook her head, and laughed awkwardly, making him feel uncomfortable.

The receptionist then called Vani's name to have her picture taken. Approaching the desk, Vani requested a moment and allowed the next student to step forward.

"Where is Abby?" Joey asked anxiously.

"You mean you don't know?" Vani shot back incredulously.

Puzzled, Joey muttered, "What do you mean? What happened to Abby?"

"She is flying to Italy to have an abortion."

"Yeah, right."

Taking a deep breath, Vani said, "I'm being serious, Joey. Her mother is escorting her to Italy for the procedure; they leave tonight. She had no say in the matter."

Feeling numb and heartbroken, Joey sank back into his seat and briefly closed his eyes, covering his face with his hands. He then grabbed his bag and hastily exited the admissions office, making his way towards the underground car park to his Hyundai.

While there was little Joey could do, he felt compelled to see Abby one last time. Parking a few blocks away from her house in Queens, he sought refuge near Mr. Callum's house, which stood across from Abby's residence, and hid behind an enormous sequoia tree.

From this vantage point, he watched helplessly as the woman he loved climbed into her father's red pickup truck. Abby appeared frightened, sorrowful, and devoid of vitality, a stark contrast to the confident and resilient girl he once knew.

As he witnessed them drive away, Joey realised the depth of his mistreatment of Abby. He vowed silently to God that hurting Abby was never his intention; he only wished she could understand how remorseful he truly was.

Standing alone in the middle of the road as tears streamed down his cheeks, Joey made a solemn promise never to fall in love again. With newfound determination coursing through his veins like wildfire consuming dry brushwood on a hot summer day, he resolved to pick up the shattered pieces of his life and find strength, knowing he had to forge ahead without looking back at the girl who had slipped through his fingers.

CHAPTER 19

Abby struggled to adjust to her new living situation, feeling as though the walls were closing in on her, suffocating any remaining shreds of hope. Her confinement caused her to spiral into a deep state of depression and resentment towards her baby and her own family, whom she longed for with aching nostalgia. The absence of her parents' familiar arguments echoing through the kitchen, the comforting scent of freshly brewed coffee wafting through the house, and Micky's cringeworthy jokes that never failed to elicit a smile served as painful reminders of happier times.

The realisation that her relationship with her parents had deteriorated ached Abby's heart, forcing her to sever ties with them to protect herself from the judgmental gossip that surrounded their strained dynamic. It pained her deeply that they had pushed her into a corner, compelling her to fabricate stories and hide herself just to maintain appearances. If only they had taken the time to truly listen and understand her feelings and concerns, perhaps she wouldn't have been trapped in isolation for what already felt like an eternity.

Standing at the hallway entrance on the upper west floor, Abby was met with an oppressive silence. The absence of any sound reminded her she was in a secluded monastery where nuns roamed quietly, observing a vow of silence and obedience. Each footstep she took echoed loudly through the empty space, prompting thoughts of whether she could endure such solitude for eight long months, or if doing so would prove her resilience against any future hardships.

But Abby's history was marred by sorrow and heartache, causing her sleepless, restless nights as she came to terms with this this new lifestyle. The ache in her chest from a shattered heart only intensified in the face of such profound loneliness.

One morning, after yet another night spent tossing and turning, Abby was greeted by Sister Mary Louise entering her room with kindness in her big brown eyes. In that momentary exchange, locked in mutual gaze, there was a sense of connection—a flicker of hope amidst the darkness.

"It's nearly five in the morning. You have ten minutes to freshen up and get dressed. I'll be outside waiting while you change." She turned, bearing a resemblance to Sister Mary Rosetta Mancini but with a gentler demeanour. She closed the door on her way out.

Abby scowled in frustration and pulled the thick, cosy blankets tightly around her shivering body, seeking warmth as she closed her tired eyes. Shortly after, Sister Mary Louise once again graced the room with her gentle aura, but Abby remained hidden beneath the covers, stubbornly ignoring the kind nun's soft pleas for attention. Sister Mary Louise's repeated calls of her name echoed through the quiet chamber, but Abby remained unmoving and silent in her cocoon of solitude.

Frustrated by Abby's unresponsiveness, Sister Mary Louise eventually sighed in resignation and reluctantly left the room.

A few hours later, as the faint light of dawn filtered through the windows, Abby stirred from her slumber to find a new figure standing solemnly at the foot of her bed: Sister Mary Rosetta Mancini. Although known for her unwavering dedication to discipline and order within the monastery, even Sister Mary Rosetta Mancini could not hide a hint of annoyance that flickered across her usually composed features as she approached Abby's bedside.

With a weary sigh, Abby sat up and listened attentively as Sister Mary Rosetta Mancini sternly emphasised the importance of punctuality and attendance at mass at five o'clock sharp.

Running her fingers through her tangled hair in a gesture of defiance, Abby, with her head held high, said, "I was exhausted, and my body needs more sleep. Or did you forget I was pregnant?"

Unmoved by Abby's sarcasm, Sister Mary Rosetta Mancini maintained an air of calm authority but her steely gaze bore into Abby with a clear warning. "Sarcasm, gossiping, and disrespect have no place within these sacred walls. Your presence here was not extended by invitation; rather it was facilitated by your parents' generous donation towards your accommodation. You are expected to adhere to all rules of this monastery and show reverence towards your superiors. Any directives given must be followed without question. The monastery has strict guidelines regarding social conduct and any form of insubordination will not be tolerated. Should you persist in this manner, I'll have no choice but to expel you from our sanctuary, a fate neither of us desires."

In response to her reprimand, Abby rolled her eyes dismissively before averting her gaze. "Got it!" she muttered half-heartedly as Sister Mary Rosetta Mancini briskly exited the room.

Alone once more in her sparse room that resembled a prison cell, Abby reclined against her pillow with a deep sigh and whispered softly to herself before succumbing to sleep once more: "I despise this place."

Over time, despite her initial reluctance and resistance to early morning rituals, Abby gradually acclimated to rising at 4:50 am every day to join Sister Mary Rosetta Mancini for mass promptly at 5 o'clock in the dimly lit hallway. She would then return to her quarters at 6:00 am for a brief respite until 7:50 am before heading off to breakfast alongside fellow sisters within the monastic dining hall.

Abby discovered the other sisters residing in the monastery harboured a deep-seated resentment towards her, their disapproval evident in the piercing gazes they cast her way and the hushed whispers that followed her every move. These interactions laid bare vulnerabilities she had previously kept hidden. The tension in the room was so thick she could practically taste it, a constant reminder of her outsider status within the tight-knit community. It was no secret why Abby had sought refuge within the walls of the monastery; she carried a reputation of being sinful, a rebellious spirit who defied societal norms and was thus deemed unworthy of acceptance by her peers. She desperately yearned for even a glimmer of kindness from those around her, but some among them showed no compassion or empathy towards her plight. Amidst this sea of hostility, Abby found support in the unlikely companionship of Sister Mary Francis and Sister Mary Josephine. Through shared moments spent together in the warmth of the kitchen and while honing their skills in tapestry-making, bonds of trust and friendship formed between them. In their presence, Abby felt a sense of security and belonging that had eluded her since her arrival at the monastery.

The daily routine unfolded like clockwork, providing a sense of stability in an otherwise tumultuous environment. After completing her duties in the kitchen each afternoon, Abby would retreat to her quarters to freshen up before embarking on a leisurely stroll through the manicured grounds surrounding the monastery. Here, she enjoyed nature's embrace as she gazed out upon the tranquil waters of Centina Sea, losing herself in contemplation as she basked in the sun's gentle caress and felt the cool breeze brush against her skin.

As night fell and silence descended upon the monastery, Abby would steal away from her room under cover of darkness, mindful not to disturb the sleeping sisters as she made her way to a secluded spot at the back of the building. Wrapped in a blanket against the chilly evening air, she would sit in quiet contemplation as she watched the sun dip below the horizon, its fiery glow casting an ethereal light over the waters below. Completely enthralled by the sea's beauty, she remained unaware of a mysterious woman lurking in the darkness, silently observing Abby with great curiosity.

CHAPTER 20

In the initial stages of Abby's pregnancy, Sister Mary Rosetta Mancini demonstrated affection and comfort towards her, serving as a pillar of support during what was undoubtedly one of the most trying times in Abby's life. Going above and beyond the call of duty, she assumed the role of a nurturing mother figure, offering understanding and a shoulder to cry on.

Abby's struggle with insomnia exacerbated her already tumultuous emotional state, leaving her tossing and turning into the early hours of each morning with thoughts of Joey, her friends, and Yale. The relentless ticking clock served as a constant reminder of time slipping away while Abby remained ensnared in a cycle of incessant overthinking. The resulting lack of sleep took a heavy toll on her mood and cognitive function, often forcing her to seek refuge in her room for much-needed rest during the day.

There were moments when Abby would lie awake for hours on end, succumbing to uncontrollable fits of weeping that only served to deepen her sense of isolation and despair that accompanied her pregnancy fears. These symptoms conspired to prolong Abby's misery in her dimly lit room, permeated by an atmosphere thick with silence.

In this gloomy setting, Sister Mary Rosetta Mancini often sat in a chair beside Abby's bed. Some days, she simply offered an empathetic ear to Abby's grievances and heartache; on other occasions, she extended a hand imbued with warmth and tenderness.

As Abby's bouts of nausea intensified and grew more frequent, Sister Mary Rosetta Mancini stood by her side, assisting with cold towels on her forehead and soothing rubs to her back during her trips to the bathroom. Even with the sudden urges that could not be thwarted in time, Sister Mary Rosetta Mancini never uttered a word of complaint as she dutifully cleaned up after Abby.

Remedies such as ginger and mint tea to combat the persistent nausea proved ineffective for Abby, but Sister Mary Rosetta Mancini tirelessly sought alternative solutions. She dispatched Sisters Mary Francis and Josephine on vital missions aimed at preparing various types of nourishment that might assuage Abby's symptoms. However, as aversions grew stronger and every food option became unpalatable for Abby, she was ultimately admitted to hospital for intravenous treatment infused with essential minerals and vitamins.

During the most challenging and arduous period in her life, Abby faced a harrowing pregnancy. Her physical form felt delicate and vulnerable, plagued by sharp pains that radiated through her pelvic region. The fatigue and dizziness left her drained and irritable, exacerbating an already trying situation.

When Abby attempted to terminate the pregnancy through a dangerous fall down the stairs and then later through an overdose on Panadol discovered hidden away in the kitchen cupboard, Sister Mary Rosetta Mancini intervened swiftly and decisively. She was as a beacon of hope in a dark sea of despair, helping her overcome her daily struggles. Through Sister Mary Rosetta Mancini's constant presence and care, Abby's world gradually regained its colour and vibrancy. Laughter once again echoed within her walls, dispelling the notion that joy had been lost forever. Furthermore, Sister Mary Rosetta Mancini imparted valuable lessons on faith and reliance upon God for strength.

Sister Mary Rosetta Mancini's profound love and concern for Abby nurtured a sense of security within her troubled heart. Going above and beyond to ensure Abby's happiness, Sister Mary Rosetta Mancini took great care of her, baking her favourite cake and adding nice pictures to her living space. Their leisurely walks together saw Sister Mary Rosetta Mancini encouraging Abby to cling to her aspirations of becoming a lawyer. Each night before bed, she knelt beside Abby to pray for comfort and protection.

Abby eventually confronted the truth: she was about to become a mother. She could no longer deny or evade this reality. The first moment she felt her baby's movements occurred as she lay in bed on her back just before drifting off to sleep. A series of jabs and kicks from her little one startled her awake. Surprised, she stared at her stomach with wide eyes. "Oh my goodness! What the hell was that?"

This occurrence repeated itself as she scolded her baby in a high-pitched tone, saying, "Stop that! What are you doing? Settle down!"

With gentle pressure from her palm against her belly accompanied by slight shifts in position alleviating the discomfort caused by kicks near her ribs, abdomen, and vulval area, it all seemed incredibly tangible now more than ever. "You're quite energetic, aren't you," she said, chuckling occasionally.

She devoted time to serenading her baby with soothing songs, engaging in conversations to welcome her child into the family dynamics. "Hmm, let's see... hello there. I am your mother, Abagail. Initially, I had plans to study Law at Yale University but that was disrupted by your arrival, seems unfortunate timing, doesn't it?"

Pausing momentarily, anticipating a reaction, she continued. "Ah, so no kick today, huh? Well, that's fine, now you know why my career is on hold; once you're out, I can focus studying law here in Italy. Um... there's Uncle Micky, he is incredibly intelligent, even though I don't always understand his jokes. I only laugh to make him happy. We have a really great relationship; everyone loves him because of his kind heart. Your grandparents are also very loving, kind people, but right now I am not on good terms with them, so I'd rather not talk about them."

She was about to say more when a group of sisters appeared. "Don't mind us," they said.

Abby blushed and bit her bottom lip, wondering how much they had overheard. She did tend to share too much with the unborn child but never brought Joey up.

Finding peace by the sea's calming embrace became a sanctuary for Abby. Drawing parallels between her own experiences and mythical tales of mermaid lore, she wove narratives of hope and resilience for both her and her unborn child. Gradually shedding initial doubts to make room for burgeoning affection, Abby discovered that love had found its way into unexpected corners of her heart through the miraculous bond forged between mother and child.

On the dreary Sunday morning, Abby stayed in her cosy cocoon of blankets as the gentle pitter-patter of raindrops against the window created a melancholic backdrop that distracted her from her busy mind. Mass was scheduled for 10:30 am instead of 10:00 am. Now in her second trimester, Abby's abdomen had noticeably swelled. The relentless waves of nausea had finally subsided, allowing her taste buds to reawaken and celebrate this momentous milestone in her pregnancy journey.

Taking her place at the podium alongside her fellow sisters, Abby gazed down upon the congregation of villagers and guests gathered within the chapel walls. Her eyes were inevitably drawn to Sister Mary Rosetta Mancini seated in the front row, a subtle smile on her face. Abby scanned the room and met the loving gazes of her parents seated five rows back. Their expressions shifted from concern to joy as they locked eyes with their daughter following the end of mass.

"Hi Mama, Papa," she said.

Unable to contain their emotions, Abby's mother began crying uncontrollably.

Abby cried, too.

Her mother embraced her tightly and whispered softly, "Abby, you look absolutely beautiful, and your singing was amazing." She then gently placed her hand on Abby's belly. Looking up at her daughter, she said tenderly, "We've missed you so much, darling." She brushed a strand of hair away from Abby's face and planted kisses on each cheek.

As she observed her father, it became apparent the stress and sadness from her pregnancy had prematurely aged him. Taking hold of her hand and placing it against his chest, his eyes brimming with sorrow, he confessed tearfully, "Abby, my heart shattered the day you left, and I bear all the blame." Drawing her into his arms, he continued regretfully. "I am sorry... so very sorry." Cupping her face in his hands and sobbing openly, he added, "I have missed you immensely," before playfully rubbing noses with her, a cherished childhood habit.

His raw display of emotion left Abby speechless as floods of tears smudged the mascara gifted to her by Sister Mary Rosetta Mancini. "Papa... I missed you, too." They held each other tightly, weeping on each other's shoulders; today was indeed a special day where she felt immense happiness having both parents by her side.

They escorted her back to her room and gathered around her bed as the rain outside intensified, prompting deep breaths as Abby attempted to release the tension in her shoulders.

Taking after her mother's meticulous and thoughtful demeanour, she delicately unpacked a bag bursting at the seams with gifts for Abby. Within the bag lay maternity leggings, tops, bras, jeans, and pants, all specially designed with adjustable bands to accommodate Abby's ever-changing body. Accompanying these clothing items were some of Abby's favourite chocolates, a range of vitamins aimed at supporting her health, as well as various body and face creams. Prominently displayed on the bed were unopened letters from loved ones, Vani and Micky.

At lunch, Abby's father and mother opted to dine in the guest area due to the chilly weather outside. This gathering marked a rare moment for their family to reunite in such a manner after a prolonged period apart. Abby felt a deep sense of connection and closeness as they shared in this joyous reunion.

"Where is Micky?" Abby asked. "I thought he'd be here."

Her father flashed a smile. "He wanted to come, darling, but he is studying for midterms, and he has managed to find himself a girlfriend."

Abby didn't believe them at first. However, her parents laughed and confirmed it was indeed true. Eagerly showing Abby a photo of Andrea, Micky's girlfriend, her mother described them as a perfect match.

Abby was a little envious as she looked at the photo on the phone, despite trying to move on from Joey. She longed for their relationship to have taken a different turn. "Wow, she's gorgeous!" said Abby.

Abby's excitement peaked when her father said, "Micky and Andrea will be visiting in two weeks."

"That's wonderful news! I can hardly wait to see them." Feeling relieved and happy, knowing Micky was thriving and enjoying his life brought immense joy to her heart.

Her mother leaned closer towards Abby. "How are you feeling, Abby? Have you been sleeping well? Are you eating properly?"

Before Abby could respond, her mother tenderly touched her dry face. "Use the lotion and moisture in the bag, apply it both in the morning and at night."

"Gabby, relax," said her father, growing visibly frustrated by his wife's overbearing presence.

Brushing off his remark dismissively with a wave of her hand, she said, "Quiet! I haven't seen my daughter; we have many matters to discuss."

Adriano shot back with a smirk. "Then let her talk."

It dawned on Abby how much she missed the entertaining dynamics between her parents and their constant arguments; they remained her favourite couple who always managed to bring laughter into their interactions.

"Please stop arguing, Mama and Papa!" said Abby. "I'm actually doing fine. I've been eating well, getting proper sleep, and Sister Mary Rosetta Mancini along with the other sisters have been incredibly supportive."

Her father nodded approvingly before leaning in closer towards Abby, gently placing his hand on her belly.

Unable to contain herself any longer, Abby excitedly blurted out: "Guess who's here to sing lullabies for you now, little one? It's your nonno!" She looked back at her tearful father, whose joy was palpable.

"You told the baby about me?"

With a nod, she said, "Of course!"

He hugged Abby and kissed her on the cheek. "I love you."

As the lullaby continued to play its soothing melody, he suddenly felt a tiny kick from the baby. Letting out a burst of excitement in a high-pitched voice, he cried out, "Gabby, the baby is kicking!"

In response, Abby's mother moved closer and tenderly placed her hand on Abby's stomach, tears of joy streaming down her face. "Oh, my darling!"

Adding to the emotional moment, Abby chimed in. "This is your nonna. I also shared stories about you too, Mum."

The radiant expression on her mother's face illuminated the room as she too could feel the kicks against her palm. Abby was grateful her parents were there to share in this extraordinary experience with her, their first as grandparents.

"I want to raise this child while studying my law degree. Maria will support me." Her parents were taken aback yet deeply touched by her words. With caution in their voices, they asked, "Abby, are you absolutely certain about this?"

Abby replied firmly. "Yes, this child is mine and my responsibility. I hope you can accept my choice."

Her father reached out for her hand and locked eyes with hers. "Abby, your mother and I will stand by whatever decision you make. We are immensely proud of you, and I will do everything in my power to provide financial assistance for your studies." Pulling her close for a comforting embrace, he added, "You are destined for great things, kid. We believe in you."

Tears flowed from Abby's eyes as she clung tightly to her parents, underlining how much those tender words meant to her and how they filled her heart with newfound confidence.

Amidst the aura of love, Sister Mary Rosetta Mancini stood standing at the door, casting an unwavering gaze upon Abby. Undeterred by the nun's stern demeanour, Abby held eye contact until Sister Mary Rosetta Mancini swiftly exited the room with a serious face.

As much as they wished for time to stand still in that moment, it was time for Abby's parents to go. Though Abby longed to return home with them to the States right then, deep down she knew it wasn't possible.

With a final hug with her father, who promised a swift return with Micky and their mother in two weeks, Abby bid a tearful goodbye.

In the tranquil atmosphere of the monastic grounds, Abby stood alone, watching her parents drive away in a taxi, she found herself immersed in deep contemplation about the intricate and fragile bonds of their relationship. She held onto a glimmer of hope that with the arrival of dawn, clarity would emerge and provide an opportunity for reconciliation and healing.

It was only after a brief moment had passed that Abby began to comprehend the extent of her personal growth and progress. For the first time in what seemed like an eternity, a profound sense of tranquillity came over her, enveloping her in a state of peace and contentment.

CHAPTER 21

Abby retired to her room earlier than usual, feeling the day's burdens on her shoulders. She gathered her night clothes and personal items before making her way to the bathroom. She filled the bathtub with warm water and added bubbles, transforming it into a serene oasis for relaxation and rejuvenation. Once submerged in the soothing water, Abby felt clean and revitalised, allowing herself to let go of the day's stresses.

After twenty minutes, she pulled the plug and carefully stepped out of the tub. She reached for a large towel adorned with crucifixes, wrapping it around her rotund body and another around her head. It was in this moment that she caught a glimpse of herself in the mirror. She leaned in closer and noticed her acne scars had miraculously vanished. Puzzled by this unexpected skin improvement, she stared at her reflection in the dimly lit room, recalling her past insecurity and self-consciousness. Memories flooded back of hurriedly applying concealer and foundation during high school days when every glance in the mirror would deflate her heart as she realised her imperfections were still visible.

The late-night hours found Abby unable to fall sleep due to the pregnancy-induced changes in her body. Elevated levels of estrogen and heightened libido resulted in increased blood flow and soreness in her breasts, alleviated only slightly by the bras sent by her mother. The pressure on her uterus led to frequent trips to the bathroom, leaving Abby questioning whether these experiences were normal during pregnancy.

With a strong desire for intimacy conflicting with feelings of embarrassment and uncertainty, Abby wanted to seek guidance from her mother or Sister Mary Rosetta Mancini. Reflecting on societal expectations surrounding female sexuality, she believed schools should have provided more education on navigating such intimate experiences. Doubts lingered about engaging in self-pleasure during pregnancy, as her concerns for potential risks to the child caused hesitation. Returning to her room for privacy, Abby locked the door in search of relief for a restless night's sleep. In a vulnerable moment alone, she found pleasured herself as a means of reconnecting with her changing body.

Embracing sensations previously unfamiliar yet deeply satisfying brought a newfound sense of empowerment and connection within herself. With each touch bringing waves of pleasure and release, Abby felt calm, relaxed, and ultimately relieved from her pent-up sexual frustration. Clutching onto a pillow for comfort as sleep beckoned, she closed her eyes, feeling content.

Having turned vulnerability into strength, Abby drifted off to sleep feeling like the best version of herself, a woman embracing both physical changes and newfound desires with grace and acceptance.

The following morning, Abby awoke with a deep sense of shame and self-blame. She berated herself for resorting to using her own body as a means to achieve sexual gratification, even with the undeniable pleasure she had experienced in that moment because this was the only way she could release her pent-up desires.

Contemplating the morality of her actions, Abby pondered whether it was selfish or inherently wrong for her to engage in such intimate acts within the sacred confines of the House of God. She tried to reassure herself there was no inherent sinfulness in seeking physical relief through self pleasure. Still, she lamented at the absence of a loving partner to share these deeply personal moments with.

Closing her eyes, Abby allowed memories of Joey, their shared life and past experiences, to flood her mind. Even after all this time, she still obsessed over a man who had long since left her behind. Doubts surfaced as she questioned why her heart continued to yearn for someone who had abandoned her.

In an unexpected surge of anger, Abby wanted to confront Joey for his perceived betrayal. She then rummaged through her nightstand in search of a collection of letters from Vani, whose words never failed to evoke anticipation and intrigue in Abby's heart. As she carefully unfolded one letter, Abby felt a rush of emotions, enveloping her in a wave of longing and nostalgia.

> *My dearest Abby,*
> *It's 10 am, I find myself composing this letter on the campus lawn. The architecture surrounding me is truly*

breathtaking, with stunning stone and sculptures on the walls. It's a sight unlike any other I've ever seen. The student body here is diverse, ranging in age from 17 to 70. However, unlike high school, there is no drama or backstabbing.

Unfortunately, my roommate Karen is a constant source of disturbance, with her loudness, snoring, and untidiness. I cannot continue living with her. Fortunately, I have saved up enough money to move out and am hoping to secure a studio apartment before the next semester begins. In the meantime, I plan to invest in noise-cancelling headphones.

Krish and I are still doing the whole couple thing, and guess what? We finally decided to play the horizontal tango for the first time! Let's just say it was more awkward than a giraffe on roller skates because Krish was a bit of a newbie at it. But hey, practice makes perfect! After a few more tries, we were riding the wave of comfort and pleasure haha.

Abby chuckled as she read this line and momentarily forgot where she was, covering her mouth in surprise. She realised she hadn't laughed in a long time. Trying to stifle her laughter, she continued reading:

I think I may be addicted to sex.

As she turned the page over, Abby chuckled softly and shook her head.

143

Your father has agreed to let me visit you in two weeks, and I'll be travelling with them. I'm looking forward to seeing you. I miss you terribly!

Being your closest friend, I feel I have an obligation to keep you updated on Joey's situation whether or not you want to hear about it. After all, he is still the father of your child.

Abby breathed deeply and made her way to the rocking chair in the corner. With bated breath, she read several more sentences while her heart beat heavily.

Joey suddenly vanished from Yale, and poor Krish was left scratching his head, totally confused about where Joey had gone. Joey had cut ties with just about everyone—he even changed his number! It was like he just vanished into thin air. But, as luck would have it, I bumped into him at the admissions office. I mentioned that you were in Italy for an abortion, just casually in conversation, you know?

A few days later, Joey came up to me and said he'd swung by your place. He caught sight of you leaving in your dad's truck, heading straight for the airport. He couldn't help but notice you seemed, well, kind of out of it, like the light had gone out of your eyes. He admitted he felt absolutely powerless at that moment. Joey also confessed he deeply regretted walking away and failing to cherish your love when he had the chance.

Abby stood before the mirror, her reflection a stark contrast to the bright and cheery image she usually projected. Instead, what stared back at her was a visage of sorrow, with tears streaking down her cheeks and heavily smudged mascara. Her hands shook as she clutched the letter, its contents like a dagger piercing through her heart and dragging her into an abyss of despair.

"He came to see me," she whispered, her voice barely above a murmur. "But why did he not fight for our relationship? Why did he not approach my parents and plead for their forgiveness? Why did he not come to my aid when I needed him most? How could he simply stand by and watch as I walked away? How could he abandon his own flesh and blood in such callous disregard?"

The weight of these unanswered questions bore down on Abby, bringing her great sadness as she sank onto her bed. Tears flowed as the betrayal and abandonment she felt cut deep, leaving wounds that seemed impossible to heal.

The following morning, Abby awoke to the presence of Sister Mary Rosetta Mancini, who was seated at the foot of her bed with a tray of food. The sight of the nun in her black attire and with a warm smile caught Abby off guard as she tried to discern how long she had been there. It wasn't until the nun whispered, "Happy Birthday, Abby," that she remembered.

How could she have forgotten her own birthday? Sister Mary Rosetta Mancini chuckled at Abby's reaction before confirming that it was indeed her special day. In a gesture of kindness and love, Sister Mary Rosetta Mancini reached into her pockets and presented Abby with a beautiful heart-shaped necklace crafted from gold.

"This is for you," she said.

Engraved with "You possess strength, beauty, and bravery," the necklace served as a reminder of her resilience and courage during tough times.

Sister Mary Rosetta Mancini placed the necklace delicately into Abby's open palm. Speaking softly but earnestly, she added, "We all face moments of weakness, but always remember your inner strength and courage. Know that God is forever by your side." With a radiant smile, she leaned in and gently kissed Abby's cheek. This simple gesture filled her heart with joy.

"You didn't have to get me anything," Abby said. "But this is absolutely perfect! I adore it. Thank you so much for this wonderful gift."

"Let me assist you in putting it on. May I?" asked Sister Mary Rosetta Mancini.

She fastened the necklace around Abby's neck. "It suits you perfectly," said the nun as she held out her hand to offer support.

"How long have you been sitting here?" Abby asked.

Sister Mary Rosetta Mancini smiled. "Around thirty minutes."

"That long? Why didn't you wake me up?"

Pointing at the array of breakfast items laid out on the tray, Sister Mary Rosetta Mancini said, "Please make sure to eat your breakfast."

Abby nodded. "Thank you."

With grace and poise, Sister Mary Rosetta Mancini rose from her seat and exited the room silently.

Holding up the exquisite necklace, in awe of its design and weightlessness, Abby read the inscription repeatedly while savouring each word. Turning her attention towards the food, she reached out for a slice of bread smothered in jam. Chewing thoughtfully on each bite, she simultaneously sifted through a stack of letters until she found one written by Micky. Her focus was abruptly interrupted by a sharp knock on the door as Sister Mary Louise entered the room.

"Abagail, there's an urgent call for you in Father Michiel's office. Please dress quickly and come with me."

Abby swiftly swung her legs out of bed, the cool floor beneath her feet sending a shiver down her spine as she hastily donned her clothes. Following closely behind Sister Mary Louise, she made her way to Father Michiel's office, where the faint scent of old books and dusty manuscripts filled the air. As soon as the sister had departed and closed the door behind her, Abby reached for the phone on Father Michiel's cluttered desk. Pressing it against her ear, she said, "Hello?"

"Happy Birthday!" came a raucous of voices. She recognised them as her parents and Micky.

Her father quickly apologised, saying they hadn't meant to scare her, while her mother scolded him for suggesting the idea.

Abby managed an emotional smile. "Thank you for the birthday call."

Micky chimed in, expressing his joy at hearing her voice.

After talking with her parents for a while and making plans to visit in less than two weeks, they passed the phone to Micky.

"Hello, tubby," he said.

Abby couldn't help but chuckle at her brother's eternal silliness, even if it sometimes grated on her nerves. Despite her doubts about him ever growing up, she adored him nonetheless.

"Wow, a message from Micky—how did I get so lucky?" she teased, her voice dripping with playful sarcasm. "Seriously, how on earth did you find someone to date? Did you bribe her with endless jokes?"

Micky's laughter bounced through the room, warm and infectious. "I see your wit hasn't dulled a bit! I was worried you might have taken a vow of silence when you went all monk-mode," he teased, grinning from ear to ear. Despite their banter, the love between the siblings was as clear as the sparkle in their eyes.

Abby responded with seriousness, saying, "That's not fair, Micky!"

Rolling her eyes, Abby's tone turned serious. "I need to talk privately with you about Joey. Can you please step away from our parents?"

"Mum and Dad just left, but I don't think discussing Joey is a good idea."

"Please, Micky, it's my birthday wish. I don't want any presents from you; I just need an update on Joey."

"It's unusual for you to reject a gift." He chuckled momentarily before adding, "No, Abby, forget about Joey!"

Taking a deep breath, she steeled herself for what was likely to be an emotionally charged conversation regarding Joey's welfare. "Micky... please! I promise this will be the final time I ask about him."

"Okay, Abby... what do you want to know?"

"Everything... what happened to Joey?"

"Joey's been pretty caught up with his studies at MIT, and we haven't seen him at family gatherings for quite a while now. Tony just shared some news: Joey landed an internship at Glencore, the biggest mining company in the world. On another note, I don't think the Giovannis know about your pregnancy yet. Mom and Dad told them you got a scholarship to the University of Sydney in Australia and are living on campus there."

As the call came to a close, a profound sorrow settled within Abby, enveloping her in the painful realisation of Joey's new life ventures that no longer included her. Each step back to her room seemed heavier, as though the weight of her heart was too much to bear. Nearing her room, an unexpected surprise awaited—her parents had arranged for a delightful chocolate sponge birthday cake, its surface beautifully coated with white frosting. Yet, the sweetness of this gesture seemed distant to Abby, her heart and mind consumed by the haunting absence of Joey in her world.

CHAPTER 22

As the twenty-eighth week of her pregnancy approached, Abby's morning sickness finally began to subside, much to her relief. However, in its place came a new set of discomforts that tested her endurance: muscle soreness, causing her lower abdomen to ache with cramps and throbbing pains. Uncertain if these symptoms were typical of pregnancy, she also experienced sharp, fleeting pains in her vulva.

Despite these challenges, Abby remained committed to maintaining her usual eating habits and engaging in daily exercise alongside Sister Mary Rosetta Mancini. Together, they sought joy in their leisurely walks through the monastery garden, where the tranquil sounds of nearby waterfalls and crashing waves provided a soothing backdrop for their conversations.

During moments when the rest of the monastery was asleep, Abby stealthily made her way to the kitchen for a late-night snack before venturing out to the cliff overlooking the vast expanse of the ocean. It was during these solitary moments that she felt the full extent of her intense back pain unlike anything she had ever encountered before. The pain radiated down her legs and intensified as her pregnancy progressed, placing additional strain on her lower back.

With exhaustion becoming a constant companion due to sleep disturbances and frequent trips to the bathroom, Abby's frustrations grew. She also experienced peculiar dreams that blurred the boundaries between reality and fantasy. One particularly bizarre dream involved Princess Diana whispering softly in her ear, urging Abby to name her unborn baby girl Ruby.

Abby's heart found solace in the gentle presence of Sister Mary Rosetta Mancini, who stood by her side throughout her pregnancy with a loving grace. Their conversations, peaceful and profound, gradually softened the edges of Abby's grief and fears, helping her to find peace in the seemingly mysterious plan that God had woven for her life. As she began to embrace the wonder and excitement of the new life growing within her, fleeting thoughts of adoption surfaced, only to be swept away by an overwhelming sense of responsibility and love.

Determined to see her unexpected pregnancy as a divine gift, Abby redirected her focus, spending time wandering the gardens and offering prayers for guidance. With each step, each whispered prayer, she absorbed Sister Mary Rosetta Mancini's lessons on acceptance and resilience, allowing them to strengthen her heart.

Though shadows of uncertainty hovered over the future, Abby moved forward with a steadfast spirit, buoyed by the unwavering support surrounding her. Then came a day of profound transformation, one she would forever cherish, when she was joined by her loving parents for a second ultrasound. Their anticipation filled the air as the doctor's voice broke the silence with gentle revelation.

"Abby, this is your baby's heart," the doctor announced, as tears welled in Abby's eyes and cascaded down her cheeks.

At that moment, hands intertwined in a sacred bond, the miraculous sound of life echoed through the room, turning previous fears into an exquisite miracle. Filled with awe, Abby exclaimed, "Oh my God, this is my child!"

The doctor's words followed like a melody, "Abby, you are having a little girl."

A wave of pure joy enveloped the room, touching every soul present. Emotions surged, voices quaked, and jubilation spilled from all corners as this new blessing was celebrated. Overwhelmed with happiness, Abby turned to her parents, her voice filled with warmth and love, "We are having a girl!"

Papa Adriano stood by his daughter with the biggest smile. "Yes, yes indeed," he said.

And there they stood united in love, three souls connected beyond measure by one beating heart.

"Doctor, I need to know, is my child healthy? Does she have all her fingers and toes? Is there anything we should worry about?" Abby's voice trembled as she spoke, while she felt her father's reassuring yet increasingly tense hand on her shoulder. He too was desperate for the doctor's affirmation.

The doctor's eyes softened as he took in the love and concern enveloping the room. "Your baby is perfectly healthy, a little miracle in every way. She has all her fingers and toes, and everything is just as it should be."

Abby's newfound fear of losing her baby gripped her for the first time during her pregnancy, proving to herself that she did not want to adopt or abandon the child. Love overwhelmed her senses, prompting her to gently place a hand on her swelling stomach and whisper, "I cannot wait to meet you, Ruby." She felt an intense bond with her unborn child that surpassed all expectations. This connection had seemed almost unattainable. "You are part of me, you are my own."

Glancing at her parents, Abby saw her father draw nearer and kiss her forehead. "Ti Voglio bene."

Gratefully acknowledging his sentiment, she smiled and said, "I love you, too, Papa."

As the due date loomed closer, Abby's parents relocated to a quaint house near the monastery gardens where they dedicated themselves entirely to each other. Every moment spent together was cherished as lasting memories were created.

Micky frequently visited her with his infectious smile and contagious laughter. Feeling more pronounced movements from her baby, Micky gently touched Abby's belly to provoke reactions from the unborn child. He even exposed their little one to heavy metal music under the belief it would have a positive influence on her development, although Abby didn't quite comprehend his reasoning.

Nonetheless, she treasured these moments with her family and acknowledged the sacrifices made for her. Grateful for their caring and nurturing ways, Abby finally accepted and understood their authoritative parenting style and genuine concerns regarding community gossip. Preparing now to embark on motherhood herself, Abby was acutely aware of how she wanted to raise her child, incorporating elements of family tradition while embracing different parenting styles in moderation.

CHAPTER 23

The contractions were coming thick and fast, vivid and real. Though the due date was two weeks, her baby was already on its way. It measured larger than average, and the doctor expressed concerns about her ability to deliver naturally due to her small build. Still, after discussing her options, it was decided that delivering the baby naturally would be best, with a caesarean section option if necessary.

"Argh!" Abby groaned through the increasing intensity of the contractions, trying to focus on breathing and recalling the techniques shared by her mother. With a sharp inhale, she forced her eyes open. "I can't handle this!" she moaned as the waves of discomfort grew stronger. Clutching her legs tightly together, she slowly manoeuvred them off the side of the bed using both arms for support as she struggled to sit up, placing a trembling hand on her swollen stomach. "Ruby, please wait just a little longer so Mama can get up."

With great effort and determination, Abby managed to hoist herself out of bed and took tentative steps towards the door. As she swung it open, anxious thoughts flooded her mind as she braced for the possibility of her water breaking at any moment. Standing before her on the other side was Sister Mary Rosetta Mancini, summoned to provide assistance in Abby's time of need.

Locking eyes with Sister Mary Rosetta Mancini, Abby managed a weak smile. "I'm so grateful you're here. I believe my baby is ready to make an appearance. Please call my parents."

In that moment, another surge of pain overtook her, and she cried out while gripping onto Sister Mary Rosetta Mancini's arm for support.

Excitement filled Sister Mary Rosetta Mancini's voice. "The miracle of life awaits us!"

Heading down the hallway towards the monastery hospital, they had to pause halfway as Abby could not continue walking due to the unbearable pain coursing through her body. Through gritted teeth and tears streaming down her face, she whimpered, "It hurts so much!"

"Abby, take deep breaths!" said Sister Mary Rosetta Mancini reassuringly. "You can do this; let's breathe together." Calling out for assistance, Sister Mary Louise and Sister Mary Josephine swiftly arrived to support Abby through the imminent childbirth.

As perspiration dripped from Abby's flushed face and panic set in when fluid gushed from between her legs, signalling her water had broken, she cried out in desperation. Without the aid of Sisters Mary Louise and Josephine steadying her weakened form, she feared she might collapse onto the floor. A cold cloth pressed against Abby's overheated forehead provided some comfort as a gentle voice coaxed soothing words into her ear: "Breathe deeply now, everything will be alright."

Moments later, Sister Mary Rosetta Mancini returned with a wheelchair, hastily assisting Abby into its seat alongside Sisters Mary Louise and Josephine for additional support during their journey towards the hospital.

"Hurry!"

Abby nodded as perspiration dripped down her face. She didn't want to give birth in the monastery hallway. "Oh my god, it's happening!" she said, her skin flushed and hot.

Another excruciating contraction gripped her, sending waves of panic through every inch of her being. Abby's hand clenched desperately around Sister Mary Rosetta Mancini's, as she fought against the consuming agony. Every breath felt like a struggle, her mind racing with anxious thoughts. Sister Mary maintained her calm, her voice a lifeline amidst the chaos. "Abby, breathe in through your nose and out through your mouth," she instructed gently.

Abby's mind briefly drifted to her mother's visits, laden with books on pregnancy: guides like "A Guide to Pregnancy and Birth," "Parent to Be," and "What to Expect When You're Expecting." They lined her shelves, meant to offer solace in knowledge, to quell the deep worry gnawing at her. But in these moments, all the preparation faded, leaving her grappling with the raw, unknown journey ahead.

Panic clawed at Abby's mind, her heart thundering in her chest. Sweat mixed with tears, marking her face with the raw emotions churning inside her. She clung desperately to the bedrail, each contraction surging through her like a storm she struggled to weather, knowing the ultimate climax was yet to come. The hospital gown felt like a flimsy shield, its delicate blue motif stark against her vulnerability.

A nurse approached her with sterile efficiency, instructing Abby to lean back. As the needle slipped into her arm, a sharp pang drew a gasp from her lips, her fingers curling instinctively into the sheet beneath her. Anxiety gnawed at her, the sterile room closing in as time seemed to stretch into an eternity.

Then, the midwife gently urged her to stand, her voice a balm against the rising tide of fear. With Sister Mary Rosetta Mancini lending her strength, Abby struggled to her feet, her body trembling as the effort intensified. Suddenly, the doors burst open, and her parents entered, accompanied by Dr. Lucio. Relief washed over her, momentarily eclipsing her anxiety. "Mama! Papa!" she cried, her voice a lifeline in the swirling chaos.

Immediately, her mother rushed over and reached out for Abby's hand while on the opposite side of the hospital bed, Abby's father stood and stroked her hair reassuringly. "Abby, it's going to be okay," he said. "I'm going to go and wait outside. Call if you need me."

The contractions intensified, becoming more challenging and enduring for longer periods. At this point, it was necessary for Dr. Lucio to examine her cervix by inserting his fingers into her vulva to assess its dilation. "Abby, I need you to remain calm," said Dr. Lucio, emphasising the importance of slow breathing.

"Abby, look at me!" Mama said. "Inhale... exhale; once more inhale and exhale."

They synchronised their breathing patterns in unison as a soothing rhythm enveloped them momentarily.

"She is dilated six centimetres," said the doctor, prompting Abby to push, and within moments she had fully dilated to ten centimetres, exerting herself with piercing screams.

"Arghhhhhh!" she screamed in agony, her body drained, her skin matted in sweat, and losing a significant amount of blood. "I can't do this anymore! I just want to go home!" Abby looked wearily at her mother.

"Yes, you can, my dear, I am right here beside you," said her mother.

Her blood pressure plummeted drastically, indicated by beeping monitors causing loss of consciousness in Abby, leading to a frantic scream from her mother. "Abby!"

"We need to take the baby out, she is haemorrhaging," said the doctor.

Abby's mother pleaded desperately for the doctors to save her daughter's life, gently caressing her forehead as she lay unconscious. "Please, wake up! wake up, Abby, please!" She prayed, asking God to intervene and save the baby.

Consciousness slowly returned to Abby following intensive medical intervention, including blood transfusions and oxygen support, to her mother's relief. She gave Abby words of encouragement, urging one final push towards delivering her child safely into the world.

"Abby, please make one more push!" the doctor urged.

Her mother and Sister Mary Rosetta Mancini stayed by her side, saying, "Abby push, you can do it!"

As the resonant sound of her mother's booming voice reverberated through Abby's ears, a sudden cry escaped from her lips. The urgency in her mother's tone was unmistakable as she fervently exclaimed, "It's nearly finished, just one more effort, puuuuuush!" Sister Mary Rosetta Mancini yelled, "PUSH!"

With every ounce of strength she could muster, Abby pushed with all her might.

And then, in the blink of an eye, it happened. One moment she wasn't there, and the next she was. The midwife triumphantly held up the newborn baby before Abby's eyes. Turning to Abby's mother with a pair of scissors in hand, the doctor asked, "Grandma, would you like to do the honours?"

Tears glistened in her eyes as she replied with a choked-up "Yes," taking hold of the scissors proudly.

With steady hands, she cut the umbilical cord, symbolising the entrance of this new life into a vibrant and colourful world.

The midwife swiftly took Ruby away for measurements and a cleanup before swaddling her up and returning her to Abby's waiting arms. Gazing down at the tiny face cradled in her embrace, Abby whispered softly with overflowing joy. "Hey there, it's me. You are absolutely beautiful." She gently clasped and kissed Ruby's delicate hand

A few moments later, Abby's father and Micky entered the birthing unit bearing gifts: a breathtaking bouquet of flowers and an oversized teddy bear.

In that moment between her parents and their grandchild, nothing else mattered. The once-pervasive anguish was replaced by pure happiness as they celebrated and embraced this new addition to their family.

Despite her fervent desire not to miss even a single instant of this profound occasion, exhaustion overtook Abby. Drifting off after the exertion of childbirth, she knew their newfound treasure belonged solely to them, a miraculous gift bestowed from above that inundated their hearts with boundless joy.

CHAPTER 24

One month after Ruby was born, Abby made a solemn return to the peaceful monastery to gather a few belongings and bid a bittersweet farewell to Father Michiel, as she prepared to embark on a new chapter in her life. She had made the bold decision to embark on a law degree at the esteemed University of Rome and was ready to begin her new life as a mother.

Little did she anticipate her visit to the monastery that day would lead to the discovery of a long-held secret held by Sister Mary Rosetta Mancini, causing an overwhelming surge of sorrow to engulf her.

Standing outside Father Michiel's office with the door slightly ajar, Abby inadvertently became privy to a conversation unfolding between two unfamiliar voices. The discussion seemed to revolve around matters closely related to Abby, piquing her curiosity. Intrigued by the exchange, Abby stealthily edged closer to the door to eavesdrop. However, due to the limited visibility afforded by the narrow opening, she struggled to discern their identities with any clarity.

One voice, gruff and tinged with emotion said, "I saw Sister Mary Rosetta Mancini holding little Ruby with such tenderness. It seemed to stir something deep within her."

The second voice expressed confusion and said, "What exactly happened to Sister Mary Rosetta Mancini?"

"Before her life here with us at the Convento de Santa Maria, Sister Mary Rosetta Mancini was a dance and music instructor in the vibrant city of Munich. She later discovered she was pregnant with her fiancé's child. One day, on her way home from work, she stopped at a local drug store and bought shoes for their future newborn, intending to surprise her partner during their dinner date that evening. Her fiancé, who was studying to become a doctor and nearing the end of his medical degree, was a wonderful man full of enthusiasm for life. To celebrate their joyful news, they opened a bottle of red wine and drank perhaps a bit too much. Although he insisted he was capable of driving, a drunk driver collided with their vehicle. In that single moment, Sister Mary Rosetta Mancini lost her beloved fiancé and the child they were so eager to welcome.

The second voice responded with sadness and shock laced in her tone. "Oh my Lord."

Abby covered her mouth in shock and quickly fled, not wanting to be seen listening in on other people's conversations. She gathered her belongings and left.

With her monastery days behind her, Abby focused on her studies. It gave her a renewed sense of purpose. It served as an example for Ruby that one should never give up on their dreams and aspirations, no matter what life threw at them. As a single mother, Abby felt a newfound sense of empowerment and capability as she stepped out of her comfort zone and completed her enrolment. Recognising that by earning her qualification, she would be able to provide for Ruby without relying on financial assistance from her parents was empowering. Having led a comfortable life under the care of her parents, Abby yearned for even greater comforts and opportunities for Ruby's future.

With the invaluable support of Maria, a friend of her mother's, Abby was able to navigate the challenges of balancing motherhood with her academic commitments. However, she understood she could not lean entirely on Maria, who had her own responsibilities managing art collection orders for numerous clients.

Even though she excelled academically with top grades, Abby noticed her concentration and memory were not as sharp as they once were due to the inevitable sleep deprivation that came with caring for Ruby. Juggling tasks such as changing diapers, breastfeeding, and soothing Ruby when agitated alongside studying, completing assignments, preparing for exams, and attending evening classes posed a formidable challenge.

Throughout her first year at university, much of her reading, writing, and assessments were completed during those precious moments when Ruby was asleep, resulting in countless late nights. Desperate to complete her degree despite the obstacles in her path, Abby dedicated her time to both studying and mothering, leaving little room for social interactions or romance.

As a full-time student committed to balancing motherhood with university and an internship at a law firm several hours per week, there were no shortcuts in Abby's life; only the constant demands placed upon her by Ruby's needs alongside her pursuit of higher education. To maintain equilibrium between these aspects of her life, Abby made sacrifices in terms of social engagements, instead living vicariously through Vani's experiences while focusing primarily on nurturing Ruby and excelling in her studies.

Vani was embarking on a promising career path as a junior public relations specialist at Paramount Plus. It was not solely her academic achievements that paved the way for this opportunity, but rather a fortuitous connection through her father's network. As Vani delved deeper into the world of public relations, she quickly discovered her ambitions were leading her down a tumultuous and unpredictable path. Her personal life mirrored this instability as she found herself constantly moving from one romantic relationship to another.

One such relationship that dominated Vani's life was with Krish, a partnership marked by its toxic and dysfunctional nature. Their on-and-off romance became notorious within their social circles due to its destructive patterns. The cycle of breaking up and reconciling seemed never-ending, fraught with heated arguments, heart-wrenching moments of betrayal, and possessive behaviour. Despite the negative reputation their relationship garnered, Vani and Krish inevitably found themselves drawn back to each other time and again. Their reunions were characterised by intense physical intimacy, grand plans for future vacations together, and discussions about the possibility of marriage. In essence, Vani's journey from academia to the professional world was coloured by the rollercoaster ride of her turbulent relationship with Krish. This constant state of flux tested her resilience and forced her to confront the complexities of love, passion, and commitment in ways she had never imagined.

Vani finally arrived in Italy, her heart brimming with excitement to meet little Ruby for the first time. As she cradled the tiny bundle in her arms, she marvelled at Ruby's enchanting green eyes and light brown hair. "Oh, Abby, she's absolutely gorgeous," she gushed, the warmth of her words wrapping around them both.

The afternoon unfolded with laughter and heartfelt conversations, as they savoured the rich, complex flavours of Red Al Grenache wine. Spread before them was a delightful array of crackers topped with cheese, salami, and olives, and a bowl of luscious chocolates that added a dash of sweetness to their gathering. Amidst this heartwarming scene, Vani, with a sparkle in her eyes and a tender smile, voiced a heartfelt dream: her strong desire to become a mother. Her words hung in the air, filled with hope and love, deepening the bond between them.

Abby sympathised with Vani and glanced at Ruby sleeping peacefully in her crib. "She is an angel."

"I am envious of you, Abby," she said with sadness in her eyes.

Abby let out a soft, almost imperceptible chuckle under her breath as she spoke in a hushed tone. "Wait, are you saying you're envious of me? Why?" "I've always looked up to you for your unwavering determination and focus. Even with the challenges of pregnancy, your goals remained unchanged and look at how far you've come! You even managed to secure an internship. I am genuinely proud of everything you've accomplished, and what strikes me the most is how content and happy you seem with your life. It's something I wish I had, too."

Abby's gaze turned sombre as she reflected on her own feelings of envy towards Vani, realising she had failed to consider her friend might have struggled with similar emotions.

Abby reached out and clasped her hand gently before opening up about her own insecurities. "I have envied you, Vani. You had the opportunity to live your life fully, attending Yale, exploring the world... meanwhile, I faced a period of darkness, alienation, and loneliness beyond anything I could have imagined. The man I loved walked away from me. The thing is, I don't regret any of it because now I have Ruby. But this was never how I envisioned my life unfolding."

Abby's eyes glanced over at Ruby sleeping peacefully nearby before she continued. "It has taken me a long time to find inner peace and acceptance with where my life has led me. There were moments when I thought I would never make it to this point."

As tears welled up in her eyes, Abby wiped them away with the back of her hand, revealing the depth of emotion that clung to her words.

Vani nodded. "I understand."

Abby's head bobbed in agreement as she absorbed Vani's words. "I understand you want all this for yourself, Vani, but to achieve it, you must cut ties with Krish and start anew with someone who genuinely loves and appreciates you."

Vani nodded sombrely, signifying her understanding of Abby's counsel. Yet, deep down, Abby harboured a sense of unease, knowing all too well that once Vani returned to New York, she would inevitably be drawn back into Krish's embrace and resume traversing the same treacherous path.

As their conversation lingered in the air, Vani reached for the bottle of Red Al Grenache on the table and poured herself another generous glass, watching as the crimson liquid cascaded until it brimmed dangerously close to spilling over.

Anticipating a long evening ahead filled with heartfelt discussions and introspection, Abby observed Vani closely as she settled back against the plush cushions of the sofa. Suddenly, a spark ignited within Vani's eyes as she straightened up abruptly, her demeanour shifting from contemplative to resolute.

"Abby!" Vani began tentatively, enveloping herself in a cosy blanket draped around her shoulders like a protective shawl. The flickering light from the nearby candles cast dancing shadows across her face as she prepared to express her thoughts. Meanwhile, Abby tore her gaze away from her phone after receiving a text message from Micky detailing his upcoming rendezvous with Andrea.

"Do thoughts of Joey ever cross your mind?"

To which Abby responded with, "No, not anymore," which was not entirely truthful. There were moments when she pondered about his whereabouts and the memories they once shared. With Ruby now a prominent figure in her life, it seemed impossible to completely erase Joey from her thoughts. Nevertheless, one thing remained clear in Abby's mind: she harboured no desire to reunite with him.

Abby often found herself feeling isolated and detached from the ordinary rhythm of life. Her academic pursuits served as a lifeline connecting her to the world beyond her own solitude. The frequent visits from her family provided much-needed comfort and companionship during these trying times. Joining a student club offered Abby an avenue to interact with peers and forge meaningful relationships. Even with her busy schedule, Abby discovered the art of crocheting.

After five years of dedication and hard work, Abby graduated with top honours, basking in a newfound sense of freedom and accomplishment. Her bond with Sister Mary Rosetta Mancini had left an indelible mark on her soul. Their unexpected friendship illuminated Abby's darkest days, filling them with warmth and hope. The absence of regular interactions with Sister Mary Rosetta Mancini left Abby yearning for their intimate conversations and strolls through the garden.

The wise nun always made Abby feel valued and encouraged her to believe that brighter days lay ahead. She helped Abby view her pregnancy as a source of joy and taught her the essence of genuine love. Through Sister Mary Rosetta Mancini's guidance, negative emotions such as anger and resentment dissipated over time, leaving room for acceptance and affection to flourish. Under her mentorship, Abby's self-assurance blossomed as she realised her intrinsic strength as a woman who charted her own path in life.

Through this transformative journey, Abby discovered how to embrace self-love and appreciate the blessings bestowed upon her. The profound connection shared between them resonated deeply within Abby's heart, evoking a surge of emotions. In an unexpected twist of fate, within the confines of a monastery, Sister Mary Rosetta Mancini assumed the role of a fairy godmother, imparting wisdom and guidance that enabled Abby to rediscover her true essence.

Still, Abby could not forget the conversation she had overheard, and how hard it must have been for Sister Mary Rosetta Mancini. Holding Ruby in her arms must have been extremely harrowing for her. Overwhelmed with empathy and sorrow, Abby contemplated the fragile nature of life and the injustices that often accompanied it. In that moment, she couldn't help but feel disillusioned by the harsh realities of existence, questioning whether true fairness could ever truly exist in this world.

CHAPTER 25

Return to Queens, Boulevard NYC

The scene at JFK airport on that Sunday afternoon was nothing short of chaotic, with families bustling in every direction, taxis forming orderly queues, and hired drivers holding signs aloft as travellers and backpackers awaited shuttle buses outside the terminal. Amidst this hectic atmosphere, after a five-year absence, Abby found herself back in her homeland with her child, embarking on a journey that would forever alter the trajectory of her life as she sought to mend her broken and bruised heart.

In the midst of all the noise and commotion at the airport, Abby sensed Ruby's nervousness and gently squeezed her hand. "Are you alright, sweetheart?"

"So many people are here, where are they all going?" she asked.

"Some people are travelling back home to see their families and friends, while others travel for work or visit different countries for vacations."

"Are we going to stay with Grandpa and Grandma forever?" Ruby asked.

"Not forever, just until we find our own place."

"Do you think I will like New York?"

"Well, yes it's one of the most exciting cities in the world. That's why there are so many people at the airport. If it was boring, the airport would be empty."

Ruby smiled.

"Mama, does Uncle Micky and Aunt Vani live here, too?" Ruby asked.

"Yes, they do, baby."

They made their way through the crowd towards the exit. Just then, her father's truck pulled into the no parking zone, risking a fine. Observing her father step out of the truck and walk towards the boot, Ruby let go of her mother's hand and sprinted excitedly towards her grandfather.

A smile graced Abby's face as she witnessed her papa's delight upon seeing his granddaughter, a truly heartwarming sight.

"Ruby, don't run, be careful!" Abby yelled, shaking her head.

But Ruby couldn't contain her excitement. "Nonno!"

Abby's father extended his arms and hugged Ruby, picking her up. Ruby held onto his neck as he playfully swung her around.

Abby felt happy, knowing her father was also joyful and nothing else mattered. As they walked towards the truck, her mama turned to her husband.

"Why are you parked here, it's illegal?"

He quickly pecked her on the cheek, but she rejected it.

"Adriano, you might get fined," she said as she got into the car with Ruby.

"Looks like some things haven't changed," said Abby, raising her eyebrow.

Her father smiled and winked at her. "It's good to have you back, kiddo," he said with teary eyes. He held onto her tightly for a moment, and Abby rested her head on his shoulder.

"I'm happy to finally be home, Papa," she replied.

"Hurry up before we get caught and receive a fine!" Gabriella barked from the backseat.

"Relax, woman! You nag like an old lady!"

Abby and her father exchanged glances and burst into laughter. Abby noticed her mother didn't find it amusing and sighed. She didn't bother arguing back; it seemed pointless when she was so delighted to be home.

Abby inhaled deeply, entered the front seat of the truck, and patiently waited for her father to load their luggage in the boot. Then he started the engine and began their journey to Queens.

Abby soon became accustomed to life as a New Yorker once more. Having established her career as a lawyer in Italy, she couldn't shake the sense of hopelessness that pervaded her thoughts about the future. Determined to counterbalance each painful memory with moments of positivity and love, Abby cherished her time spent with Ruby, creating enduring memories that served as beacons of light in an otherwise tumultuous existence.

Every time Abby gazed upon Ruby's innocent face, she couldn't help but be reminded of the love that had once betrayed her heart so cruelly. The wounds inflicted by past betrayals remained raw even after years had passed, haunting Abby with fleeting moments of anguish that underscored the irrevocable loss she had endured. Nevertheless, driven by an unwavering commitment to shield her daughter from the same heartbreaks that had marred her own past, Abby resolved to go to great lengths to protect Ruby from any harm Joey might bring into their lives.

Abby needed time to adjust and acclimate to her unfamiliar living situation, striving to strike a harmonious balance between the significant milestones and the seemingly trivial moments that made up her new reality. Initially, she and her mother took on the responsibility of aiding Ruby in acclimating to school life and arranging their shared living spaces. Meanwhile, Abby diligently searched for job opportunities to support herself and Ruby.

It was during this period of transition that Abby stumbled upon a promising opportunity at a law firm in New York City, courtesy of her papa's acquaintance, Ray Williams, a seasoned criminal lawyer who had dedicated his entire existence to his career and passion for fishing, eschewing marriage and parenthood along the way. Despite his reservations about taking on a newcomer like Abby, Mr. Williams ultimately extended an offer to her, paving the way for a fortuitous turn of events.

As Abby navigated through the whirlwind of changes unfolding in her life, she couldn't help but feel immensely grateful for the blessings that came her way. Little did she know, amidst all the newfound opportunities and experiences awaiting her in the city that never sleeps, there lurked unexpected encounters and blurred lines between truth and lies that would soon challenge everything she held dear.

To protect their loved ones from prying eyes and wagging tongues within their close-knit community, Abby's parents resorted to extreme measures to keep certain truths concealed from public scrutiny. Their primary concern revolved around safeguarding

Abby and Ruby from potential gossip mongers at any cost, even if it meant resorting to artifice and deceit as a means of self-preservation.

Adding yet another layer of complexity to the already intricate tapestry of their lives was Ruby, a distant cousin who tragically lost both of her parents in a devastating accident. To maintain appearances and uphold a facade of familial unity within their household, Abby's family concocted an elaborate narrative detailing a strong bond reminiscent of a mother-daughter relationship between Abby and Ruby, one they projected outwardly for all to see.

This charade continued unabated with Abby willingly assuming the role of a nurturing caregiver for Ruby, whose emotional scars ran deep following the loss of her mother. Through tender gestures like openly referring to Abby as "Mama" or holding hands in public, Abby sought to fill the void left behind by Ruby's late mother while convincing those around them of their unbreakable bond.

However, their carefully constructed facade began to unravel when Angela Giovanni, an astute observer with keen instincts expressed doubts regarding Ruby's sudden reappearance in their lives. Unfazed by such revelations and armed with unwavering determination, Angela set out on a quest to unearth the truth behind this mysterious cousin whom no one seemed to have heard of before, thereby throwing into disarray the fragile story maintained by Abby's family.

CHAPTER 26

Abby sighed as she rummaged through her handbag, her movements frantic yet familiar. Relief washed over her when her fingers finally curled around the cigarette pack tucked inside. With a small, victorious smile, she made her way down the hallway towards the back door, eager to indulge in a moment of solitude on the patio. The calming ritual of smoking offered her a brief escape from the whirlwind of her hectic life. However, Abby couldn't ignore the fact that Ruby absolutely hated her smoking habit. It was a topic of tension between them, and Abby often made half-hearted promises to quit. Somehow, the promises always faded away as the days wore on.

Stepping into the gentle embrace of the evening, Abby placed a cigarette between her lips and struck a match, the small flame briefly illuminating her face. The familiar sensation of the first deep inhale brought a sense of tranquillity, and she exhaled a thick plume of smoke, watching it dissipate into the night. Just as she began to settle into her quiet moment, Ruby's distinct and spirited voice pierced the darkness, calling out to her from the back door.

"MUM...! What are you doing?" Ruby's disapproving gaze bore into Abby, clearly upset by her mother's filthy habit.

With guilt, Abby tossed the half-smoked cigarette and turned to face her daughter, bracing for what was sure to be an uncomfortable conversation.

"You said you stopped," Ruby said disdainfully.

"I know, and I will."

"When?" As if on cue, a gust of wind blew over them followed by a sudden flash of lightning overhead. Shivering slightly from the cold, Abby sighed. "It's not that simple. But I promise I'll stop soon, okay?"

"I don't believe you!" she said frowning with her hands on her hips.

"Let's go inside and finish this conversation, baby," she said as the wind intensified, and Abby shivered as the cold seeped through her clothes.

Just as they headed indoors, the doorbell rang unexpectedly. Abby turned towards her papa. "Are you expecting any visitors tonight?"

Before he could respond, the front door swung open, and Mr. and Mrs. Giovanni entered unannounced.

Abby's stomach dropped as she watched them march into their home. She knew eventually she would have to face them, but she was completely unprepared at that moment.

Anxiety gripped her as Mr. Giovanni exchanged pleasantries with Papa while Mrs. Giovanni fixed an intense gaze upon Abby that sent shivers down her spine.

Mr. Giovanni knelt in front of Ruby, "What's your name?" he asked, pretending not to know, causing her to shyly mutter, "Ruby," before seeking safety behind her grandfather as Frank burst into laughter, then darted off to play elsewhere, away from all the attention.

Abby released the breath she was holding, which had turned her face pale. "Hello, Mr. and Mrs. Giovanni." She kissed them on the cheek.

Mr. Giovanni's smile was genuine and full of warmth as he gazed at Abby, pride evident in his eyes. "You've reached a remarkable achievement by becoming an attorney," he said, his voice carrying both admiration and affection. "Your mama and papa are incredibly proud of you." He settled into the couch comfortably, taking the glass of fine whisky offered by her father, and raised it slightly in a gesture of celebration.

A choked sound escaped her throat as she uttered, "Thank you so much."

She followed them into the living room and sat opposite the Giovannis. Ruby copied and sat beside her mother. "Mama, who are these people?" she asked with a curious expression on her face.

Abby glanced at Mrs Giovanni when she laughed, knowing it was because Ruby had called her mama when, according to their cover story, she wasn't. "The Giovannis are our closest friends," Abby said, deeply on edge. "It's time for bed now since you have school tomorrow."

Mrs. Giovanni asked if Ruby could stay a little longer. Ruby, full of energy and resistance, vehemently protested. "No, Mama! It's too early for bed. I want to stay with Nonno and Nonna." She leapt off the couch and climbed onto Nonno's lap.

Perspiration formed on Abby's hands as she observed Mrs. Giovanni's narrowed gaze. Rising from the couch with a sense of resolve, Abby sternly reiterated to Ruby it was bedtime and Nonno had no say in it.

"Okay, Mama, but I want Nonno to tuck me in," said Ruby. She then kissed Nonna goodnight, whispering, "I love you, Nonna," before returning to Abby and wrapping her arms around her neck.

"I love you too, honey," Abby replied with a smile as Ruby held onto her a little longer.

With smiles, everyone bid, "Goodnight Ruby" before Mrs. Giovanni directed turned to Abby. "Why does Ruby call you mummy?"

"I remind her of her mother in many ways." She maintained a composed expression as she maintained the lie they had spun. "It caught me off guard initially, but I have grown accustomed to it."

"Your mother told me you had taken her under your wing," Mrs. Giovanni said warmly. "I just didn't realise how deeply you cared for the child."

"In the aftermath of her mother's passing, I felt a strong pull," Abby replied softly. "Ruby needed someone to lean on, someone to offer her the nurturing care and stability she had lost so abruptly. I paused...stepping into a motherly role was the least I could do... to ease her pain and wrap her in the comfort of a loving home."

Mrs. Giovanni nodded, her face warm with understanding. "You've done more than that. It's a rare gift to care so deeply for someone not born of your blood."

Mrs. Giovanni leaned forward eagerly, disbelief etched across every line of her face. "But... my dear Abby, you must consider how this decision may impact your prospects for marriage," she said.

"I am not worried and have no immediate plans of getting married."

Mrs. Giovanni's laughter came out effortlessly, resonating with a familiar sense of zeal as she interlocked her hands joyfully. "Oh, darling, don't have such thoughts, you're an incredibly beautiful young lady; it's time to consider settling down."

Abby experienced a wave of discomfort that settled uneasily in her heart and stomach.

Suddenly, a clap of thunder reverberated around the house followed by a streak of lightning that momentarily disrupted the power supply before it was swiftly restored, catching everyone off guard.

Startled by the unexpected occurrence, Abby leapt up from the couch and ran upstairs upon hearing Ruby's distressed cries from her bedroom.

"Mama, Mama!" Ruby wailed inconsolably, tears cascading down her delicate cheeks. Without hesitation, Abby rushed to her daughter's side. "Mama's here, baby, it's okay, it's okay!" With gentle strokes and comforting pats on her back, Abby calmed Ruby until she eventually fell asleep in her mother's arms. The distant thunder continued to loom ominously outside, prompting Abby to hold onto her daughter even tighter.

After twenty minutes, Abby returned to the living room.

"How's Ruby? Is she okay?" they all asked.

"The thunder frightened her; she was so scared."

A few minutes later, her papa entered the room with a flashlight in hand, preparing for any more power outages. "Seems like we're in for a rainy Christmas," he said as he added more logs to the fire.

Mr. Giovanni agreed as he inched closer to the fireplace.

Abby joined the women in the kitchen and assisted in setting the dining table for dinner. When she finished, she stuck her head out of the kitchen door and called out, "Dinner is ready!"

In response to Abby's call, the men made their way into the kitchen, whisky in hand. Taking their seats at the table, Abby sat at the far end, distancing herself as much as possible from the scrutinous eyes of the Giovannis, though she was filled with a mixture of gratitude and nostalgia at seeing them once again, and soon became lost in memories of Joey.

"Abby, it's great to have you home with us," said Mr. Giovanni. "We truly missed you."

Abby smiled. "It feels wonderful to be back. I missed all of you, too." A stray strand of hair fell across her face, which she tucked behind her ear.

Everyone fell silent as the rain gradually subsided.

Mr. Giovanni looked across at Abby. "I must confess, I am truly amazed and filled with pride to see you embracing a maternal role with Ruby. It demonstrates tremendous character. You truly are a kind-hearted person, Abby."

"Thank you."

Surprised by his heartfelt words, Abby exchanged glances with Mrs. Giovanni, who seemed less than convinced. As conversation flowed around the table, Mrs. Giovanni extended an invitation for dinner with the children over the weekend, catching Abby off guard.

Abby's heart raced as she unintentionally dropped her fork, causing a momentary disturbance. With a nervous chuckle and an apology, she tried to regain her composure but found it difficult.

"Thank you so much for the invitation," said Abby's father, "but we already have plans this weekend.

Mr. Giovanni had just finished his meal and polished off his whisky before reclining in his chair. "Cancel your plans; you will join us for dinner."

Abby's mother chimed in. "Let's leave it for another time."

Mr. Giovanni sat upright. "All our children are here for Christmas holidays; it has been so long since we celebrated together. I won't take no for an answer!" Abby exchanged glances with her parents and waited for their response.

"Okay, we'll come," said her papa.

Mrs. Giovanni turned towards Abby, seeking confirmation "You'll be joining us, too?"

Abby shook her head. "Unfortunately, I can't. I'm sorry but we've already committed to a birthday party hosted by one of Ruby's classmates."

Mrs. Giovanni smirked. "It's alright, Abby, we'll wait for you."

Abby paused before responding. "No really, it's not necessary. Go ahead without us. I'm sorry, but we can't make it."

Mrs. Giovanni shook her head. "Nonsense."

Even as pressure mounted from all sides including an implicit directive from her own father, who muttered under his breath affirmatively "She will be there," Abby fought stubbornly, staring blankly at her father's face, wondering what he was doing.

"Absolutely perfect!" Mrs. Giovanni said, her hands clasped together in a gesture of delight as she settled comfortably into her seat.

Abby hid her nausea by taking small sips of water. She shifted her focus back to Mrs. Giovanni, uncertain about the woman's request and its potential implications. Abby couldn't help but wonder if Mrs. Giovanni had any inkling about her relationship with

Joey. The fear that Joey had divulged their secret affair caused Abby extreme anxiety.

Abby excused herself and impulsively bolted from the kitchen, leaving her half-eaten plate in the sink as she hurriedly made her way to her bedroom, slamming the door shut behind her. Memories and thoughts flooded her mind as she reached into her pocket for a pack of cigarettes. Opening the window to let in the chilly breeze, she took a long drag, reminiscing about her last conversation with Joey.

"Abby, it's over," he had said. "I believe we should go our separate ways, and I don't want this baby.... You should have an abortion."

Fighting back tears, Abby prayed Joey wouldn't show up that weekend. Lost in contemplation, she failed to notice when her mother knocked on the door, bearing a tray of coffee and cake. Hurriedly stubbing out her cigarette, she opened the door to greet her mother with a forced smile and muttered, "thank you" as she accepted the tray. Knowing it wasn't the right time to argue about her father's reckless behaviour during dinner, Abby decided to bide her time until after the Giovanni's departed before voicing her opinion on the matter.

For the next hour, she hustled her way through some administrative tasks while enjoying slices of her mother's lemon cake. As she pondered how she could wriggle out of attending Sunday dinner at the Giovanni's house without raising suspicions, she absentmindedly played with her hair. Feeling increasingly confused and unsure about Mrs. Giovanni's awareness of Joey and Abby's relationship, Abby found herself contemplating ways to avoid facing any uncomfortable setting.

The weekend snuck up on Abby more quickly than she expected, and she was resolute in her decision to miss Sunday dinner at all costs.

"Dad, can you please tell them I'm feeling unwell?" she pleaded while sitting in the kitchen untangling Ruby's hair.

"Mama, that hurts!" Ruby piped up unexpectedly.

"Oh, sweetie! I'm sorry," said Abby, leaning forward to kiss Ruby's head.

Glancing over at her father engrossed in his morning newspaper and coffee across from them in silence, Abby said, "Dad! Please!"

She then picked up the brush from her lap and combed Ruby's hair before styling it with a ribbon. "Is this better?"

"Yep," Ruby responded with a nod.

"All done," Abby muttered.

Ruby rose from the floor and turned to face her mother.

"Beautiful as always," said Abby after brushing Ruby's cheek gently with one hand and placing kisses on both cheeks.

"Enough, Mum!" Ruby darted off into the living room, leaving behind a bemused yet radiating smile on Abby's face. She let out a quiet chuckle and moved closer to her father.

Closing his newspaper with deliberate care, he removed his glasses. His eyes focused intently on Abby with an unwavering intensity that seemed to pierce her soul. Speaking in a soft but firm tone, he asked, "Are you afraid of Joey?"

Abby's stomach twisted into knots. With a shaky voice betraying her inner turmoil, she said, "No, father, I'm not. Once he sees us, I'm afraid the truth will be revealed."

He reached out and clasped her hand firmly. "We stick to our version of events, nothing changes," he said with a smile.

Rising slowly from his seat, a grave expression settled upon his face as he looked back at Abby. His voice took on a stern edge as he issued a warning that cut through the air like a sharpened blade. "If he causes any trouble, let me know immediately."

Abby nodded but couldn't shake off her fear. She attempted to smile but failed. Sensing her distress and unease, he enveloped her in a tight embrace. "Abby, everything will be alright."

Clutching onto him tightly, Abby released a sharp breath. Her words carried a weight of longing for peace and certainty as she whispered softly against his chest. "I truly hope so, Papa."

CHAPTER 27

Three days before Christmas, Abby stood outside the Giovanni residence, her nerves tightly wound in anticipation of encountering Joey after five years. The mere thought of coming face to face with the man who had shattered her heart and callously abandoned her caused an ache in her chest she could not ignore. Countless regrettable memories flooded her mind, causing her to hesitate momentarily before realising it was too late to turn back now. With a heavy heart, she released a sigh that seemed to echo through the crisp winter air.

Abby had changed outfits several times before settling on a stunning French red V-neck dress paired with an elegant Gucci coat. The faint scent of French cologne clung to her fingers after she had delicately applied perfume along the base of her throat. The cost of her entire outfit amounted to three monthly pay cheques, yet she knew true beauty came from within and was merely an accessory to her strength and independence as a woman.

Ruby wore a precious pink velvet dress with cream stockings that accentuated her innocent appearance, complete with her long curly hair and adorable little boots. Taking a deep breath and exhaling slowly, Abby finally mustered up the courage to press the intercom button.

Mr. Giovanni greeted them at the door. "Abby, Ruby, you made it!" His voice was filled with excitement.

"Hello, Mr Giovanni," she responded, leaning in to give him a kiss on both cheeks.

He furrowed his brow and looked down at little Ruby, whom he picked up in his arms and kissed on the cheek. "Hello, Ruby."

"Hi," she replied softly.

As they stepped over the threshold, they were met by Mrs. Giovanni, who wore an apron and showered each of them with kisses while expressing genuine happiness at Abby's attendance.

Abby expressed her gratitude towards Mrs. Giovanni for welcoming them into her home, and assisted Ruby in removing her coat. A wave of relief washed over Abby as her parents and Micky entered the room, their presence providing a sense of comfort.

"Nonna!" Ruby joyfully shrieked as she darted towards her grandmother with open arms, enveloping her in a tight embrace around the waist. Her grandmother's head turned, and her eyes widened with excitement. "Oh, darling, you're here! And don't you look beautiful in that dress!" She wrapped her arms around Ruby and kissed her head.

"Hi, Mama," Abby said, approaching her and kissing her on the cheek.

"Hi, honey, what took you so long?"

"There was a lot of traffic on the road today."

"Ah, indeed, we're just three days from Christmas, a typically stressful time. Many people often wait until the last minute to buy gifts."

"I am also guilty," said Mrs Giovanni, raising her hand. "I just finished wrapping my gifts yesterday."

Abby stood in the kitchen, staring restlessly at Mrs. Giovanni. "What can I do to help?"

"Honey, we have it all under control here, why don't you take Ruby and join the others in the living room."

"Are you sure?"

"Yes, darling."

Abby nodded. "Alright."

She reached out and gently clasped Ruby's hand, leading her down the hallway to the living room. Suddenly, her steps came to an abrupt halt as her gaze drifted upwards towards the array of framed photographs on the wall, stopping at one featuring young Joey. A flutter of anticipation coursed through her veins, causing her heart to skip a beat in response. Just then, raucous laughter resonated from within the living room, prompting Abby to rush in. "What did I miss?"

Eyes sparkling with delight, Ruby said animatedly, "Uncle Micky!"

Without hesitation, she bolted across the room and flung herself into his waiting arms, clinging tightly to his neck. The bond between Ruby and Micky was heartwarming; he effortlessly embodied the role of a caring and hip uncle, showering her with endless affection and participating in a myriad of enjoyable activities together. Whether playfully tossing her into the air, an activity she relished wholeheartedly, teaching her how to ride a bike or swim, or treating her to movie outings, Micky never failed to keep his promises. He remained steadfast in his support by attending school events alongside Ruby's grandparents and remembering significant dates without fail.

Ruby sometimes pondered why other children her age had fathers, and this curiosity touched a tender spot in her heart. Her mother, Abby, sensed the silent emotions Ruby felt growing up without a father figure. Abby carried her own bittersweet memories of Joey but lovingly decided to wait until Ruby was older to share their family's story, ensuring Ruby would be ready to embrace the truth with understanding.

During this time, Abby's father stepped in to fulfill the role of a father figure in Ruby's life. His presence was a comforting anchor, wrapping Ruby in a cocoon of warmth and safety. He became a guiding light, offering not just boundaries and advice but also a deep well of affection and support. This nurturing relationship became a cornerstone of Ruby's development, offering her security and confidence. Her grandfather's steadfast protection and unwavering love ensured Ruby felt cherished and emotionally secure, forming a bond that strengthened her well-being and will help her grow into a resilient young lady.

Once, after returning home from school, Ruby had approached her with a question that had been on Abby's mind since. "Is my dad dead?" Her voice trembled with confusion as she looked at her mother with a pained expression. Alarmed by Ruby's distressing query, Abby knelt to meet Ruby at eye level, taking hold of her hand. "Ruby, who told you this?"

Ruby tried to speak but no words came out; instead, tears filled her eyes.

It broke Abby's heart to see Ruby in such a state. With tears, Abby implored Ruby to reveal who had told her this information.

Eventually, Ruby confessed. "A boy from my class." She then lowered her eyes to the ground.

"Baby girl," Abby said gently yet firmly, "Look at me!"

Ruby looked up at her mother as tears rolled down cheeks.

"Your father is not dead!" Her voice quavered with emotion as she fought back tears. "If he repeats those words again, I will contact your school and arrange a meeting with his parents."

Ruby nodded solemnly, and Abby enveloped her tightly. "Damn you, Joey!" she muttered soundlessly, trying to suppress the intense hatred towards him.

"Abby," squealed Tony in a high-pitched voice when he arrived at the Giovanni's home. "I'm glad you came." He threw his arms around her. "It feels like ages since we last caught up."

"Wow, look at you! I forgot how beautiful you are," he added with a chuckle. Taking hold of her hands, he spun her around lovingly, making her blush. She had always been aware of Tony's infatuation towards her. He was a hopeless romantic, constantly trying to catch her attention with sweet words and gestures. He would go out of his way to bring joy, sharing food, tutoring sessions, letting her win at board games. He longed for her heart but ceased efforts when he realised long ago that her feelings were not reciprocated, especially when he attempted to kiss her during a family trip to Italy and Abby pulled away. However, none of that seemed important now as they embraced each other and laughed like childhood friends, rediscovering their deep connection.

With a slightly jealous tone, a woman approached Tony and asked, "Who is this?"

The woman, whose eyes were the bluest she had ever seen, was petite, and her long hair was jet black. With an assertive grip on Tony's arm, she said, "Tony, why haven't you introduced me yet?"

With a strangely guilty face, Tony faced her and cleared his throat. "Francesca, this is Abagail, a close family friend."

Francesca's cold stare scanned Abby from head to toe.

Tony faced Abby. "This is Francesca, umm, my girlfriend."

Abby stretched out her hand. "Lovely to meet you. I hope we can become friends."

She gave a faint smile. "Hi." She raised her wine glass to her lips. After taking a deep sip, she turned and made her way back into the crowd.

"She seems... lovely," Abby said.

Tony smiled uncomfortably. "I apologise for her. She tends to get jealous." He shook his head nonchalantly. "But I love her, so I tolerate it."

They shared a chuckle.

"Mummy, look what Uncle Micky got me!" said Ruby, interrupting Abby and Tony as she tore open the box and revealed a baby doll.

"Did you say thank you?" asked Abby.

"Yes, I did."

Abby realised Tony and Ruby had never met her daughter before. "Ruby, please say hello to Uncle Tony."

Tony knelt and extended his hand. "Nice to meet you, Miss Ruby."

"You are not my uncle. I only have one uncle and his name is Micky." She dashed off to the fireplace to sit beside Micky, Andrea, and Francesca.

Tony chuckled and stood up. "She's feisty and sweet," he said. "Like you."

"Tony, I apologise for Ruby's insensitive comment. She didn't intend it to come across that way. I honestly can't understand where she gets it from."

"It's actually quite endearing," he replied, and went on to express admiration for Abby raising Ruby as her own.

"Thank you, Tony. I can only do my best, right?" She shifted her attention to Ruby, who was holding her crotch.

"Mummy, I need to go to the bathroom."

"Tony, let's catch up later, okay?"

"Of course, go ahead... and hurry!"

She tightly held Ruby's hand and rushed down the hallway when she heard the front door close with a bang. She turned her head slightly and regretted it immediately when she glimpsed Joey standing at the entrance. Fear surged through her, causing a knot to twist uncomfortably in her stomach, making it difficult to breathe. Seeing him after so many years made her desperately want to escape.

A young woman with striking blonde hair whispered something into Joey's ear while he remained completely still, fixed on staring directly at Abby as she rushed ahead towards the bathroom, reassuring Ruby they were almost there.

When catching sight of herself in the mirror hanging on the wall nearby, fear and panic combined in Abby's eyes. She tried to compose herself by running her shaky fingers through her tousled raven-laced locks before silently reciting affirmations like "You've got this!".

"Mummy, I've finished," said Ruby.

This was followed by a knock on the bathroom door. It made her jump. In a strained voice, she called out, "The bathroom's occupied!"

"Abby, it's your mother!"

After washing Ruby's hands and opening the door slightly, Abby noticed her mother's distressed expression before she closed her eyes tightly and massaged her temples. Abby clutched her mother's hand reassuringly and uttered, "Mama, don't worry. Everything will be fine." She wanted to believe her own reassurance but struggled.

"Avoid him at all times and keep your distance, do you hear me?" her mama whispered.

Abby just stared at her mother's anxious face. "Mama, please relax! I've got this."

She nodded and returned to the kitchen.

Abby took a deep breath, opened the bathroom door, and rejoined Ruby in the living room. She walked in with a calm manner until she spotted him with his back towards her, in deep conversation with the blonde woman. She had forgotten how tall and broad he was, like a football player, towering over the woman. Unaware of Abby and Ruby's presence, they moved to the sofa. Abby half-listened to Francesca speaking passionately. "Because all men are true narcissists," she said, locking eyes with Tony.

"Oh, come on, Franny," Tony playfully taunted with an embarrassed smirk.

Just then, Mrs. Giovanni entered the room through the sliding doors. "Dinner is ready, kids. Let's continue this discussion in the dining room."

Then Joey turned to face the room. Abby felt a sudden loss of air as if it had been sucked out of her lungs. An icy dread gripped her heart as their eyes met, but she looked away. Still, she could feel his eyes burning into her like laser beams, making her skin heat up. Unable to keep up the pretence of ignoring him, she ultimately swung her eyes back and remembered how deeply in love she once was; he was the only man who had held that place in her heart. Memories of their past flooded her thoughts. She noticed how incredibly attractive he had become, with a short beard and those captivating eyes that immediately caught any woman's attention. His smile still possessed the ability to charm beautiful women, the ideal man perhaps, until one fell pregnant and then he bolted for the nearest door. Something about him hinted at a sinister side. He was more powerful than her, fearless in the face of anything, except fatherhood, obviously, and lived by his own rules. His confidence was infectious, mixed with a hint of arrogance, dressed impeccably in Armani clothing that no woman could resist. He exuded danger. His green eyes continued to lock onto hers, and his expression was inscrutable. His eyes were peculiar yet familiar to her. The silence between them was raw and intense. There was something commanding about the way he looked at women. Despite this distraction, he attempted to turn his focus back to the woman beside him but failed. This wasn't the Joey she used to know; now he stared at her defiantly, almost challenging her. Was that resentment in his eyes? Abby remained rooted to the spot, returning his gaze with a burning desire to strike him but unable to move. His menacing eyes scanned over her face and body, pausing on her chest and widening into perfect disks when he saw Ruby.

As they progressed towards the dining area, his female companion edged closer and positioned herself behind them in the line.

"I'm Joey's girlfriend, Christine Pace," she said. As she observed Abby, it was evident from her artificial blonde hair, enhanced chest, and exaggerated lashes that she was someone who liked attention. Was this the type of woman Joey was attracted to? Someone who was interested in casual encounters and would playfully tease you all day while wearing a short skirt and consistently sporting red lipstick with every outfit.

"I'm Abagail Giovanni, and this little cutie is Ruby," said Abby.

Christine couldn't contain her excitement. "Abagail Giovanni!" Her eyes widened before fixing on Joey. Suddenly, her expression shifted dramatically as she gasped and covered her mouth.

It dawned on Abby that Joey must have told Christine about their previous relationship.

With a slight movement, Joey shifted closer to Ruby and quickly glanced at her. Despite the depth of his eyes, his expression remained stoic.

"Hello, Abby," Joey said, fixated on her face. "Long time no see."

Abby replied, "Hello, Joey." Her emotions were all over the place, but Joey seemed relaxed and unfazed. Abby took a step back, creating some distance between them, and decided to skip the waiting line, swiftly making her way towards the dining room alongside Ruby.

"She was eager to get away from you," Christine said with a hint of amusement, but Joey was not amused. "You never mentioned that she had a child."

"She is not the child's birth mother," he replied.

Christine paused. She may have looked like a blonde bimbo but looks could be deceiving. "Hmm, alright, but the child bears a striking resemblance to her, don't you think?"

CHAPTER 28

The dining room was buzzing with conversation as the two families enjoyed their meal and copious amounts of wine. Silencing the lively atmosphere, Frank gave a speech that brought a smile and laughter to Abby's face, until she noticed Joey glaring at her. His eyes darted between her and Ruby and back to her.

She sensed a change in his temperament. Had he figured out he was her father? Her heartbeat accelerated rapidly, causing her breathing to become laboured. Feeling nauseous and struggling to eat dinner, Abby took a deep breath when Ruby quietly asked, "Mummy, can you get some more bread?"

Without hesitation, she replied, "Of course, darling." She picked up the tongs and transferred the bread onto Ruby's plate.

Abby tried to ignore Joey but became aware of his mother giving her a suspicious glance from the corner of her eye.

When Micky approached Joey and inquired about his recent endeavours, Joey's expression turned sour. Abby overheard Joey had achieved enormous success as an entrepreneur in the steel industry, specifically for oil and petrochemical sectors, and it was Abby's signal to exit the room.

"Sweetheart, I need to use the restroom. Are you alright staying here with Grandma, Grandpa, and Micky? I won't be gone for too long."

Ruby nodded and started eating her lasagna, while Abby, her head pounding even worse than her strained thigh muscle from her early morning run, excused herself and hurried to the bathroom.

Joey discreetly followed her under the guise of making a phone call. Unaware of the ambush awaiting her, Abby felt a hand on her shoulder and was forcefully steered inside one of the bedrooms.

Startled by his sudden aggression, Abby gasped. "What on earth, Joey?"

As the door ominously clicked shut behind them, trapping them in the tiny room furnished only with a bed pressed against one wall and an antiquated brown dresser against another, panic surged through Abby. She bit her lip nervously and tried to make for the door, only to find Joey blocking her path.

"Move aside, Joey!" she said.

"Enough of this," he said sternly.

"What are you on about?" But she knew exactly where this conversation was headed.

"Let's cut the crap, shall we?" he said.

She shifted backwards and could feel the bed pressing against the back of her knees as he approached her. "Joey, what are you doing?"

"Tell me honestly—is Ruby my child?"

"You, of all people, have no right to treat me like this!"

With a serious expression, he gazed deeply into her eyes, leaning forward to delicately cradle Abby's face within his hands. "Abby, is Ruby mine?"

Regret for ever having felt affection for a man so cruel, a man who had once captured her heart only to later chew it up and spit it out, seeped through her. She despised him more than ever. "Stop it, Joey!" She pushed him away.

He seized her shoulders firmly, compelling her to maintain eye contact with his unyielding gaze.

"Let me go! Ruby does not belong to you, you despicable man!" Her anger made her voice tremble as she delivered a powerful slap across his face.

Abby speculated that the slap didn't infuriate him because she believed deep down, he knew he deserved it.

"I don't trust anything you say!" Joey said, drawing nearer to her.

"Release me, Joey!" she insisted, pushing him away once more. "Right now!"

"Damn you, Abby, tell me the truth!" He gripped her arm and pushed her against his firm physique. As she met his piercing green eyes, she realised she couldn't trust herself in his presence.

"Let me go! Now!"

He refused and tightened his grip around her waist. Despite her desperate pleas and attempts to break free, tears streamed down her cheeks whilst she remained steadfast in his grip. Instead of letting go, he kissed her and groped her breast before moving his hand towards her hips. He silenced any cries or objections with the pressure of his lips upon hers. Although she tried not to respond, she couldn't resist his touch; it had power over her, and his kiss left a lasting mark upon her soul. She could have chosen to put an end to it, but secretly she found pleasure in the unfolding events because deep inside, she craved it.

His hand glided down her thigh and lifted her dress, his fingers tracing the edge of her stockings over her mound, tenderly caressing and teasing her flaps. Pressing his lips against hers once more elicited soft moans from Abby as he nuzzled against the curve of her neck just like he used to. Inhaling his manly scent, she found herself unable to speak, so caught up in the moment.

Moaning softly into each kiss led him towards penetrating her stockings to create an opening, allowing him to feel her warm, wet folds brush against his finger. Exposed and vulnerable, she whimpered as he increased the speed and intensity of his affection. Eager for what was to come, she yearned for the forthcoming pleasure.

Joey also whimpered in response, his beast rising as he confirmed the anticipation reflected on her face.

She lacked the courage to keep her eyes open throughout the encounter, and it only fuelled his own inner beast, pushing him to take control of the situation.

"Abby, consider this your final warning!" he murmured softly into her ear as he lifted her up and then swiftly retreated. "You're free to leave!"

Abby opened her eyes with a sense of disappointment. Her expression became blank as she mulled over the sudden change, leaving her puzzled and uncertain about what had just occurred. It took a moment for the realisation to sink in that once again, Joey had deceived her.

Fool me once, shame on you; fool me twice, shame on me, she thought to herself with a mix of anger and regret. Allowing him to manipulate her with kisses and wandering hands had been a foolish mistake. The betrayal pierced through her heart like a sharp dagger, the rejection cutting deep into her soul. It became painfully clear he didn't care about how she felt.

"Abby," he said, as she adjusted her dress and prepared to unlock the door. "This is not the end. I will uncover the truth." His gaze turned icy and malicious; his lips firmly pressed together.

She tried to respond but found herself unable to speak again, merely staring at him with cold silence. Without further hesitation, she opened the door and escaped to the bathroom, seeking refuge.

A short while later, she heard Christine through the bathroom door. "Babe, what is taking you so long?"

"Sorry, love, I had to make an overseas phone call," Joey lied.

"Okay, let's go back, darling."

She heard them leave with great relief.

Abby stared at her own teary reflection in the ornate gold-framed mirror on the wall. She realised it was time to leave the Giovanni household.

After a few moments, she returned to the dining room and caught a whiff of Joey's familiar scent in the air. To her astonishment, she spotted him seated next to Ruby by the crackling firepit, roasting marshmallows.

In a calm tone, she politely said, "Ruby, could you please step away from the fireplace?"

She grabbed Ruby's arm and pulled her away from Joey.

"Uncle Joey was helping me toast the marshmallows."

"He is not your uncle!" said Abby, and turned sharply towards him, eyes blazing with anger. "Keep your distance from Ruby, do you understand?"

The sincerity in her eyes caused him to recoil. As painful or uncomfortable as the truth was, Joey needed to know.

Without waiting for his response, Abby took Ruby's hand and led her towards the kitchen, saying, "Time to go home!"

Unaware of the attention she had attracted from the guests in the room, Abby knew the best way to avoid Joey was to leave, and that was what she did. She expressed her gratitude to the Giovanni's for a pleasant evening before heading home with Ruby.

CHAPTER 29

Abby returned home after eleven and put Ruby to bed. Forty-five minutes later, she collapsed on her bed, consumed by anger over her encounter with Joey. The memory of his kisses and touches sent her heart racing with a mix of emotions. Why? It was impossible not to notice the way he looked at her tonight; why did he have to be there? Why couldn't she resist him? Even after the misery he had put her through and the long passage of time, she succumbed easily to his advances. She longed to hurt him and avenge the unbearable pain he had caused her. Suppressing a cry of disgust, she swallowed hard.

She had been navigating her new life one day at a time, working towards healing from the emotional scars of her past and finding a new direction for herself. Tonight, she couldn't stop thinking about how every part of her body numbed when he touched her. His repulsive and detestable hands violated her innocent body, but it was more than just a physical sensation; it affected her on a deeper level, reaching into her very core. Mentally, Abby berated herself for allowing this to happen.

Her intense dislike for him was counterbalanced by the fact she yearned for his touch. In frustration, she clutched her pillow tightly and released a scream into it.

When Abby's parents returned home long after midnight, a storm was raging; the windows shook and objects from the garden flew in every direction. Sitting up in bed, she pulled her knees to her chest and stared into the darkness. Although lonely and heartbroken, she knew better than to let him deceive and take advantage of her. She didn't want to forget how he abandoned her and Ruby. It didn't matter what her heart desired if her soul, body, and mind wanted him. She would ignore the quiet temptation and focus her energy on keeping the truth hidden. She cracked open a window slightly, allowing a burst of cold air into the room before lighting a cigarette and wrapping herself tightly against the chill. Unable to withstand the onslaught of conflicting emotions any longer, she extinguished the cigarette before shutting the window. Moments later, she knelt at the edge of her bed to pray, but her efforts seemed pointless as she begged God for assistance in resisting Joey's advances. Fears that Joey would discover their secret and put them in danger remained ever-present.

* * *

Joey, once more finding himself suffering from insomnia, lay tossing and turning in his bed as the night stretched on endlessly. The rhythmic crash of waves against the shore provided a calming backdrop to his troubled thoughts, which were consumed by memories of Abby. A sense of unease gnawed at him, although he struggled to pinpoint exactly what she had done wrong.

Even after the passing of five years since their tumultuous split, vivid images of a tearful and wounded Abby remained etched in Joey's mind. He couldn't shake the guilt for pushing her away in pursuit of his own selfish ambitions, ultimately driving him out of town. It was hard to admit he had been extremely selfish and even more difficult to accept.

In the dark of night, Joey's thoughts turned to the authenticity of his biological connection to Ruby. If she truly was his own flesh and blood, he was determined to seek retribution by ruining Abby for concealing this truth from him over the years. He would spare no effort in uncovering his own version of the truth, regardless of the personal costs involved. Even if it meant dedicating his entire life to this quest, he refused to allow himself to be deceived any longer.

The idea Abby may have deprived him of experiencing fatherhood struck a deep chord with Joey, filling him with profound sadness at the thought of his child growing up without his comfort and protection. His anger towards Abby burned fiercely in his chest, propelling him towards actions he believed were necessary for justice to prevail.

As sleepiness set in, he cast a fleeting glance at Christine sleeping peacefully beside him in the bed. As he looked at her, he remembered she had made advances towards him tonight, but he had rejected her. While he appreciated her in his life, he didn't feel a deep romantic connection to her, making it difficult for him to fully commit. Still, she was a constant in his life. He admired her qualities such as her intelligence, humour, and physical attributes.

He also felt pity towards Christine. The scars she bore both physically and emotionally from past abusive relationships tugged at Joey's heartstrings, preventing her from fully embracing life on her own terms. She believed she loved Joey, although his actions didn't align with her idea of love. She often hinted at engagement and held onto the hope he would propose someday. But Joey had always been content with their casual arrangement.

If he left her, she'd be heartbroken, but he knew how to keep her dancing to his tune, on a leash just long enough that she did not bite.

His thoughts irrevocably swung back to Abby, despite his efforts to forget her. A powerful tension existed between them. He felt an uncontrollable desire to kiss and hold her tightly. He understood why she had allowed him to embrace her, as evidenced by the way she looked at him. She had awakened his deepest longings and ignited a passionate flame. Her beauty and ardour were impossible for him to resist. He was entranced by her softness and curves, which triggered his primal instincts. They fitted together perfectly, with her hips cradling him, and he had treasured each moment of their connection and became completely immersed in her touch, surprised she had welcomed it instead of fearing him as he had anticipated. A mischievous grin spread across his face.

He could have ripped open her dress and made love to her on the bed, tantalising her soft delicately scented skin. She made him feel more of an animal than a man. She was small, but she could bring so much pleasure to a man, making his blood pound.

There was fiery passion in her, and he had felt it again after all these years, recalling the sensation of her fingertips over his back and scratching him, almost begging him for more in her own needy way. Her warmth and softness relived in his mind as their bodies moved together. By nature, she always came across as shy, but she was far from it. Joey felt captivated by the way she had stirred his thoughts and wanted her so badly. He wanted to possess and play with her. He realised he could spend all his nights with his face buried between her thighs. He pressed his groin and growled at the thought but felt conflicted. He had betrayed her and broken her heart, but he hadn't expected he would be wanting her again. He longed to reclaim her and have her surrender herself to him completely. In his eyes, she had blossomed into a stunningly beautiful woman, captivating in both sensuality and exotic charm. Deep down, he knew he didn't deserve her, but if Ruby truly belonged to him, he swore vengeance, promising to break her heart anew.

CHAPTER 30

The following morning, Abby awoke with a sense of unease and trepidation. The events of the previous night had left her embarrassed and vulnerable, prompting her to seek refuge beneath the covers, where she could shield herself from the harsh light of reality. As she lay there, consumed by her own thoughts, she became acutely aware of the ragged rhythm of her breaths and her thoughts felt scattered like glass fragments.

In a fit of frustration, Abby cast aside the blankets and swung her legs over the edge of the bed, determined to shake off the shame that clung to her like a second skin. Before she could gather herself enough to embark on her morning routine, she was interrupted by Ruby.

"Mama, when are we going Christmas shopping?" Ruby's sweet voice aroused her from her thoughts. Abby mustered a smile as she bent down to kiss Ruby's forehead before gently cradling her face in her hands.

"Good morning to you, too, my darling," Abby replied in a soft and tender tone that belied the storm raging within her.

Ruby giggled in response, basking in the warmth of her mother's affection. Then, with a mischievous smile, she asked, "So, when are we going Christmas shopping?"

Abby chuckled at Ruby's eagerness and made a mental note to savour this moment of maternal connection. "We shall go after I have showered and had my coffee," she told Ruby with calm authority.

"I already had my breakfast with Grandma and Grandpa."

"But I haven't had my coffee yet."

Ruby nodded to show she understood and happily skipped down the hallway while humming, "Jingle bells," which made Abby laugh.

Abby locked the bathroom door and filled the tub, adding bubble soap. She tested the temperature with a toe, hung her robe on a hook, then slid in, submerging herself. Wiping bubbles from her eyes, she leaned back against the rim. It was wrong to entertain these thoughts of Joey, but these had been five long, sexless years, and the lack of physical connection had taken its toll.

She was so desperate that she even considered giving John Sarani a chance for some fun or possibly more. John was thirty years old and renowned for his promiscuous behaviour and penchant for cycling through romantic partners. Patricia, employed as Abby's legal assistant, learned this during a rendezvous with John's cousin Andrew, who divulged the truth about his relative's amorous exploits. John had a Mediterranean look, standing tall with an attractive countenance characterised by light brown wavy locks. His piercing, leafy green eyes and meticulously braided long brown beard was accompanied by a stylish moustache. With his winning smile, John possessed an innate ability to captivate women and draw them towards him. His sartorial choices often consisted of Black Label tailored shirts with the sleeves rolled up to reveal his Scorpio tattoo, paired effortlessly with blue-washed denim jeans. It was undeniable that John emanated an irresistible aura of sensuality, emitting a magnetic energy that enticed females from all walks of life. Abby had sensed his disappointment when she turned him down. Now the thought no longer repulsed her. The physical touch of a man warmed her inside. Damp lips pressed against hers, she was ready to be romped but felt guilty for thinking and feeling this way. Her vulva cried for pleasure, and Abby decided to indulge. She swept her wet hair to one side, draping it over a shoulder. Taking hold of the showerhead, she positioned it between her spread legs and turned the water on. She threw her head back, closed her eyes, and gasped as the pulsing water stimulated her clitoris.

She visualised Joey's member pressed against her moist vulva, his voice low. "Do you like it?" Drops of water ran down her ponytail, twisted over her shoulder. She pictured Joey's fingertips trailing the path to her breasts.

"Yes," she whispered, changing position to spread a leg over each side of the bathtub, opening herself wide to him. Her vulva, hips, thighs responded to his imagined touch, massaging her breasts, lowering himself for a sensual kiss.

A soft moan escaped her throat.

"I want to taste you," he murmured, eyes narrowed and shifting, drawn towards her dripping vulva. She couldn't prevent him, not that she wanted to.

As he kissed between her legs, he curved one hand beneath her buttocks and sucked on her vulva pleasurably while his other hand caressed one of her breasts. He was losing control, listening to her moans growing louder and harder.

He lifted her from the bathtub and threw her onto the bed, water droplets trailing from the bathroom. Abby responded eagerly to his touch, heart racing as she surrendered herself spreadeagled, a rush of cold air through her pubic hair giving her goosebumps.

"Touch yourself for me," he said, his sensual smile taking an edge off the command.

Shocked but compliant, she started with gentle strokes, then forcefully stimulating herself until she became consumed by the intense pleasure she evoked. She focused intently on her own expression, the movement of her body, keeping her mouth open as she locked eyes with him. He pressed firmly on her clitoris with the heel of his hand, massaging her inside with a finger, eliciting moans of approval.

"Beautiful," he said with a grin, shuddering.

She wrapped her legs around him, pulling him closer, accepting his erect member into her vulva with a whimper of pleasure. He was larger than she remembered. Closing her eyes and moaning his name, she tightened her legs around his waist, holding his shoulders tightly as they kissed and panted together with each thrust.

She followed his rhythm fervently, writhing with pleasure, head thrown back, as he reached the depths of her soul. Her toes curled until her excited cries blended into a long groan.

Abby opened her eyes, and her breathing slowly returned to normal. She was still in the bathtub, with the showerhead running and water overflowing onto the floor.

After a soothing forty-five minutes in the bathroom, she emerged less tense, more satisfied, and slightly guilty for allowing thoughts of him to enter her mind. She was dressed in a white lacy bra and matching underwear, paired with Ralph Lauren jeans and a cosy red jumper from Macy's.

As she sat at the edge of the bed, slipping on her socks, her peaceful moment was abruptly interrupted by the buzzing of her cell phone on the bedside table.

Turning to check the message, she saw it was from an unknown number. Initially assuming it might be a client reaching out, she hesitantly opened the text. To her dismay, it was a message from Joey that read, "Abby, we need to talk. Let's meet today or I'll come to you."

She believed he was hell-bent on uncovering her secret and exacting revenge. Knowing he would stop at nothing to get what he wanted, she realised she needed to create distance between them to protect herself and, most importantly, her daughter.

With determination in her heart, she made the decision not to meet him and promptly deleted his message. Gathering herself, she rose from the bed and made her way down the hallway towards the stairs. Entering the kitchen, she found it deserted, which piqued her curiosity. Glancing into the family room, she spotted Ruby helping her parents decorate the Christmas tree with twinkling lights.

Joining them in the festive activity after grabbing a cup of coffee, she greeted her parents with a kiss and smiled warmly at them. "Good morning, Mama and Papa." Excitedly, Ruby rushed towards her for a hug, almost causing her to spill her coffee. Carefully, she settled down on the sofa next to her father and watched as her mother and Ruby busied themselves decorating the Christmas tree.

"Nonna, you're doing it wrong; the red tinsel should always go around the bottom part of the tree," Ruby said in her bossy manner.

Abby retorted sharply, "Nonna can place the tinsel wherever she pleases."

"But Mum, it looks better this way."

Abby sighed and shook her head as she observed her mother wrapping the red tinsel around the bottom of the tree.

Abby leaned in closer to her father and quietly said, "She wants to have control over everything. I honestly can't fathom where she gets it from because I was never like that, Papa."

Her father let out a soft chuckle before responding, "Oh, Abby, my dear. You were once a determined child as well, who enjoyed tackling tasks independently and had quite the influence on your peers."

"But Papa," Abby interjected with furrowed brows, "she can be so overwhelming at times."

The two shared a knowing laugh before her father's tone shifted to one of seriousness. "Abby, there is something important I need to discuss with you," he whispered solemnly.

Abby's heart sank as dread washed over her. "What is it? Is something wrong with you or Mama?"

"Let's go to the kitchen where we can talk in private," he muttered, leading the way.

Abby followed him into the kitchen. Taking a seat at the kitchen table, she looked into her father's eyes. "Please tell me what's going on, Papa," she implored earnestly.

Her father nodded gravely. "Last night, your mother and I had a serious discussion, and we believe it's time for the Giovanni's to learn the truth."

A look of shock crossed Abby's face. "What! Are you serious? Why now... just because Joey is back?" Her voice quivered as she stared blankly at her father.

"Yes, that's part of the reason. But also... to be truthful, our sense of right and wrong is pushing us towards this decision. Ruby's also their granddaughter, and they deserve to spend time with her."

"Papa, you're joking right?"

Before any more words could be exchanged between them, Abby's mother entered the room with a grave expression. "Abby, we are completely serious about this. Joey was fixated on Ruby throughout the entire evening; it is only a matter of time before he discovers the truth."

She observed them silently for a moment. It hadn't occurred to Abby that perhaps her parents were burdened by the weight of this lie they carried within them all these years.

"Abby," her mother said soothingly, clearly trying to calm the storm brewing within their family dynamic.

Taking a deep breath, Abby stood with clenched teeth. "No!" she snapped. "I don't want anyone else knowing about Ruby."

Helplessly seeking support from her father, tears welled in her eyes. "Papa, we had an agreement."

"Abby," her father said.

Abby looked at them, expressing disappointment on her face. "No, Dad!" She paused for a moment. "No, we can't share this with anyone else! We're done talking about it!"

Just as her mother prepared to speak, Ruby innocently entered the kitchen. "Mummy, when are we leaving?"

Abby took a moment to reply. "We're leaving right now, sweetheart. Go get your coat and boots."

"We're in for some bad weather," her father observed, as he switched on the television. The reporter conveyed the news of a significant winter storm causing widespread disruption across the country. The public was urged to exercise caution due to the approaching blizzard, which is expected to bring freezing temperatures and possible power outages.

Abby's mother gently rested her hand on her shoulder, her tone serious. "Abby, we have reason to believe that Angela may be aware of our circumstances. Your father and I are convinced of it, which is why she extended an invitation for dinner last night."

Displaying her disapproval, Abby said, "But it doesn't change anything." She shifted her gaze from her mother to her father. "Let's stick to our original plan, otherwise my five years in Italy was a complete waste of time and effort." Leaving her words hanging in the frigid air, she swung open the back door and ventured outside into the chilly weather with Ruby trailing closely behind.

A heavy downpour fell from the heavens accompanied by a fierce gust of wind that shook the windows. The roads were congested, and they were nowhere near reaching the Queens' shopping centre. Her mind was busy processing the conversation with her parents. She could not fathom why Joey had chosen to return to Queens after such a prolonged absence. For a fleeting moment, she stole a glance at Ruby and couldn't help but smile. Ruby was the only positive outcome of her turbulent relationship with Joey, and she was determined not to lose this battle.

After a forty-minute journey, they arrived at the shopping centre only to be met by a chaotic, congested parking lot. Eventually, after fifteen minutes of searching diligently, they secured a spot close to the entrance. The mall buzzed with activity as people scurried about frantically purchasing last-minute Christmas gifts. They spent hours meandering through various stores selecting presents and trying on clothing and footwear. They dined at Mr. Chi's restaurant, a favourite spot for Ruby, indulging in an assortment of delectable dishes including noodles, egg rolls, and stir fries while relishing in dipping dumplings into savoury sauces.

"Mama, do you think Dad will come home for Christmas this year?" Ruby whispered.

Abby sank into her chair, feeling deflated by the question. She shifted uncomfortably and looked at her daughter, uncertain of how to answer.

"I want to give him a hug," Ruby said sadly.

A worried expression appeared on Abby's face.

Ruby stopped eating. She was now quiet, displaying an anxious anticipation as she waited for her mother to respond.

Abby, already feeling drained, wanted to wait until Ruby was older and settled before revealing the true reason for her father's absence. However, she saw this as an opportunity to be honest with her daughter and answer her questions in a sensitive manner. After pausing briefly, Abby softly responded, "No, sweetheart, Daddy won't be coming home for Christmas. But I want you to know he loves you very much and always thinks about you. Daddy lives far away because he needs time to work through some personal things that I couldn't help him with. Mummy and Daddy agreed it would make everyone happier if we lived apart."

Abby held Ruby's hand. She felt pathetic but continued. "I understand how you feel. It's normal to feel angry or sad sometimes. Please remember this is not your fault, darling. Every family is different. Some children live with their grandparents because their parents can't take care of them; some live in orphanages without anyone to care for them. There are also families with two dads or two mums, or no dad or mum at all. But Nonna, Nonno, and Uncle Micky love you very much, okay?" She despised Joey for putting her through this difficult situation, feeling a tightness in her chest.

"I understand, Mum." Ruby's voice was barely audible through her sobbing.

Abby rose from her seat and knelt beside Ruby, wrapping her in a comforting embrace while gently patting her back. They exchanged kisses before embarking on their journey back home together.

CHAPTER 31

On a frosty Christmas Eve, the Di Manos family valiantly ventured out into a raging blizzard to attend the evening mass at St. Mary Cathedral. Following the spiritual service, they were supposed to meet the Bianchi Family for a festive dinner gathering, but as the snow continued relentlessly, the hallowed halls of the cathedral transformed into refuge for the homeless and those in need.

Driven by age-old customs and familial obligations, Abby displayed remarkable courage as she strode into the cathedral alongside Ruby, initially sticking close to her parents before inadvertently getting separated in the throng of congregants. Undeterred by the intense scrutiny of onlookers, Abby navigated through the sea of faces with poise and determination until she found a vacant seat upon one of the polished wooden pews.

During the midway point of the mass, Abby noticed that familiar pale expression on Ruby's face, a sign something was wrong. It was a sight that had haunted her for the past five years. Halting mid-song, Abby turned towards Ruby, grabbing her arm. "Baby, what's wrong?"

"I'm feeling sick," Ruby uttered weakly.

Instantly seizing her daughter's clammy hand, Abby apologised profusely as they wended their way through rows of worshippers, all eyes fixated upon them, including Joey, who sat beside his parents and Christine at the rear of the church.

Opening the heavy oak doors, Abby ushered Ruby swiftly towards the bathroom. "Sweetheart, we're almost there!"

Ruby leaned over a stall with her head bowed low, she vomited while Abby rubbed her back, listening with sorrow as her daughter sobbed uncontrollably.

Abby hadn't noticed Joey had trailed after them. She turned just as Joey walked into the bathroom.

"Is Ruby alright?" he asked.

"Joey! You shouldn't be here!"

He brushed past her and approached Ruby. "Are you feeling any better?" Joey asked while locking eyes with Ruby and then glancing at Abby, who remained silent.

Abby nodded. "We're fine now, Joey. Please go!"

Joey delicately grasped her chin, compelling her to meet his gaze. "I'll be waiting outside, alright?" He then turned and left through the door.

Snatching up paper towels from dispensers nearby, Abby tenderly dabbed Ruby's damp face. "Sweetheart, let's go home," she said, ushering Ruby towards the exit with an acute sense of history repeating itself.

Gazing at Ruby, she attempted to offer a comforting smile, but it was more sorrowful than comforting. With her heart racing and anxiety filling her stomach, Abby couldn't ignore the same distressing circumstances unfolding once more.

Ruby had suffered from Hydronephrosis since birth, a condition necessitating future kidney transplant for a normal life, heightening Abby's anxiety whenever Ruby fell ill. Each instance of fever, cough, stomach-ache, and fatigue inflicted unbearable pain and sorrow upon Abby's heart. She would stay up late at night, taking care of Ruby until she fully recovered. She was willing to sleep anywhere, including on the floor, just to be close to her baby girl.

When Ruby was just a tiny toddler, her little body was engulfed by a vicious fever that seemed to steal the very warmth from her soul. The fever clung on relentlessly, and when she finally surrendered to its grip, losing consciousness, sheer terror enveloped their home. Panic turned into chaos as she was whisked away to the hospital. Abby's heart shattered as wave after wave of sobs wracked her body, making it almost impossible to catch a breath. Desperation clawed at her insides as she turned to the doctors, eyes wide and pleading. "Oh, please, save my baby! I'm begging you, please, just save my baby! Oh Lord, don't let her slip away from me!" Her words tumbled out like prayers, flooding the sterile room with the raw anguish of a mother on the brink of losing her greatest treasure.

Doctors and nurses worked tirelessly and swiftly to provide care for Ruby. They inserted tubes and IVs into her delicate arms as Abby's distress continued to escalate, especially when the nurses tried to guide Abby away from the emergency area, but she vehemently pushed past them to reach Ruby, her cries piercing the sterile corridors.

As Abby caught a glimpse of Ruby's frail form, lying weak and defenceless in that hospital bed, emotions overwhelmed her; she screamed and wept uncontrollably. Days seemed to drag on slowly as Ruby remained in the ICU until, finally, on the fifth day, there was a glimmer of hope when she opened her eyes. By the tenth day, Abby was able to sit by Ruby's side and shower her with affectionate cuddles as her condition gradually improved.

"Mama," Ruby's voice trembled as she clung desperately to Abby's coat, snapping her back into a harsh reality. "I d-don't feel well," she whimpered, her sobs piercing the air and sending a jolt of terror through Abby's heart.

An overwhelming dread gnawed at Abby, her throat tightening as tears welled up, threatening to overflow. Her entire body tensed as fear wrapped around her like a vice, barely able to maintain her composure. "We're going home now, honey," she murmured, her voice quivering, as she gripped Ruby's hand with a fierce, unyielding urgency.

In their haste to leave the bathroom inside the cathedral, they completely forgot about Joey standing outside with his back against the wall. He approached them with concern etched on his face. "Abby, what's wrong? Why are you both crying?"

Ignoring Joey, Abby brushed past him. When he attempted to grab her arm, she jerked away forcefully. "Joey, go away and leave us alone!" They rushed outside and headed towards the parking lot, but Joey trailed after them despite Abby's attempts to distance herself from him.

No matter how hard she tried to push him aside, he never gave up. "Mum, it hurts, really hurts," Ruby whimpered, clutching her stomach.

"Baby, I know you are in pain. See, we are almost there." She pointed at her papa's truck, quickening her pace.

Joey's voice grew louder as he continued trailing after them. "Abby, what the hell is going on?"

Abby rummaged through her bag, frantically searching for the truck keys.

Finally locating them, she managed to unlock the truck just when Ruby began losing consciousness and collapsed. Panic surged through Abby as she shot a terrified glance in Joey's direction. "Joey!"

Without hesitation or delay, Joey sprang into action and scooped Ruby up into his arms before carrying her gently towards the back seat of the truck. As he shut the door securely behind him, Abby rushed towards the driver's side only for Joey to snatch the keys from her "I'll drive, you take care of Ruby."

Realising time was of the essence in getting Ruby immediate medical attention at St. Andrew's Hospital without further delay, Abby accepted his assistance before settling into the back seat alongside Ruby, who lay still and unconscious.

"Which hospital?" Joey asked briefly as he started up the engine.

"St. Andrew's," said Abby, keeping a watchful eye on Ruby.

"Baby, we are on our way to the hospital now," Abby said, sobbing with tears.

Joey had one eye on the road and the other on his rear-view mirror, staring at the girls. "Abby, what's wrong with Ruby?"

Placing her hand on Ruby's forehead, Abby felt relieved to discover her temperature was normal. "Ruby isn't well. She has a condition called Hydronephrosis, a blockage in the urinary tract that impairs her kidney function."

Joey was rendered speechless despite his usual loquacious nature, as his mouth both opened and closed simultaneously. His jaw tightened and his eyes softened.

Stopping at the red traffic light, Joey turned towards Abby, "How is this even possible?"

"She was born with it, okay!" she snapped, glaring at him with anger.

"Okay... I'm sorry, Abby. I was just asking..." His voice trailed off when the driver behind them honked aggressively as the traffic light had turned green. Joey quickly released his foot off the brake and accelerated.

Abby breathed out heavily through her nostrils. "Can you please stop asking so many questions and concentrate on getting us to the hospital quickly?"

Casting a tender glance at Ruby cradled in her arms, she whispered, "We're almost there, baby."

Retrieving her phone from her handbag, she composed a text message to her mother: *Hi Mama, Ruby and I are on the way to St Andrew's hospital. Joey is with us, too.*

CHAPTER 32

Upon arriving at the hospital, they parked their vehicle in the designated emergency lane, where Joey swiftly exited the truck and made his way to the back passenger door. With urgency, he gently lifted Ruby and hurried through the entrance.

Abby hurried to the triage desk. "I need to see Dr. Matthew Denver right away. My daughter here, Ruby Di Manos, is his patient and needs immediate medical attention!"

The receptionist collected Ruby's information but instructed Abby to take a seat while she processed it. Abby remained standing, keeping a vigilant eye on Ruby as she observed the receptionist jotting down notes before engaging in casual conversation with her colleagues about her weekend plans.

Filled with frustration and anger, Abby felt her face flush and her heart race faster as she witnessed what seemed like indifference towards Ruby's urgent situation. Approaching the information desk once more, Abby took note of the woman's name tag, which read

Karen. "Listen, Karen, I need you to notify Dr. Denver that Abby Di Manos is here with Ruby and in need of immediate medical attention!"

Karen cleared her throat. "Madam, I will certainly relay your message to Dr. Denver, but please remember there are other patients ahead of you also waiting to see the doctor. We will call you when it's your turn. Would you please move to the side so I can attend to the other patients standing behind you?"

Anxious about Ruby's deteriorating condition, Abby quickly assessed her daughter's condition and noticed alarming symptoms, such as weak breathing and a pale complexion. Overwhelmed with concern, she instructed Joey to find a seat while she contemplated their next steps.

Growing increasingly panicked and frustrated by what she perceived as negligence towards her daughter's urgent medical needs, Abby shook her head in disbelief before decisively approaching the triage desk once more. In a raised voice, she said, "What kind of hospital is this? My daughter is hanging on by a thread and you are not doing anything about it. Karen, please call your supervisor!" Slamming her hand forcefully onto the counter caused the glass window to rattle and startled Karen out of her seat. Karen moved quickly towards the adjacent room.

Meanwhile, Joey remained seated, his eyes following her with curiosity. The sudden commotion caused heads to turn among the other patients in the room, their eyebrows raised as they engaged in hushed conversations about the public scene.

Joey rose from his seat, gently cradling Ruby in his arms as he made his way towards the front desk. "Abby, please calm down!"

Abby glared at him intently. "Are you serious?"

"Security might kick us out if you're not careful," said Joey.

Finally, after what seemed like an eternity, the supervisor arrived on scene. Abby took a deep breath and explained the circumstances calmly and rationally.

To Abby's surprise and relief, the supervisor showed empathy and understanding towards her situation. Hope blossomed in Abby's eyes as she nodded gratefully and continued to share her concerns about her daughter's well-being.

With a nod from the supervisor, the emergency doors were unlocked and swung open automatically.

"Thank you so much," Abby said to the supervisor, and flashed a smile before composing herself. She led Joey and Ruby towards the sliding doors while casting a disdainful glance back at Karen.

As they walked down the seemingly endless hallway, each step echoing loudly in Abby's ears, her heart raced with mounting anxiety. The harsh fluorescent lights above seemed to flicker ominously, casting eerie shadows along the walls. When she finally spotted Dr. Denver deep in conversation with a red-haired nurse, Abby's nerves twisted even tighter. She could barely breathe, fear gripping her chest. But then, when Dr. Denver turned and met her gaze with a warm smile, a rush of relief washed over her like a tidal wave, momentarily soothing her frayed nerves.

Dr. Denver, tall and lean, was in his late thirties, possessing eyes that were an intriguing mix of grey and green. His strikingly handsome features left a memorable impression on Abby, and his gentle and approachable demeanour earned him the trust of many patients. Whenever Abby was around him, she felt a sense of safety and security. However, this connection between them caused Joey to frown with concern.

On one particular evening, Dr. Denver invited Abby to join him for a movie. Respectful of their professional boundaries, she declined, wanting to maintain clear distinctions in their roles as patient and doctor. Undeterred, he suggested they meet again, this time as friends outside of the medical setting. Once more, Abby politely turned him down. It wasn't until this moment she realised true happiness could only be achieved by letting go of the past and embracing a new beginning. However, she found herself unable to open her heart to Dr. Denver despite this realisation.

Meanwhile here now at the hospital, Joey observed Dr. Denver closely, his gaze fixed intently on him before shifting to Abby. Without uttering a word, Joey's lips pressed tightly together, and his brow furrowed, reflecting a sense of intense concentration and contemplation.

"Abby, could you explain what's happening?" Dr. Denver inquired gently, his voice full of empathy, as he watched Joey carefully place Ruby on the bed following the nurse's instructions.

"She's been complaining of stomach pain and just threw up," Abby explained, her voice unsteady with worry. "She suddenly passed out and has been in a semi-conscious state for the last thirty minutes or so. Please, you have to help Ruby!"

Dr. Denver reached out and gently held Abby's hands, his gaze steady and reassuring. "We'll do everything we can to help Ruby," he promised. "We need to run some tests, take some blood samples. Try to stay calm, okay?"

Abby's efforts to smile were futile. She briefly shut her eyes before nodding.

"Hello, Miss Ruby," said Dr. Denver, greeting her with a smile. "I have missed you." He revealed a colourful lollipop from his jacket.

Startled yet pleased, Ruby looked up and formed a smile as she accepted the lollipop. In a gentle voice, she said, "Thank you."

Meanwhile, Nurse Gretchen prepared the blood pressure monitor for Ruby while Dr. Denver focused on arranging the necessary tools and donning disposable gloves. After snapping on the gloves, he injected pain relief medication and extracted blood from Ruby's left arm. "Baby, it's almost over," said Abby as she gently stroked Ruby's hair.

Ruby remained still without shedding any tears.

"Ruby, I'll return a little later to check up on you," Dr. Denver said, giving her a playful wink as he gingerly removed his gloves and discarded them in the appropriate receptacle.

Nurse Gretchen swiftly retrieved the tray of medical instruments and exited the room. Before leaving, Dr Denver turned to Abby. "Can we have a moment to talk?"

Abby nodded.

"Darling, I will be back shortly, Mummy needs to talk to the doctor okay, I will be just outside the room, alright?"

Ruby responded with a nod of understanding.

"I apologise for not having had the opportunity to introduce myself earlier," Joey said politely, extending his hand and offering a warm smile. "My name is Joey Giovanni."

"Doctor Matt Denver," he replied. "Pleasure to meet you, Mr. Giovanni. Are you a relative?"

"Abby and I are close friends, we grew up together."

Dr. Denver acknowledged with a slight nod.

The two men chatted briefly until they heard Abby approaching. Simultaneously, they turned their heads towards her as if synchronised by some unseen force. As she joined them, studying each man with curiosity and pondering why Joey was still there, she focused on Dr. Denver.

"Abby, I will return shortly with the results of the tests. The sedative should help her relax; she should soon drift off to sleep."

"Thank you," Abby said with a nod as he turned and walked away.

"What is your connection to Dr. Denver, Abby?" Joey asked, raising an eyebrow and crossing his arms while scrutinising her expression.

It took a moment for Abby to process his question when anger flashed in her eyes. "You have no right to ask me that question! It is none of your concern." She stormed back into the room where Ruby lay in the hospital bed connected to monitors and with a cannula in her fragile arm.

Seeing Ruby in such a vulnerable state tugged at Abby's heartstrings as she struggled to comprehend why they were facing such hardship. She sank into a nearby chair, burying her face in her hands.

After a few minutes, Joey entered the room and stared at Ruby before tracing his finger along her cheek and cute little nose. Dropping down on one knee beside Abby in his church attire, he gently grasped her hands. "Is Ruby my daughter?"

Abby struggled to look at him. "Look at me!"

Reluctantly removing her hands from her face and locking eyes with him, Abby shook her head. "No, Joey... Ruby is not your daughter."

"Abby, if there's even a slight possibility that Ruby may be my daughter. Please, if there is any chance at all, do not keep me in the dark. I swear on everything I will protect her."

227

Despite his heartfelt plea, Abby remained indifferent, refusing to acknowledge his presence or respond to his pleas.

"Wow!" she said, clamping her hand over her mouth to silence her mock-laughter. "Your promises hold no value to me anymore. I'm well aware you are incapable of keeping them."

With a swift movement, he rose from the floor and distanced himself from Abby, yet his unwavering gaze remained fixed upon her. Attempting once more to appeal to Abby's sensibilities, he said, "Abby, I—"

Just then, Abby's parents burst into the room, their voices pitched with panic as they screamed, "Ruby!"

Abby watched as her parents hurried towards the hospital bed without noticing Joey on the other side of the room.

"What happened?" asked her mother. "Where is Dr. Denver? I must speak with him immediately."

Rising from her seat, Abby relayed the information regarding Ruby's condition. "She fell ill at the cathedral and has been experiencing stomach discomfort. Dr. Denver ran a few tests on her, and now we're just waiting to hear back on the results."

"We?" asked her mother.

"Hello, Mr. and Mrs. Giovanni," said Joey as he approached the bedside.

Abby's father gave Joey a shocked look and politely told him to wait outside in the emergency room.

"I'm not going anywhere. You can't hide this from me any longer. I know Ruby is my daughter, and I will stop at nothing to unveil the truth.

Abby's father angrily interrupted, raising his voice. "Ruby is not your child!"

Abby's mother stood motionless, her eyes widening in disbelief. Abby herself was left speechless, staring at Joey with intense hatred. She watched the men argue with great pain while her mother desperately tried to calm them down.

Suddenly, Joey turned to Abby. In that moment, she became completely lost and unsure of how to react or respond. Charging out of the room, she hurried down the narrow hallway.

"Wait, Abby!" said Joey, stopping her in her tracks. "I apologise, okay?"

"Joey, I need you to go away." The expression on her face conveyed she didn't truly mean it. "Go tend to Christine; your phone won't stop ringing."

Letting out a heavy sigh, Joey attempted to reach for her hand, only for it to be swiftly withdrawn as if his touch was a searing flame. Retrieving his phone from his pocket, he held it up. "She doesn't matter to me, alright?"

A tense silence hung between them as they maintained eye contact. "I want to make it clear that you are not needed here. You are not Ruby's father, so please leave us alone!"

Joey stood motionless. "Fine!" he said, uttering a vulgar curse that shocked her.

She watched him finally leave the emergency room.

CHAPTER 33

Joey left the hospital, unable to stop thinking about Ruby, whom he now firmly believes is his offspring, lying in a vulnerable state in the hospital bed.

As soon as he entered his apartment, he was greeted by Christine, who appeared visibly distressed as she paced about the room clutching her phone in one hand and a glass of whisky in the other. The bottle was partially depleted on the coffee table.

Immediately bombarded with her questions, Joey remained too preoccupied to answer them.

"Are we back to drinking?" Joey asked.

Angered by his comment, Christine glared at him.

Joey approached her and took the glass from her hand before grabbing the bottle and walking towards the kitchen to tip the contents down the sink.

Christine followed angrily behind him into the kitchen. "How could you abandon me at the church and leave with her?" she yelled.

Joey turned to face Christine, pausing as he contemplated his reply. She was visibly struggling to hold back tears and maintain composure. "What is happening, Joey? Tell me!"

Breaking the silence between them, Joey finally said, "Ruby is unwell, so I took them to the hospital."

She stared back at him, swaying and pointing at him. "Is Abby the reason we moved back here?"

Joey shook his head. "Why are you drinking again, Christine?" He passed her a glass of water, urging her to drink it.

"I don't want a glass of water!" she shouted, yanking her arm away from him, causing the glass to fall and shatter on the floor.

Joey's expression hardened; his eyes grew cold and dark.

"Joey, answer my question!"

"We moved here for my work, okay?"

"Bullshit, you moved here for her. Is Abby the reason we moved back here?"

"Chrissy, stop this now!"

"We were so happy in Los Angeles. Why did we have to leave?"

"I don't know what you expect me to say, Christine."

"Well, start by being honest with me!" she yelled.

"I am being truthful; we moved here for my work, and it has nothing to do with Abby."

As tensions rose between them, Joey softened his tone, grasped her hand, and gave it a comforting squeeze. "Christine, I'm sorry for not calling you and leaving you at the cathedral."

Christine moved towards the kitchen window and looked up at the dark sky as wind battered the window and the silence encompassing them.

Joey stood behind her. "Chrissy, don't be afraid, I am with you."

She spun around to face him, wiping away tears.

"Chrissy, I won't leave you," he said.

She went on tiptoes and hugged him tightly, confessing her love for him.

Joey's response was not one of reciprocity, but rather a display of confusion and inner conflict as thoughts of both Abby and Ruby took precedence. After an uncomfortable pause, Christine released her grip and asked about his love for her, her voice cracking with emotion as she placed her hands firmly on her hips.

Initially hesitant, Joey eventually mustered the words, "I do."

"You do what?" she asked.

"Babe, please stop this now! I am exhausted and want to take a shower and retire for the night."

Christine sat in silence, staring down at the floor while Joey proceeded to the refrigerator, retrieved a water bottle, closed it forcefully, then stormed out of the kitchen towards the living room.

She trailed after him. "Can you recall our last intimate time together? Because I certainly can't."

His expression turned into one of anger as he faced her squarely. "Christine, you are intoxicated. I refuse to have sex with you in this state. Is this what you want to hear?"

"Screw you, Joey!"

With a barely contained smirk, he said, "Hmm, very mature."

"I have been sober for two and a half weeks now, yet you have made no effort with me. Every opportunity we have, you withdraw."

For a moment, Joey remained silent, avoiding direct eye contact with Christine. Her observation rang true; at times, he would create excuses to avoid intimacy with her since reconnecting with Abby had stirred up long-buried emotions. He could not help but replay their initial encounter over and again in his mind these past few weeks. Since reconnecting with Abby, he had emotionally distanced himself from Christine, despite trying ardently to push aside his lingering feelings for Abby after all these years. The guilt ate at him incessantly and couldn't be silenced by any argument.

Unbeknownst to Abby, he had yearned for her passionately in his dreams for five years and regretted each mistake he had made deeply. Joey desperately sought closure from the past to move forward with his life but found it challenging as memories of Abby lingered stubbornly.

How can I forgive myself if Abby cannot find it within herself to forgive me? he pondered silently.

"Are you even listening to me?" Christine's voice suddenly pierced through his reverie as she raised her volume.

"Yes, Christine, I am." He ascended the stairs to their bedroom, and she followed closely behind him.

"Why are you avoiding this conversation?" Christine persisted as they reached the bedroom door.

Joey finally reached his breaking point and abruptly turned around. "Enough! Or I'll leave this house tonight!" His ultimatum carried a tone of intensity and finality as he exited the room and slammed the door behind him.

CHAPTER 34

Abby sat beside her parents, the anticipation of Dr. Denver's imminent arrival stirring a mixture of eagerness and apprehension within her. Meanwhile, her father's face was contorted in agitation.

"Why is he here?" Abagail whispered, not wanting to further complicate the already strained relationship between her father and Joey. "I tried asking him to leave, but he insisted on staying. He won't give up until he uncovers the truth."

Unexpectedly, Abby's parents experienced a sudden shift in their perspectives towards their shared secret. Her mother, suddenly angry, voiced her concerns while anxiously patting her chest. "We cannot allow this to happen, Adriano. If the truth comes out, Abby's reputation will be tarnished."

"I know," Adriano replied.

"Please, Mother, stop this archaic thinking! It is not a crime for women to engage in sexual activity before marriage; it is very common in today's society, you know."

"In the eyes of God, it is considered a grave sin."

Staring intently at her mother, Abby shook her head vehemently. "I am an adult capable of making my own decisions and living my life without your protection or judgment. I refuse to be constrained by outdated societal norms."

"Abby!" her mother interjected. "The sanctity of a woman's purity holds great importance in the eyes of God."

"Mother, women can have sexual experiences and still hold onto their faith. I know you may not grasp this concept, but in today's society, sex is seen as a natural aspect of life and is increasingly accepted as the norm. So, please stop persisting on this issue. And anyway, whether I tell him or not, it doesn't change anything. God will regard me as a sinner."

"That's enough!" said Abby's father, glaring intensely at his two girls, just as Dr. Denver knocked on the door and entered with a troubled expression.

A few months ago, Abby couldn't help but remember the same expression when Ruby was rushed to the hospital with abdominal pain.

With a sombre expression, he said, "I have some unfortunate news for you, Abby."

She froze. "What is it?"

"Ruby's kidney is declining at a rapid rate and her iron levels are below the acceptable range. This could be causing her weakness and fatigue, in addition to her glomerular filtration rate being only fifty-five percent. A normal GFR typically ranges from 90-120%, which indicates possible issues with Ruby's kidney function. Unfortunately, it seems she will need a kidney transplant. I'm sorry, Abby."

Abby's mother gasped in shock and rushed to her daughter, wrapping her arms around her waist. "Oh, my Lord!" she said, her voice muffled as she tried to hold back tears.

Abby stood there crying. Meanwhile, her father slumped onto the couch and covered his face with his hands. With tears pooling in her eyes, Abby released herself from her mother's embrace and looked at Ruby on the hospital bed. She clasped Ruby's hand, planting delicate kisses on each finger before turning to Dr. Denver with a choked sob. "What happens now?"

"In an effort to explore potential matches for Ruby, she will be placed on the waiting list for a kidney donor. However, the timeline for when a suitable donor may become available is uncertain, ranging from as soon as one year to possibly several years. Nevertheless, I am fully committed to exhaust all possible avenues to find her a compatible match."

"So, it could potentially take a long time?"

"In certain cases, family members and close acquaintances can present themselves as viable candidates for donation. A series of comprehensive tests including blood work, tissue analysis, cardiac and pulmonary assessments, as well as genetic testing are conducted to determine compatibility between potential donors and recipients."

Abby's father stood up eagerly from the couch. "I volunteer to undergo testing first." Following suit, Abby's mother stepped forward clutching her rosary beads tightly. "I would also like to be tested."

"We will arrange for blood samples, imaging scans, and oral swabs for genetic testing," said Dr. Denver with a nod towards Abby's parents before turning his attention back to Ruby. "Ruby will be relocated tonight to the Kidney Transplant unit on Level Ten." After a brief pause, he directed his next words specifically at Abby. "Could we perhaps have a private chat?"

Her heart raced with anticipation as she agreed and followed him out of the room. She couldn't help but wonder what else he had to share on this matter.

Dr. Denver proceeded at a leisurely pace so Abby could keep up with him as they made their way through the corridors. "Would you care for some coffee?" Though not particularly in the mood for it, she nodded gratefully while wiping away her tears and runny nose as they made their way down to the cafeteria located on the ground floor of the hospital building.

Taking a seat at a table, Dr. Denver ordered two cups of coffee from the counter while Abby, her mind filled with daunting thoughts that seemed to suffocate her, sat lost in thought as waves of pain rolled over her.

Returning to their table with drinks and a chicken sandwich, Dr. Denver gently placed them before Abby. "Here you go."

"Thank you," she said, gratefully accepting the warm cup of coffee, feeling its heat seep into her cold hands and provide some semblance of comfort.

When he extended the offer of the chicken sandwich, Abby politely raised her hand. "I'm not hungry."

"That's alright; save it for later. By the way, there is an assistance program available at the hospital for families with young children facing illness and undergoing treatment."

"I do not need a social worker!" she snapped but quickly regretted her outburst. "I'm sorry, Matt." Tears cascaded down her face. "Please concentrate on finding a donor for Ruby."

Dr Denver reached out and squeezed Abby's hand gently. "Abby, I apologise for upsetting you. My intention was to inform you about the available support groups in case you need someone to talk to. Finding a donor for Ruby remains my top priority. Additionally, the transplant coordinator will visit tomorrow to discuss further details."

Abby nodded and quickly wiped away her tears.

* * *

Joey turned away from Christine with a visible expression of discontent. Slowly shifting onto his side, he stared at the wall, desperately seeking to silence the cacophony of thoughts racing through his restless mind through deep and measured breaths.

Glancing back towards Christine, whose serene form lay beside him in peaceful repose, a profound wave of guilt struck him. Here was a woman of unparalleled beauty who had consistently provided him with unwavering support and unconditional love; her devotion knew no limits, as evidenced by her willingness to fulfil any request he made without hesitation. Cursing quietly in frustration for entertaining such conflicted thoughts, Joey longed to be by Abby's side at that very moment as she navigated the lonely corridors of the hospital.

Rummaging through the clutter on the bedside table, he grabbed his mobile phone and started typing. *"Hey Abby, how is Ruby doing? What did the doctor say?"*

He hit send and awaited eagerly for Abby's response.

In five minutes, his phone emitted a series of pulsating vibrations. Expecting to see a text message from Abby, he was disappointed to see another spam email. He hurled the phone onto the soft surface of the bed in an act of despair.

Feeling a boiling impatience bubbling inside him, Joey couldn't bear to simply sit and wait for Abby's reply. Decisively, he grabbed a weathered New York Yankees cap, slipped into his old, comfortable denim trousers, and shrugged on a woolly sweater that lay abandoned nearby. As he stepped outside, a fierce gust of icy wind sliced through the air, nearly knocking him off balance. He hastily clutched at his collar, pulling it up to fight off the biting cold that clawed at his neck.

Forty minutes later, St. Andrew's Hospital loomed as Joey pulled into the underground car park and swiftly made his way towards the emergency ward foyer.

Joey was walking down the corridor when he bumped into Nurse Gretchen, who greeted him warmly. "Hi there," she said. "If you're trying to find Abby, she's in the cafeteria with Dr. Denver."

"Thanks for letting me know," Joey responded.

He made his way to the cafeteria and quickly noticed Abby and Dr. Denver sitting together, their hands intertwined. Approaching them, he asked, "What's going on here?"

Abby swiftly retracted her hand from Dr. Denver's. She saw Joey's eyes narrow as they flickered back and forth between her and where her hand had been. A moment of stunned silence hung in the air before Abby let out a loud sigh.

The tension in the room escalated until Dr. Denver broke the silence by standing up. "Welcome back."

Joey's response was laced with suspicion. "Isn't your shift over? Why are you still here?"

The unusual question left Dr. Denver puzzled.

Joey switched his attention to Abby, who remained seated. "Is Ruby alright?"

"What are you doing here, Joey? I thought I told you to leave!"

"I've come to see our daughter," Joey replied.

Dr. Denver turned to Abby. "Is this true?"

"No, Ruby is not Joey's daughter," replied Abby.

"Are you sure about that?" he asked. "Maybe we should have the good doctor here do a DNA test."

Abby scowled at him. "What the hell are you doing, Joey? I am under enough stress right now; I don't need you, of all people, in my ear. Just leave!"

Abby rose, pushing back her chair with force. "I beg of you, Joey, please leave!"

With some reluctance, he agreed. Before going, he pressed Dr. Denver about Ruby's blood test results.

"Can I share this information with him?" Dr. Denver asked, searching for clarity from Abby. He was uncertain about her relationship status with the man standing before them. After a moment's hesitation, Abby nodded, feeling that she had no other option.

"Ruby's left kidney is deteriorating rapidly," said Dr. Denver. "We will need to perform a transplant; we are seeking relatives and friends who could potentially be suitable donors."

Joey stared at Abby with her red and puffy eyes.

"I have to get back to Ruby," she said, hugging herself tightly against the chill in the canteen.

Joey took a deep breath. "Take my coat."

Abby stubbornly shook her head. "I'm fine."

"Abby, take the coat!"

Finally relenting, she reached out for the oversized jacket, but instead of handing it to her directly, he draped it over her shoulders.

"Don't be afraid," he whispered into her ear as he pulled her into an embrace. Holding her in his arms made him worry more about her well-being. He couldn't imagine the toll it was having on her.

She seemed so delicate and unsteady, like someone who had sank one too many drinks.

"Abby, are you sure you're alright?"

"I'm fine... just feeling lightheaded."

"Let me take her from here," said Dr. Denver. "Come with me, Abby." He wrapped an arm around Abby's waist and led her towards the elevator with authority while casting a disapproving glance at Joey.

"Abby," Joey called out, his voice echoing through the corridor as he desperately tried to catch her attention.

She turned back slowly, her expression a mix of curiosity and trepidation. "I'll be back tomorrow to see whether I'm a viable donor."

Then she disappeared behind the closing elevator doors.

Joey let out a frustrated, jealous sigh at the thought of Abby seeking the comforting presence of the doctor. Despite knowing Dr. Denver was a trusted confidante of Abby and her family, he couldn't help but think they might be romantically involved.

Refusing to entertain such intrusive thoughts, Joey vehemently pushed them aside, reminding himself that such suspicions were unwarranted and baseless. He reassured himself that Abby was not one to engage in casual relations, despite the undeniable closeness she shared with Dr. Denver.

The encounter with them in the canteen made him realise his attraction towards Abby only grew stronger with every passing moment, and now more than ever before he craved her.

As he stood there in silence, contemplating his next move, his mobile phone suddenly rang. Glancing down at the screen, he saw the caller ID was blank. Hesitantly, Joey answered the call. "Hello?"

"Joey, where are you?" Christine's voice came through loud and clear.

"Why are you calling me from a No caller ID, Christine?"

"So, you'll answer my call," she replied matter-of-factly. "Where are you, Joey?"

Thinking quickly on his feet, Joey decided to fabricate a story to avoid revealing his true whereabouts. "I couldn't sleep, so I went for a drive." However, it became apparent almost instantly that Christine was not fooled. "She doesn't need you, Joey; I do!"

Caught off guard by her blunt statement, Joey struggled to find the right words to respond. "Christine, it's not just about you and me... this is bigger than just us."

"Okay, then please explain it to me!"

Realising this conversation was best held in person, Joey made up his mind. "I will see you at home, Christine."

* * *

After Joey abruptly terminated the phone call, Christine's emotional state deteriorated. Overwhelmed by a flood of emotions, she collapsed to her knees in despair. She huddled into a foetal position on the cold hard floor, tears streaming down her face and anguished cries echoing through the room.

As ten agonising minutes passed, Christine gradually regained some semblance of control and stood up.

"I have to leave this place!"

With frantic urgency, she scoured the apartment for a suitable bag. Finally settling on an old, worn suitcase, she packed her belongings and a few essentials.

She made a swift exit through the front door and headed towards her car. The engine roared to life as she sat behind the wheel. Setting the GPS system to point her south, she embarked on a journey into the enveloping darkness.

CHAPTER 35

Abby made her way to Ruby's room in the brightly decorated children's ward, bidding a temporary farewell to her loving parents, who promised to return bright and early the next day. With a heavy heart, she settled down beside Ruby on the cosy bed and together they watched a classic Cinderella movie while indulging in Ruby's beloved red jelly snacks.

After what felt like an eternity of blissful distraction, Abby finally peeled off Joey's coat and carefully draped it over a nearby chair before turning her attention to the winter wonderland outside their window. The snow fell gently, casting a serene yet melancholic atmosphere inside the room. Christmas Day was only a few hours away.

The thought of missing out on the traditional present exchanges and festive feasts with their family around the beautifully adorned Christmas tree filled Abby with a deep sense of sorrow. These were moments she cherished dearly, moments filled with love, joy, and merriment that now seemed like an unattainable dream from within the hospital walls.

Teary eyed, Abby looked down at Ruby's sweet face and felt a surge of anger at the unfairness of their situation. They were destined to spend Christmas confined to this sterile hospital instead of being surrounded by loved ones. Leaning in close, she pressed a gentle kiss to Ruby's forehead before sinking to her. After pouring out her heart in prayer, she slowly rose from the floor and shuffled over to the sofa, where exhaustion finally caught up with her. As sleep claimed her weary body, Abby held onto hope that morning would bring a glimmer of light.

The following morning dawned bright and early, rousing Abby from her slumber as she stirred on the sofa. As her eyes fluttered open, she glanced around the room with a sense of curiosity and wonderment. To her astonishment, she saw her dear parents already in the room, diligently building a tiny Christmas tree with twinkling lights and colourful ornaments for Ruby's enjoyment. The tree was surrounded by an array of beautifully wrapped presents, creating a festive atmosphere that filled the room with such love and joy.

Abby sprang up from the sofa and cast a loving gaze upon Ruby, who still lay peacefully asleep. With a heart brimming with gratitude and love, she approached her parents engrossed in their task of spreading holiday cheer throughout the room. Without hesitation, she hugged them, expressing her delight at their presence.

"Merry Christmas, Mama and Papa! When did you arrive?"

Her mother offered Abby a steaming cup of coffee from the nearby cafeteria while kissing her cheek. "Merry Christmas, Abby," she whispered.

Accepting the coffee gratefully, Abby turned to face her father with a beaming smile. "Merry Christmas, Dad."

In response, he kissed her on the cheek and pulled her into a loving embrace. "Merry Christmas to you, too, bella!" he replied.

Abby's stared at the enchanting Christmas tree standing proudly in one corner of Ruby's room. "You really didn't have to go through all this trouble just for Ruby."

"We brought the tree here because we know how much Ruby loves it," he said with a warm smile.

"I don't know what I would do without you guys."

Her mother placed a comforting hand on Abby's cheek. "Sweetheart, we will always be here for you."

Abby nodded. "I know that, Mama."

Turning towards Ruby's bedside where her mother stood vigilantly watching over her, Abby studied Ruby, gently brushing strands of Ruby's light brown hair away from her peaceful face. "Did Ruby sleep well through the night?"

"Ruby slept soundly, but a nurse came by at three this morning to check her temperature, which was stable, thankfully."

Abby's father finished setting up the Christmas tree and suggested waking Ruby.

Abby gently nudged Ruby. "Wake up, sweetheart. It's Christmas! Merry Christmas, Ruby." She kissed Ruby's cheek and watched her stir, opening her eyes to take in the festive scene before her.

Ruby opened her big, green eyes and scanned the room, her beloved Nonna and Nonno standing by her bedside with arms full of beautifully wrapped presents. Her excitement brimmed over as she tried to sit up before Abby helped her. "Are those for me?"

"Yes, darling," they said simultaneously. "They're all for you. Merry Christmas, Ruby."

With a joyful expression, she said, "Merry Christmas to Nonna, Nonno, and Mama."

With uncontainable delight shining in her eyes, Ruby eagerly tore into the presents laid out before her: a ragdoll to cuddle, chocolates, a puzzle book, a mug adorned with her favourite anime character, and the ultimate surprise—an iPad loaded with her beloved shows to keep her entertained during her hospital stay.

As Abby observed the pure happiness radiating from Ruby's face, she felt an overwhelming sense of contentment. The simple act of witnessing Ruby's unbridled enthusiasm as she unwrapped each gift brought Abby immense joy and created memories that would be treasured for years to come.

Shortly thereafter, a nurse delivered a tray of food to Ruby.

"Why don't you go home and freshen up, Abby," said her mother. "Your papa and I will stay here with Ruby. Micky and Andrea will be arriving soon."

Abby hesitated before replying. "I'm fine, Mama. I want to stay."

As Abby's father opened the wicker basket brimming with an assortment of delectable pastries, pies, cake, and juice lovingly prepared by her mother earlier that morning, he put his arm around Abby's neck. "Your Mama will take good care of Ruby."

Abby struggled against the impulse to stay, hesitating as she raised her shoulders uncertainly. "Are you absolutely certain?"

Her mother responded with a reassuring smile. "Absolutely, sweetheart, now go!"

Sitting on a nearby chair and tugging on her boots, she said, "I'll quickly gather some essentials for Ruby while I'm out."

"You don't have to do that," said her mother. "I've already packed some items for Ruby."

"Thank you, Mama," Abby said and kissed her mother and Ruby on the cheek. "Baby, I'll be back soon, okay? Listen to Grandma and Grandpa, okay?"

Squeezing Ruby's hand affectionately, Abby received a nod from Ruby as she continued munching on her meal.

"Papa," Abby called out. "I need the keys to your truck."

Retrieving the keys from within his coat pocket, he handed them to his daughter. "Drive carefully!"

She nodded, reached for Joey's jacket, and left the room.

* * *

Christine set out on her drive to her mother's house, her mind briefly drifting towards the thought of visiting the St. Andrew's Hospital. The idea lingered, and with a quick decision, she adjusted her route towards the hospital. Upon her arrival, she parked and stayed seated for a moment, absorbing the reality of where she was. She took a few deep breaths, steadying her nerves and sorting through her emotions. With newfound determination, she stepped out of the car and made her way to the children's ward, prepared to confront whatever lay ahead.

As she turned a corner within the hospital corridors, nearly colliding with Abby in the process, their eyes met. Christine tried to hide her distress, but her swollen, red eyes, cheeks devoid of colour, and her overall dishevelled appearance betrayed her. And when she noticed Abby wearing Joey's coat, her distress manifested with a piercing stare.

"Can we please talk?"

Abby hesitated momentarily. "About what?"

"Joey," Christine replied bluntly.

"Not here," said Christine. "Let's go to the cafeteria." Agreeing to her suggestion, Abby followed Christine into the elevator as they made their way towards the cafeteria. Seated across from each other, an uneasy silence hung between them.

Breaking through this tension, Abby said, "I need to return to my daughter... so can we make this quick?"

Christine gathered herself and took a deep breath before speaking; however, her voice trembled slightly as she began. "I need you to stay away from Joey," she stated before pausing momentarily. "You had your chance with him and let him go. He is my future now."

"I am not interested in Joey. I barely even like the guy; we are family friends. There's no reason to be concerned."

"But he has feelings for you."

"Christine, I need to be honest with you about something. I'm unsure about where things stand between you and him right now. However, I want to assure you that there is no romantic interest between us. If you have any concerns, I really think it's best to discuss them with him directly."

The intensity of her stare seemed to convey a warning. "Then why are you wearing his coat?"

"Last night, Joey made a visit to the hospital and met me and Ruby's doctor in the cafeteria. I left my coat upstairs. I was cold and Joey kindly offered his jacket. I understand how this could unsettle you, but I want to assure you there is absolutely no chance of anything happening between us."

Abby stood, removing the jacket and handing it over to Christine while adjusting her clothes. Accepting the coat, Christine said, "It is not about the coat, but deep down inside you already know this."

Abby remained composed even as Christine glared at her intensely. "Joey belongs to me, so you... maintain your distance."

"I understand you care for Joey, Christine. However, it's important to know I don't share the same feelings towards him, nor do I have any intentions of being involved with him or his family. In fact, please relay the message to Joey that he should refrain from approaching me or my family. He rightfully belongs to you. He is all yours." Abby walked away, leaving a stunned Christine standing there with her mouth slightly agape.

* * *

Abby's hand trembled slightly as she reached into her handbag for a cigarette. The bitter taste of resentment lingered on her tongue as she mulled over the betrayal she felt towards Joey Giovanni. She couldn't fathom how he had twisted the truth and insinuated she was the one who had ended their relationship. A surge of anger coursed through her veins as she lit the cigarette, hoping the nicotine would soothe her frayed nerves.

Starting up the engine of her father's truck, Abby took a deep drag of the cigarette, watching as smoke billowed out of her mouth and dissipated in the cold winter air. Snowflakes danced lazily in front of the windshield before melting away, mirroring Abby's own thoughts as she pondered just how much of Joey's version of their shared history was fabricated.

Christine's unexpected appearance at the hospital demanding answers about her relationship with Joey only served to highlight the depths of Christine's insecurities. Abby couldn't help but wonder what personal information Christine had gleaned from their past interactions, causing a seed of unease to take root in her mind.

Arriving at her parents' house, Abby tossed her second cigarette butt onto the ground before hurriedly making her way inside. Racing up the stairs to her bedroom, she laid out her clothes on the bed with practiced efficiency before stripping down and stepping into a hot shower.

After twenty minutes under the steaming water, Abby emerged from the bathroom with damp hair clinging to her shoulders. She blow-dried it quickly before applying a fresh layer of makeup, transforming herself from dishevelled to elegant in a matter of moments.

Traversing the hallway towards Ruby's room, Abby paused in the doorway to take in the familiar surroundings through tear-blurred eyes. Walking over to Ruby's bed, she felt exhaustion wash over her and a yearning for nothing more than to curl up and sleep for days. Grabbing Ruby's favourite blanket and Costa, a stuffed teddy bear with one missing button eye, Abby collapsed onto the bed in a flood of tears. "Why is this happening to us? Why?"

Inhaling Ruby's scent, she cried until there were no more tears left to shed.

Collecting Ruby's belongings, Abby made her way downstairs and donned her boots and coat before grabbing the truck keys and fleeing out into the biting wind. The chill stung her cheeks and froze her teeth as she rushed towards the waiting truck, desperate to escape the turmoil that threatened to ruin her.

CHAPTER 36

After parking the truck in the dimly lit underground hospital car park, Abby paced towards the elevator leading to the main hospital floor. Her eyes widened in surprise as she caught sight of Joey approaching from a distance, causing her breath to catch in her throat. The sound of her own heartbeat echoed loudly in her ears, creating a sense of urgency within her. Her first instinct was to flee from the impending confrontation, but she found herself inexplicably rooted to the spot.

Joey's approach was accompanied by an excessively large teddy bear tucked under one arm and several gifts cradled in his free hand. As he drew nearer to Abby, she breathed out heavily through her nose. "What are you doing here?"

"Happy holidays to you as well," Joey replied. He towered graciously over Abby, exuding an air of calm. "Cross match testing for a kidney donor," he added.

"Joey, I don't want you around!"

For a brief moment, Joey gazed at Abby with a pained expression on his face. "Curse me all you want; I deserve it. But don't shut me out like this."

She heard a small voice demanding to know where he had vanished to for the past five years. Her frustration grew as she recalled the countless nights she'd waited for a call, the empty promises that turned into mere echoes in her mind. Each day that passed, her anger intensified, simmering beneath the surface, as she grappled with the betrayal. How did he think he could just reappear after all this time? The heat of anger rushed to her cheeks. "Joey!" She shook her head disapprovingly. "We don't need your support, and you have no place in my family's affairs. I'm going to say this once and once only: get lost!"

Joey took a step closer and reached out tentatively to touch her shoulder. She recoiled instinctively at his touch.

"Abby, I want to apolo—"

"Honestly, Joey? Save your apology for Christine because she also deserves one. And with her, it might actually carry some meaning."

In response to Abby's pointed remark, Joey locked eyes with her. "What is that supposed to mean?"

"Ask Christine!" Abby replied dryly, brushing past him as she made her way towards the elevator. Her voice carried a hint of finality as she distanced herself from the conversation.

Joey opened his mouth, but no words escaped.

As Abby walked out of the elevator and headed along the hallway towards room 130A, anticipation filled her chest. Upon opening the door, she was greeted by a heartwarming scene— members of her extended family gathered around a table laden with

253

Mama's pastries and coffee, sharing laughter and joy as they celebrated together. Micky and Andrea had arrived early to join in the festivities, their presence bringing comfort and support to Ruby as they assisted her in unwrapping gifts.

Abby's gaze lingered on Ruby, noting her frailty and sadness. Her heart clenched at the sight of pain reflected in Ruby's eyes. Turning her attention to Micky, Abby observed his efforts to bring a smile to Ruby's face, admiration glimmering in her eyes as she watched him clown around, trying to make her laugh.

Suddenly, Nurse Gretchen burst into the room. "Why are so many people in this room?" she snapped. "Visiting hours are over, everyone out! NOW!"

"I'm very sorry," said Abby. "They are all leaving now, but my parents will stay."

"That's fine," the nurse responded.

As Abby's extended family prepared to depart, including Micky and Andrea, they took a moment to exchange brief farewells before making their way out the door. "Thank you for coming to visit, and Merry Christmas!" Abby called after them as she closed the door.

Nurse Gretchen waited at the foot of Ruby's hospital bed until each family member had left. Then she checked Ruby's vital signs and administered pain relief through her cannula. Staring at the monitor, she said, "Ruby's blood pressure is low, so I will raise the height of the bed."

She picked up the remote control and adjusted the elevation. "Make sure she drinks plenty of water, and I will get her something from the pharmacy. Also, Dr. Denver would like to see you in his office."

Abby nodded before Nurse Gretchen left the room.

After sitting at the edge of the bed, she drew Ruby closer by wrapping her arm around her waist.

Abby looked at her mother. "Mama, would you mind getting some water for Ruby please?"

"Yes, of course, my dear," she said as she hurriedly went to the bedside table and filled a cup with water.

"Mama, I feel tired," Ruby murmured.

"Please, Ruby, have some water for mummy," Abby pleaded as she held onto the glass.

Ruby reluctantly took a few sips before pulling away and shaking her head to indicate she didn't want any more. "Sweetie, Nonna and I need to go see the doctor. I'll be back in a few minutes. Nonno will stay with you, okay?"

Ruby nodded sleepily before closing her eyes. Leaving Ruby in capable hands, Abby and Nonna proceeded down the hallway towards Dr. Denver's office following Nurse Gretchen's lead.

* * *

Joey sat in his car and dialled Christine's mobile phone. Unfortunately, the call went unanswered and was diverted to voicemail. He tried again until she finally answered with a groggy voice.

"Christine! Where are you?"

There was a brief pause before Christine responded wearily, "Joey, I've returned home."

"Where is home?"

Christine let out a sigh of resignation before replying, "Our house."

"Stay there! I'll be there in forty minutes."

Pulling into the driveway, he climbed out of his car and came through the front door. Spotting Christine in the kitchen whipping up something to eat, she gaped at him incredulously.

"Follow me," he said coldly before making his way out of the kitchen towards the hallway that led to their living room. The tension was palpable as Christine nodded silently, put down her breadmaking utensils, and followed him.

Facing her in the living room, he spoke slowly. "You must tell me the truth. Don't even think about lying to me. What exactly did you say to Abby?"

Christine cleared her throat nervously. "I'm not sure what you mean." She broke eye contact and stared at the floor.

Joey did not accept her answer. He observed her and moved closer. His demeanour changed instantly. His emerald, green eyes bore into hers as he demanded answers from her without hesitation or mercy.

"You have one chance to tell me the truth!" Joey warned as he clenched his jaw tightly in an effort to contain his rising anger. "So, speak up now!"

"Joey," she began tentatively, "you really put me in an uncomfortable position. You didn't leave me any choice. I told her to leave us alone and that you belonged to me."

His expression hardened and he shook his head disapprovingly.

Her voice faltered as tears appeared in her eyes. "Don't blame this on me! It's your fault!"

"Let me be clear, Christine! I belong to no one, including you. Do you understand?" he asked with a stern, unyielding gaze.

"Why did you visit Abby at the hospital? She's going through a tough time?"

"I didn't mean it that way," Christine muttered while shaking her head in denial. Tears glistened in her eyes as she struggled to convey remorse for her actions. "I'm so sorry, okay? I had no idea what I was doing or saying. I don't want to lose you. Why are you giving that woman so much attention? It doesn't make any sense!"

Joey slowly approached the couch with Christine, and they both sat. He took her delicate hand. "There is something important I need to tell you. Ruby may be my biological daughter. She's very ill and in need of a kidney transplant."

Christine looked stunned, pulling back slightly as she stared at him. With tears streaming down her face, she screamed, "WHAT? When did this happen?"

"Five years ago, obviously."

Christine slowly sank back into the couch. "Have you requested a DNA test?"

"Not yet, but it is something I intend to do."

"Joey, this is not okay," she murmured.

"There's more..."

"What?"

With a heavy heart and a deep breath, he said, "I believe it would be best for us to end our relationship."

"What? Why?" Christine's face twisted as she stood up abruptly. She began pacing around the room, sobbing and screaming. "No Joey, we are not breaking up! You cannot do this to me! Do you understand me? You can't abandon me for another woman. I won't accept it!" She picked up a vase from the coffee table and launched it at Joey's head, but he caught it effortlessly in his palm.

"Please calm down!"

She shrieked, "NO! How dare you ask me to calm down. It's because of her, isn't it? You haven't been able to erase her from your memory this whole time. She made you do this, didn't she?"

"Abby didn't influence my decision. I've been thinking about it for a while now. I acknowledge your frustration, but let's discuss this rationally. Please, take a seat."

With a sigh, Christine sank to her knees and uttered, "Joey, this isn't fair. I don't deserve this."

Joey tried to imagine their future, married with children, a nice house, but it was incomprehensible for him. He closed his eyes and saw Abby, longing for her as he always had without truly knowing it. Now he knew. He wanted her and only her.

"You're absolutely right, Christine. Your beauty, intelligence, and affection deserve to be reciprocated by a good man who accepts everything about you. While I cannot fulfil this role, there is one truth I must admit: I am not deserving of your love or anyone's. I have committed terrible sins in my life and abandoned Abby when she needed me during the pregnancy. Even now, five years on, it still haunts me deeply, and something I'll always regret."

Joey extended his arms towards Christine, who crawled into them sobbing quiet tears. He lifted her chin and made her look at him, gripping her face firmly as he leaned in for a tender kiss. "Chrissy, I apologise for not keeping my promises. I'm sorry for disappointing you and failing to be the man you desire."

Christine remained quiet.

He pulled her close against his shoulder and wrapped his arms around her waist. "I'll miss you too."

After a few minutes, they let go of each other.

"Chrissy, if you ever find yourself in trouble, please call me, okay?" He brushed her hair from her face and tucking it behind her ear with a tenderness that belied the situation, an overwhelming sense of finality settled between them. She looked at him, her eyes reflecting a storm of emotions—gratitude, sorrow, and a hint of desperation. With a forced smile that didn't quite reach her eyes, she turned away, feeling the weight of uncertainty about what lay ahead pressing down on her shoulders. The distance between them felt insurmountable now, and as she walked away, she carried his words with her, hoping she'd never have to make that call.

CHAPTER 37

Abby, accompanied by her mother, made their way to Dr. Denver's office to convene with the medical professionals and transplant experts hailing from the donor program. Following the customary exchange of pleasantries, Dr. Kitchener proceeded to delve into the intricacies of the matter at hand.

"At St. Andrew's Hospital, we have successfully completed seventy kidney transplants within this past year alone and have determined that a transplant stands as a viable treatment option for Ruby. However, before proceeding any further, additional investigations, examinations, compatibility testing, and eligibility assessments will need to be conducted for both potential living donors and recipients like Ruby."

Abby looked on with a blank expression before exchanging knowing glances with her mother.

Dr. Kitchener crossed one leg over the other before continuing. "When a potential donor becomes accessible, patients on our waiting list undergo thorough evaluations based on various criteria such as genetic makeup, blood type compatibility, medical imaging results, physical size considerations, and time spent waiting for transplantation. It is paramount you prepare yourself accordingly and familiarise yourself with the substantial financial obligations associated with undergoing a kidney transplant. These costs encompass not only expenses related to the actual transplant surgery and subsequent hospitalisation but also extend to cover post-operative care requirements including anti-rejection medication regimes, outpatient consultations and follow-up appointments. The total cost for a kidney transplant typically ranges from $89,000 to $125,000."

The colour in Abby's face drained. "That's ridiculous! I don't have that kind of money. I'm a single mother; I can't pay that."

Dr. Denver looked at her with a sympathy smile.

She turned her attention back to Dr. Kitchener when she started speaking again. "I understand your predicament entirely, Miss Di Manos. We can provide assistance in connecting you with an experienced transplant financial coordinator who specialises in facilitating financing options, which may not be covered under conventional health insurance plans, assuming you possess one?"

"Yes, I do, but I'm not sure if my policy covers major procedures like a transplant. I will need to contact my insurance company to determine what options are available to us."

"Yes, please do that."

"But what if my policy does not cover transplant costs?"

"Miss Di Manos, if you can't afford to pay for the transplant, Ruby will be placed at the bottom of the waiting list until a suitable donor is found, which could take a year or longer."

An hour later, Abby and her mother emerged from Dr. Denver's office, the news hitting them like a forty-ton truck.

"I'll contact the insurance provider now," said Abby, still in shock. "I'll catch up with you later in the room. Can you please make sure Ruby has something to eat?"

Her mother nodded but said nothing.

With that, Abby turned and walked away.

"Abby, wait!" her mother called out.

Abby glanced back at her mother, bursting into floods of tears.

Her mother held her close, gently running her fingers through Abby's hair the way she did when Abby was a little girl. "Everything will be alright, please stop crying. We'll find a way to get the money. I'll talk to your father about taking out a second mortgage on the house."

"No, Mama, that won't be necessary. I won't allow you and Papa to do that. I won't accept any financial help from you or Dad. You've already done more than enough for Ruby and I."

Abby reached out for her mother's hand. "I have some money saved up, Mum. I'll reach out to the insurance company to see what options we have. Don't worry, I got this." She lightly patted her mother's hand, mustering a feeble smile. Then quickly turned away, rushed towards the waiting elevator, and pressed the button for the ground floor.

Sitting alone in the peaceful garden outside the hospital, Abby sank onto a bench and let herself break down completely. Overwhelmed by the weight of responsibility resting on her shoulders, she allowed herself a moment of release before pulling herself together. Dialling the insurance company's number, she engaged in a fruitless conversation with an unhelpful representative, learning transplants were not covered and that no amount of complaining would change that. The sense of hopelessness that settled over Abby was palpable as she hung up the phone and stared into space, grappling with the seemingly insurmountable challenge before her, contemplating how best to secure the funds needed to save Ruby's life.

"Abby," a soft voice called out.

She gasped and looked up at Dr. Denver, her eyes filled with tears. "Oh, I'm sorry, I didn't hear you."

Dr. Denver held out his handkerchief for Abby, who accepted it graciously and delicately dabbed her eyes while summoning a smile that did not quite reach her heart. "Thank you."

"I have been searching high and low for you," Dr. Denver said. "May I join you?"

Abby's voice was stuck in her throat as she struggled to contain her emotions, so she nodded. "I was just on the phone to the insurance company, and guess what? It seems Ruby is not eligible for significant medical procedures under our policy plan."

Dr. Denver embraced Abby tightly, sharing her grief before gently pulling back. "Abby, there is something important I wish to discuss with you. Take your time to ponder it before responding."

Perplexed but attentive, Abby asked, "What is it?"

"I would like to contribute to Ruby's transplant," he said, only to be interrupted by Abby's vehement shake of the head.

Raising a calming hand, Dr. Denver said, "Please, Abby, allow me to finish."

She nodded and listened as he continued.

"I am willing to cover the expenses of Ruby's transplant, but I understand if you are uncomfortable with this arrangement.

Therefore, I want to lend you the necessary funds and allow you to repay me in manageable monthly instalments." He paused briefly before asking, "Does this proposed payment plan suit your needs?"

"Matty, your kindness is truly appreciated, but I must respectfully decline."

"Abby, please allow me to help you."

"I am grateful for your offer and trust you will do everything possible to ensure Ruby's recovery," she acknowledged. "But I feel compelled to handle this situation independently. I hope you can respect my decision."

"I completely understand and hold in high regard the decision you have made, Abby. Please know the offer I extended to you still stands should you ever find yourself in need of it."

He reached out and gently grasped her hands, gazing directly into her eyes as he spoke. "Abby, I want you to know I will always be here for you and Ruby. You can rely on me without hesitation. Feel free to use and abuse me." It made them share a light-hearted chuckle.

Following their brief exchange, they sat together in silence for a moment. She expressed her gratitude once more before shifting her attention towards the handkerchief that lay folded on her lap. Rising from her seat, she cast a parting glance back at him and holding up the handkerchief. "It's time for me to make my way back now, but I would like to wash this before returning it to you."

Dr. Denver chuckled. "Not a problem at all; you may keep it. I have plenty more at home."

"Thank you," she replied.

Standing up alongside her, he accompanied her to the elevator. As the doors slid open, Dr. Denver bestowed upon her a kind smile.

"Abby, please let your family and friends know that the pathology centre will open today at 1:00 pm for donor testing."

"Thanks, Matty, I'll make sure to let the family know."

He grabbed her arm as she was about to enter the elevator, prompting her to take a step back and meet his gaze with a look of confusion. "Is everything alright?"

In response, Dr. Denver shook his head gently before retrieving a small gift from the pocket of his lab coat and placing it delicately into her palm while retaining his grasp on her wrist.

"I was meant to give this to you earlier." He smiled. "Merry Christmas, Abby. I hope you like it."

Overwhelmed by his unexpected act of kindness, she hesitated briefly before expressing her reluctance to accept such a thoughtful offering. "Oh no, you really didn't need to do this. I cannot accept this. Truly, I can't

"Abby, I really want you to take this, even though it's not a lot. If you don't accept it, I'll be very disappointed." He released her wrist. "I have to leave now, but we can catch up later, okay?" Then he rushed off.

She nodded and watched him jog towards the emergency corridor. A fleeting smile crossed his lips as he glanced back at her before vanishing from sight.

As she stood there, her hands trembling and her heart racing within her chest, she carefully inspected the gift now cradled in her grasp before stepping into the waiting elevator.

In that moment, she made the decision to conceal it within her coat and pondered how she would gather enough funds for the transplant. Closing her eyes, a silent prayer escaped her lips beseeching God for deliverance from this plight. She made up her mind to utilise the $70,000 she had saved up for her business and borrow an additional $55,000 to cover the hefty $125,000 cost of the transplant, acknowledging that contacting the bank and obtaining a loan was her only option.

At 1:00 pm, Abby's parents, Micky and Andrea, as well as some relatives and family friends, gathered on the fifth floor where the pathology ward was located to undergo testing.

Abby sat beside Ruby on her bed and gently held her hand. "Hey, my little star, soon a nice nurse will come to take a small bit of blood from you. After that, we'll move to another room for some more check-ups. But don't worry, when we're finished, we'll come back here to see Nonno and Nonna." There's nothing to be scared of, okay, possum?" she said with a smile.

A sorrowful expression crossed Ruby's face. "Mummy, I want to go home." She clutched Mr. Costa tightly and wrapped herself in her beloved blanket.

"I know you do, baby, and I wish the same." She longed for the comfort of their own home, where they could sit by the fireplace and enjoy the cosy atmosphere beside the Christmas tree.

Ruby started weeping, and Abby quickly picked her up and held her, gently combing her fingers through her hair. "Don't worry, baby, everything will be alright. We can't go home until you're feeling much better, can you try really hard to get better for me, please? Can you do that for mommy?" She lovingly wiped the tears from Ruby's cheeks.

Ruby nodded.

Abby held Ruby's face. "I am sorry, baby, we will be home soon I promise." She extended her pinkie finger and said, "Pinkie promise."

Ruby beamed, displaying her beautiful smile. She joined her pinkie with her mother's and sealed it, softly replied, "Pinkie promise, Mummy."

"I love you so much, kiddo," Abby said, squeezing her small body.

A few minutes passed before she remembered she needed to call the bank. She reached for her phone but then she realised banks are closed during the Christmas holiday. It became apparent that she would have to wait until after Boxing Day.

CHAPTER 38

Dr. Denver, accompanied by nurse Gretchen, returned to the room to collect blood samples from Ruby's IV line in test tubes. Shortly after, two hospital porters whisked Ruby away to the imaging ward for further examinations. After forty-five minutes, Abby and Ruby were back in their room. To her surprise, they discovered the room transformed into a lively gathering. Her parents, Micky and Andrea, and the Giovanni family had gathered, bonded over the simple joy of sharing pizza.

Abby scanned the room, her heart calming at the absence of Joey and Christine, glad to sidestep any potential tension for now. Smiling warmly, she exchanged greetings with her loved ones, her presence a stitching of comfort and calm. Gently perching on the edge of Ruby's bed, Abby began to feed her daughter, savouring a slice of pizza herself amidst the vibrant gathering.

A sudden cough caught Abby's attention as Joey entered the room bearing gifts. She suddenly became acutely aware of her withdrawn appearance as she sat up straight and saw her face in the mirror. Joey lingered near the doorway, exchanging brief eye contact with Abby before making his way over to Ruby. His presence caused a stir within her, prompting her mind to race with thoughts of what she would say upon interacting with him.

Offering Ruby a warm smile, Joey presented her with a bouquet of flowers, oversized teddy bear and an assortment of presents, wishing her a "Merry Christmas."

Ruby responded graciously with a soft "Thank you," her smile growing even brighter.

Turning his attention towards Abby, Joey whispered "Merry Christmas" before planting a gentle kiss on her cheek. Startled by this gesture, Abby pulled back slightly, feeling a rush of embarrassment wash over her. Joey then handed her a gift from his large bag, prompting a sarcastic remark from Abby along the lines of "So now you're Santa Claus?" which elicited laughter from all those present. He joined in on the laughter.

"Where is Christine, why isn't she with you?" asked Mrs. Giovanni.

Joey hesitated. "Let's talk about that later," he replied.

Persistent as always, Mrs. Giovanni pushed for information until finally Joey disclosed, "I ended my relationship with Christine" before locking eyes briefly with Abby.

The sudden silence enveloped the room as everyone directed puzzled looks towards Abby. Tony interjected, stating matter-of-factly, "I saw that coming. I never liked her anyway" resulting in a sharp look from Mrs. Giovanni. "Stop that right now, Tony!"

"Christine is such a wonderful girl who truly cares for you. Why on earth would you end things with her? I can't wrap my head around your actions, Joey. How could you treat her so badly? Is there someone else?

"Enough!" he snapped. "I don't love her, okay?"

The tension in the room escalated as each person attempted to process this unexpected turn of events. Abby kept her eyes fixed on Ruby's toy, attempting to shield herself from the intense atmosphere surrounding her.

When she looked up again, she found Joey staring at her, making her feel uneasy again.

"Angela, leave the kid alone," said Mr. Giovanni, glaring at her.

Mrs. Giovanni shook her head, refusing to accept the situation.

The noise in the room resumed, and soon after, Mr. Giovanni deftly reached for the remote control and flicked through the channels on the television screen, selecting a new program that captured everyone's attention. As the newscaster's voice filled the room, detailing a tragic and heart-wrenching event involving an innocent man who had been brutally stabbed to death by a homeless individual near a subway station in Brooklyn, a heavy silence descended upon the gathered group. The motive behind this senseless act of violence was the victim's refusal to give financial assistance to his attacker.

Abby's father, visibly impacted by the grim news unfolding before him, shook his head in disbelief as he recounted the poignant story of Benjamin Jones.

"I encountered a homeless man in his early forties, so unkempt and dirty, sitting outside the restaurant late at night while I was closing up one evening. He had worn-out shoes and tattered clothes, wrapped in a thin blanket with a sign requesting employment. Although I frequently saw him wandering the streets in our neighbourhood and occasionally resting on the bench outside our establishment, he did not come across as a beggar. On that fateful night, I extended an invitation for him to come inside the restaurant, but he appeared hesitant and scared. Eventually, he agreed. During our chat, I asked him why he always sat outside the restaurant. His response was that he loved the smell of pizza but couldn't afford to buy one. So, I prepared a piping hot pizza along with some soup for him and sat alongside him as he ate. As we conversed into the wee hours of dawn, he shared with me tales of poor decisions made during his youth which led him down his current path. There was something about his demeanour that resonated with me; his politeness and resolute determination to better himself were truly inspiring. After he finished eating and wiping away tears of gratitude, I made an impulsive decision to offer him employment and lodging above the restaurant until he could find permanent housing. Additionally, I offered him some of my old clothing and a pair of brand-new shoes. Initially hesitant yet deeply moved by my gesture, he accepted my offer with tears in his eyes. Six years have passed since that pivotal moment and Ben is still with us. Our bond has blossomed into an enduring friendship; he found love and started a family, but most significantly is the unwavering trust and faith I placed in him."

Mrs Giovanni smiled. "You have a kind heart, dear. Not many people would have been willing to lend a hand."

Her father nodded, adding, "It is indeed a rare quality to find in people nowadays."

As tears threatened to spill from Abby's eyes, listening intently to her father recounting the captivating tale of Benjamin Jones. Her gaze shifted towards Joey, who was looking at her with a gentle expression. Their eyes met briefly before Abby turned her attention to Ruby, who had already drifted off to sleep.

Suddenly, Mr. Giovanni called out Abby's name, causing her to look at him curiously. "Yes?"

Your father shared with me the details about the transplant costs, and we want to help cover them, the elderly man kindly offered.

Mrs. Giovanni nodded with enthusiasm, saying, "Yes, Abby, we see you as family. How much do you need, dear?"

Abby's father chimed in, "We're truly grateful for your kindness, but Abby has chosen to handle this herself and isn't accepting help from anyone.

Mrs. Giovanni reacted with surprise. "What!"

Everyone turned towards Abby, prompting her to confirm. "I genuinely appreciate your generous offer, but I feel I must do this on my own without financial assistance from any of you."

"You see?" said her father. "She refuses to listen, she's as stubborn as ever."

Frank and Angela glanced back at Adriano with a shock expression and shook their heads. "Abby, this isn't fair," said Mrs Giovanni. "We know you may feel uncomfortable accepting money from us, but your father wants to help. You shouldn't have to do everything on your own; family must stick together through the good and bad times."

"I don't know why she is being so stubborn about this," said her mama, giving her a stern glance.

"Abby, sweetheart, this isn't something you should handle on your own," Mrs. Giovanni gently remarked. "Let us help you." She leaned over, compassion in her eyes, and pulled a pen and cheque book from her handbag.

"Mrs. Giovanni, I cannot accept your money. Our policy covers the kidney transplant, post-care treatments, and medication; we are fortunate in that regard." She felt uneasy about the lie.

Everyone, including Abby's parents, gazed at her with uncertainty. A prolonged silence filled the room as they waited for her to elaborate or change her mind.

"I appreciate your support, but I can handle everything myself."

One hour later, nurse Gretchen arrived in the room. "It's time to leave, visiting hours are over."

A flurry of movement ensued as each visitor rose from their seats to bid their farewells one by one. This amused Abby, who let out a chuckle.

Nurse Gretchen wasted no time in swiftly exiting the room after the last visitor had departed, leaving Abby and Joey alone. Joey slowly rose out of his chair and approached her. Leaning in close, he brushed his lips against her ear in a gesture that sent shivers down her spine. "Tomorrow, I will uncover the truth about Ruby."

It caught Abby off guard.

Her shocked expression betrayed her confusion. "What do you mean by that?"

"I spoke with Dr. Denver to check if my blood type would be compatible with Ruby's. I wanted to see if I could be a donor for her."

"You went ahead and did that?"

In a fit of rage, Abby grabbed his arm and shoved him out of the room into the hallway. "You have no right! She is not your daughter! Get that through your thick skull!"

He looked at her with a teasing squint. "You've always struggled with lying. I have no idea how you became such a successful lawyer."

"Then you know I've been telling the truth."

Abby held her breath as Joey encircled her waist with his arm, drawing her closer to him, whispering, "So you have nothing to be concerned about."

She clenched her teeth in response. "Let go of me, right now!"

"You should have been truthful with me, Abby. You didn't leave me much of a choice, did you?"

"Let me go, Joey, before I scream for help!"

He burst into laughter before kissing her forehead. "I'll see you tomorrow." Then he turned and confidently walked towards the stairwell.

Abby stood there, feeling uneasy as she watched him leave. His deep voice echoed through the hallway as he said goodbye to the doctors and nurses.

She leaned her weary body against the wall, feeling the cool surface against her back. With a heavy heart, she closed her eyes, shutting out the world around her momentarily. She knew deep down the truth could no longer be concealed, looming ominously over her like a dark cloud ready to burst.

Once he found out and the Giovanni family discovered the extent of their deception, they would see through the web of lies that had been carefully woven over the years to conceal their ties to Ruby. The fragile facade of their long-standing relationship would crumble under the weight of betrayal and deceit. Regret flooded her as she realised the folly of not coming clean from the very beginning. For nothing good ever sprouted from seeds of dishonesty.

As devout Christians, they had strayed far from grace by choosing lies over truth. What consequences awaited her now that Joey was on the brink of uncovering the tangled web of secrets?

Would he seek retribution and attempt to take custody of Ruby away from her grasp? Questions swamped her mind like a whirlpool threatening to drag her into its depths.

She couldn't fathom why Dr. Denver hadn't approached her directly with his testing request. Was Joey playing an elaborate prank on her, or was this reality staring at her in its stark nakedness? Everything hung precariously in the balance with nothing but uncertainty on one side and risk on the other. Summoning courage from deep within, she drew in a deep breath and opened her eyes, steeling herself for what lay ahead. Rising from the wall, she retraced her steps back into the room and settled onto the sofa.

Fingers trembling slightly, she reached into her handbag and retrieved her phone, fingers dancing across the screen as she composed a message to Joey. "Come to the hospital tomorrow at noon. We need to talk." With a sense of finality, she pressed send before dialling Dr. Denver's number. The phone rang incessantly before finally being picked up on the other end.

"Hey, Matty, are you still at the hospital?"

"Yes, I am. Are you alright?"

"Yes," she replied quietly, anxiety clogging her throat.

"I really need to speak with you about something important."

A pause lingered between them before Dr. Denver spoke again, his tone serious yet comforting. "I'll be there in ten minutes."

* * *

Joey, upon preparing to leave the hospital, decided to make a small deviation from his original path to visit the administration office with the intention of resolving the outstanding bill. Engaging in a discussion with one of the staff members at the office, he made it abundantly clear that confidentiality regarding his personal information was of utmost importance to him. However, before he could explain further, his attention was diverted to his phone. As expected, Abby had sent him a text message that confirmed his suspicions about her deceitful actions. By persistently pushing her to be truthful and challenging her bluff regarding the donor test, Joey had ultimately succeeded in getting her to come clean.

CHAPTER 39

Abby faced a daunting task as she mustered up the courage to finally disclose a long-held secret, realising concealing it any longer was simply not an option. The uncertainty of what kind of father Joey would prove to be loomed over her, leaving her to ponder whether he would step up to support and care for Ruby or fall back into old patterns by once again abandoning them.

With a heavy heart, she gathered her clothes and toiletries and made her way into the bathroom to begin her nightly routine.

Standing in front of the mirror, Abby removed her turtleneck jumper and jeans, opting instead for comfortable sweatpants and an oversized sweater. She let her hair down, allowing its gentle curls to cascade over her shoulders. Stepping out of the bathroom, she made her way towards the chair where she had hung her coat earlier, retrieving the small gift from Dr. Denver. Seated on the sofa with her legs crossed, she began unwrapping the present only to be interrupted by Dr. Denver's unexpected appearance at the door.

"Hi, Abby," he said warmly as he noticed the partially opened gift in her hand.

Abby placed a hand over her heart. "Oh, Matty, you surprised me!"

He smiled. "You have an infectious smile, you know."

Rising from the couch with a playful tousle of her hair, Abby said, "I wish I had a reason to smile."

"Ruby is resilient. We're doing everything we can to find a suitable donor for her treatment. Speaking of which, I need you to come down to the pathology centre tomorrow for some testing."

"Absolutely," Abby replied without hesitation.

Dr. Denver pointed at the present in her hand. "Why don't you open it and find out what's inside?"

"I was." She finished unwrapping the gift and opened the box to find a gold heart pendant. "Oh my goodness..." Her eyes lit up with delight.

"Do you like it?"

Abby's gazed between the pendant cradled in her palm and Dr. Denver standing before her before. "It's truly beautiful... but I'm not sure if I can accept it."

"And why not?"

"Because..." she began, but he cut her off.

"Abby... you know how much you mean to me. Could we perhaps explore something beyond friendship? Allow me to become closer to both you and Ruby... Let me bring joy into your lives."

Abby took a deep breath. "You are an amazing man, immensely kind, but I cannot enter a romantic relationship with you... We can only be friends."

"Why?"

"Joey is Ruby's biological father... he is unaware of this."

He fell silent for a moment, locking eyes with hers. "Why are you keeping this from him? He deserves to know the truth."

"Joey and I have shared a bond since childhood, and over time, our relationship naturally deepened. We mutually decided to keep it private until we were prepared to inform our families. Upon discovering my pregnancy six weeks along, I disclosed this news to Joey urged me to terminate the pregnancy and subsequently chose to sever all ties with me. I was overcome with fear, isolation, and a sense of rejection, which greatly undermined my self-confidence. I eventually decided to confide in my parents, who regrettably responded poorly, more concerned about community perception than my well-being, leading them to send me away to a monastery in Italy for the duration of my pregnancy. After five years, I returned to my hometown with Ruby and a freshly earned bachelor's degree in law. However, the circumstances surrounding Ruby's presence in our home were not as straightforward as they appeared. To shield ourselves from potential backlash and harsh judgments from the community's gossip mill, my parents concocted an elaborate tale that Ruby was a distant cousin who had tragically lost her parents in a devastating accident, and she had come to live with us. To further bolster this facade, we orchestrated an elaborate charade wherein Ruby began affectionately referring to me as 'Mum.' The thought of anyone discovering the truth terrified me because it would not only result in community gossip but also cause damage to the longstanding relationship my parents held with the Giovanni family. I harboured doubts about whether the Giovanni family would ever be able to forgive my parents."

He reached out and gently held Abby's hand. "I'm sorry for what you had to endure, Abby. You are an incredibly brave woman."

"My time there was far from easy; it posed numerous challenges that often left me feeling overwhelmed and defeated. The stringent rules, traditions, and insular way of life left me struggling to find my place. But Sister Mary Rosetta Mancini emerged as my beacon of light. She embraced me like one of her own children and guided me through moments of anxiety, distress, and sorrow that accompanied the uncertainty of my situation. Her unwavering support and compassion sustained me through each phase of my journey; without her presence, I don't think I could have made it this far."

"It's wonderful to hear that Sister Mary Rosetta Mancini was there by your side to offer her support.," he said. "From what I've heard, she seems extraordinary."

"Indeed, she embodies the qualities of an angel."

"However, your motives for concealing the truth are far more sinister, and I believe you recognise this fact. Abby, Joey deserves to know the truth. He has a right to be informed about the existence of a sick child who may require his kidney. At times in life, we are confronted with difficult decisions, and this is one such occasion where you must ponder your choices and contemplate what is morally justifiable. I understand your reasons; people will be hurt, friendships may be tested or even broken, and your reputation is at stake. While you can control many things, there are some aspects of life that we cannot control. Therefore, you must accept the situation as it is and allow it to unfold naturally, regardless of how it makes you feel or what the outcome may bring. Abby, you have been trapped in the past for far too long; you need to let go of the pain it has caused you. To do so, you must find the courage to reveal the truth. Aren't you tired of hiding?"

"I hear you, Matty, I really do, but it's a big deal. I feel frightened and weary from maintaining this deception."

Dr. Denver acknowledged Abby's statement with a nod. "I know you are, and I understand, Abby, but I want you to know that you have an incredible strength within you, even if you don't always see it. Just take a moment to appreciate everything you've accomplished so far. If it would ease your mind, I can be there when you talk to Joey.

"Thanks, but I need to do it alone. I hope you understand."

"Of course I do."

"Abby, have you considered the possibility that Joey could be the potential donor we've been searching for? Are you willing to take a major gamble and potentially risk your reputation for the sake of your daughter's safety?"

"Yes, I am prepared to take that risk."

"I'm really glad to hear that," he said, with a warm smile.

They stood up from the sofa and Abby accompanied him to the door.

"I'll meet you at the pathology centre tomorrow," he said, hugging her.

"Of course, I'll be there," she replied, nodding and smiling.

Their warm embrace was abruptly cut short by Nurse Gretchen entering the room, her arrival completely unexpected and catching them off guard. They instinctively pulled away from each other in surprise.

"I apologise for intruding," she said, her tone slightly curt. "Dr. Denver, you are urgently needed in room 510." With a cold glare directed at Abby, Nurse Gretchen swiftly exited the room, leaving an awkward tension in her wake. At that, Abby wondered if Nurse Gretchen had feelings for Dr. Denver.

Once alone again, Abby retreated back to the sofa and wrapped herself in a blanket.

As she closed her eyes, haunting visions flooded Abby's mind— vivid images of her alone in her childhood bedroom at her parents' house with hands stained in blood. She rushed frantically into Ruby's room only to find it soaked in crimson stains.

Abby collapsed to the floor, desperately searching for Ruby but finding herself immobilised by sudden paralysis in her legs. Her cries for help echoed through the empty space until a tall figure emerged from the shadows with bloodied hands clutching a knife that dripped scarlet onto the carpet.

The man's face was partially obscured as he moved closer towards Abby, causing her to scream uncontrollably out of fear for her life and struggling to catch her breath. Locking eyes with him, she questioned if he was Joey. His voice was icy and unforgiving as he accused her of hiding his daughter from him. In that chilling moment, Abby shut her eyes and shuddered, still unable to move.

"Joey, where is Ruby? Where is my daughter?" Her sobs grew louder as panic overtook her senses.

"She's dead! I killed her and disposed of her body in the Wisconsin River." He laughed callously at her distress.

The intensity of Abby's screams startled Ruby awake, prompting two nurses to rush into the room.

Abby rose from the sofa and hurried to Ruby's bedside to comfort her daughter. "I'm so sorry, baby. I didn't mean to scare you. Mummy just had a bad dream."

She held Ruby close against her chest and gently stroked her hair. She glanced up at the nurses and apologised, her voice breaking with emotion. "I'm sorry... I... I had a terrible nightmare, which felt too real."

"It's okay. I can bring you something to help you relax," the nurse whispered.

Abby blushed. "No, thank you. I believe I'll be fine. I'm sorry again. I have a lot of my mind."

CHAPTER 40

The following morning, as the clock struck eight and the sun began to filter through the window blinds, Abby's parents arrived at the hospital. A short time later, Abby took a brief detour to the pathology centre to have her blood checked to see if she was a suitable match for Ruby.

After spending approximately forty minutes undergoing the blood test, Abby navigated through the hospital corridors until she reached the elevator that would take her up to the administration office. Once there, she sought Ruby's consent forms and proceeded to make a payment using her hard-earned savings to cover any necessary expenses.

"I believe there may be an error here... it shows that payment has already been made?" Abby asked, furrowing her brow in confusion.

"Full payment was actually made yesterday evening at 5:00 pm," said the receptionist.

"May I ask who made this payment?"

"I'm afraid I cannot disclose that information, Miss Di Manos," said the receptionist. "The individual has opted to remain anonymous, and we must respect their privacy. Unfortunately, I am unable to provide further assistance."

Abby glanced at the nametag on her uniform vest. "Lorraine, could you perhaps offer some insight? Was it an older or younger gentleman? Could it possibly have been someone employed here at the hospital? It is imperative for me to know."

Lorraine pondered for a moment and discreetly surveyed the area for any potential eavesdroppers. Leaning in closer towards Abby, she whispered, "I suppose I can divulge that he is tall with black hair. He was dressed impeccably." She flashed a knowing smile and winked mischievously.

Abby thanked Lorraine for revealing Joey had been the one to pay, still role-playing Santa it seemed.

Making her way back towards the elevator with a sense of anticipation gnawing at her insides, she anxiously awaited its descent back down to ground level after pressing the button.

As soon as the doors slid open several moments later, revealing an empty compartment, Abby let out a sigh of relief before letting out her pent-up frustration by gently stamping her feet and silently screaming behind pursed lips. The idea of being indebted to Joey weighed heavily on her mind and heart alike. Eventually, the elevator doors opened to the underground car park, and she headed towards her father's truck, psyching herself up for her conversation with Joey on the drive home.

A streak of lightning illuminated the sky as thunder rumbled and rain poured over the streets. Uncertain how long she had been driving at high speed, she eased off the accelerator. Upon reaching home, she burst through the front door and hurried up the stairs into Ruby's room to gather some clothes. Shortly after, she entered her bathroom, undressed, and stepped into the shower while rehearsing the conversation in her mind until she felt mentally prepared to confront Joey. Although she hoped not to rely on him or anyone else for support, if there was a chance someone could save Ruby and provide her with the miracle she needed, she would do anything just to see Ruby happy and healthy again. It was her desire for Ruby to have a good life filled with happiness, love, and laughter.

In a frantic search through her closet, looking for a suitable outfit, she eventually chose a pure white Chanel wrap dress that emphasised her body, fitting snugly beneath her breasts and tracing the curves of her slender waist and hips. Pairing it with tall, slim boots, she applied mascara to her lashes and added some brown eyeshadow to enhance her natural eyes. She finished off with soft red lipstick and flowing locks that cascaded from her shoulders to her waistline.

Braving a strong gust of icy wind that penetrated her coat and the scarf snugly wrapped around her neck, she hurried inside the truck, started the engine, and increased the climate control. The heavy traffic caused such a significant delay that she arrived thirty-five minutes late.

In the elevator foyer, Dr. Denver was standing with a group of doctors clad in white lab coats and drinking from Sippy cups. She reciprocated his smile before going inside the elevator with Dr. Denver and his colleagues.

"Good morning, Abby," he said with a radiant smile.

By level thirteen, they found themselves alone. Abby paused. "Matty, can we talk privately?"

"Certainly. Let's speak in my office," he suggested.

Abby nodded. "Alright."

Dr. Denver and Abby walked down the hallway towards his office. "The test results will be available later today or early tomorrow morning and will determine if any of your family or friends are suitable donors for Ruby."

"Thank you," Abby replied.

Arriving at Dr. Denver's office, he unlocked the door and gestured for Abby to take a seat at his desk.

Abby put her elbows on the desk. "I need you to be very honest with me."

"I am always honest with you. What is this about?"

"Ruby's procedure has been paid in full. Did you pay for it?"

"I actually didn't, but I'm pleasantly surprised to hear it's all settled. That's such a relief! I wonder who stepped in to help—what a kind gesture!"

Abby shrugged. "I am on a mission to find out. I have my suspicions, but the staff won't release this information. I was not prepared to accept any help from anyone, as you know."

"I can see how much this is upsetting you," he replied.

"Is there any way to confirm who made the payment?" she asked.

Dr. Denver's shoulders sagged. "Well... Abby, I genuinely want to assist you, but revealing this information would jeopardise my employment and constitute a significant breach of duty on my part. You are well aware of this."

Abby closed her eyes and nodded, needing a moment to process the magnitude of her request. "I'm truly sorry, Matty."

"Don't fret, Abby. I'll do my best to gather some information for you. The nurses here often engage in gossip. Let me see what I can uncover, alright?"

"Alright." She grabbed her bag and stood up before making her way towards the exit.

She was just about to leave when Dr. Denver called her name. Abby halted and turned back.

"It could be Joey, no?"

"I already suspect it was him," she replied. "I truly hope that's not the case."

"Why not?"

His phone suddenly rang, signalling he was needed, so she left, feeling frustrated.

Upon reaching Ruby's room, Abby surveyed the surroundings. Micky and Andrea were already there, sitting beside Ruby's bed alongside her parents. The jovial atmosphere turned subdued as they discerned the seriousness of Abby's expression.

Abby's parents rose from their chairs and approached her. "What's the matter, Abby?"

Her hesitation stretched to almost ten seconds. "It's nothing. I just had a conversation with Dr. Denver, and our blood test results might be made available later today or tomorrow morning."

"Excellent," her father responded before returning to his seat and crossing his arms over his chest to resume watching the television news.

Her mother approached her. "Abby, I have faith that God will find a donor for our little Ruby. Stay hopeful."

"I hope so, Mama," she replied, taking a deep breath. However, deep down she was uncertain.

CHAPTER 41

The moment of truth had finally arrived, filling her with nervous tension. Hours spent meticulously analysing and replaying the conversation with Joey in her head had led to this juncture, leaving her in a state of frenzied anticipation. After dutifully tending to Ruby's needs by giving her a shower and braiding her hair, Abby leaned in close to whisper softly, "Hey sweetie, I'll be back in about an hour, alright? Nonna and Nonno will take care of you while I'm gone, okay."

Ruby responded with a nod as Abby bestowed upon her a fleeting hug and kiss on the cheek before discreetly leaving the room.

As she waited for the sluggish arrival of the elevator, time seemed to drag on endlessly, exacerbating Abby's growing impatience. Glancing down at her watch and realising she had less than five minutes to reach the cafeteria, she opted for the stairs instead. Breathless and slightly dishevelled upon reaching the cafeteria, Abby's eyes immediately spotted Joey seated at a table wearing a sleek blue Armani suit.

In that moment, she was reminded of Joey's innate charm and allure that never failed to stir butterflies in her stomach. In an effort to remain calm, Abby silently coached herself to take deep breaths as she approached his table.

Rising from his seat with a warm grin, Joey greeted her with a soft, "Hello, Abby."

Seating herself at the table as he handed her a cup of coffee, their eyes met in an intense gaze.

"How is Ruby?" he asked.

"She's eager to return home," Abby replied.

"Any updates on the donor match?"

Abby maintained unwavering eye contact as she responded. "The results should be available either later today or tomorrow."

"I hope one of us turns out to be a match," he remarked cryptically, his lips curling into an enigmatic smile.

An internal voice urged caution as Abby grappled with divulging the truth. Steeling herself with another deep breath, she mustered up the courage to speak. "There's something I need to tell you."

"Go on."

With bated breath, she revealed what had long been concealed within her heart. "Ruby... is your daughter!"

"What did you just say?"

"Ruby is... yours!"

The terror on his face deeply affected her as she witnessed his mouth contort and his gaze fixate on her in an unyielding silence. He was rendered speechless, and his true emotions showed when he slammed his fist onto the table, causing their coffees to spill.

"Joey, please calm down!" Abby pleaded softly.

This unfamiliar display of raw emotion from Joey left her reeling; gone was the carefree eighteen-year-old boy she once knew replaced by an imposing figure radiating anger and hurt.

"Don't you dare tell me to calm down!" he replied coldly. "I knew it! I asked you repeatedly, and yet you lied to me! I always suspected Ruby was mine... I knew it all along! What the hell, Abby!"

Abby bore witness to his anguish tinged with guilt and shame as tears welled up in her eyes. "Joey... I'm sorry I kept this from you for so long," she confessed tearfully. "But when I needed your support the most... you abandoned me. You will never know how much you hurt me, or what I went through after you left."

"What did you anticipate my response to be? Should I have confessed to my parents that I impregnated you, risked ruining both our lives?"

"You should have stood by me when I needed you most," Abby implored through choked sobs. "It takes two people to create life... but only one faced the consequences alone. Our families would have understood; they would have helped us. Mine did. We would have found a way to make it work. I didn't get a choice about being a mother, but this is what God wanted even if I didn't want to go ahead with it at the time. I didn't get that choice either. I didn't have the option to walk away, like you." She wiped tears from her eyes with the back of her hand.

A heavy silence hung between them.

"Support you? Abby, I was young and had no idea what I was doing. You want to know what my first thought was when you told me you were pregnant? I didn't want to be a father. It freaked me out. How could I have financially supported you and Ruby when I had less than twenty dollars in my bank account?"

Abby found herself incapable of answering him. Instead, she sat in hushed stillness, staring down at the table.

"Abby, we both knew we were too young for marriage or parenthood. Our dreams would have been impeded by having a child. We might have grown to resent one another."

"Well, because you left me, I grew to resent you. You completely broke me. You left me to fend for myself. My parents sent me away to a monastery in Italy for eight long months, where I had no contact with the outside world. I was frightened, alone, and carrying our child. Yet, where were you? Enjoying life, partying, drinking, sleeping around."

She saw he lacked any remorse, displaying no regret or embarrassment for his previous misdeeds. Her words had little effect on him. She believed he derived pleasure from her anguish and distress; it was like a competition to him, and he was winning. She hoped for some form of apology, but he was unemotional and devoid of shame.

* * *

Joey was drowning in a sea of guilt and remorse, his love for Abby consuming him. The weight of his emotions was crushing, but he staunchly refused to apologise or even express his feelings to her. A profound sense of heartbreak and humiliation ate at him. Compounding his pain was the realisation of how much he had missed out on Ruby's life, causing a deep well of sorrow to bubble up inside him.

For years, Joey had carried a heavy burden of anger and guilt, deeply regretting his past actions and harbouring the belief he did not deserve forgiveness from Abby. His disappointment in himself grew exponentially as he saw himself as a failure, unable to meet her expectations. This led him to make a solemn vow to never love again, convinced he was unworthy of love or incapable of sustaining a committed relationship. Marriage, children, and happiness seemed like unattainable dreams for someone like him.

Seeking temporary solace in physical relationships with other women over the five years only served as a superficial balm for his emotional wounds. Consumed by a desire for vengeance against Abby, he sought ways to inflict pain upon her until he finally acknowledged that deep down, he still loved her.

Words alone could not heal the profound hurt festering inside him; instead, he concocted an intricate plan to punish her and compel her submission. Believing there was no alternative for her but to bend to his will, Joey laid out his ultimatum to Abby with chilling resolve.

"What have you disclosed to Ruby regarding my whereabouts?" Joey demanded sternly, locking eyes with Abby.

"I sat down with our daughter and told her, "You know how sometimes in school you get a really tough math problem and you need a little time to figure it out, well, your dad needs a little time like that right now. He's working through some things and needs a bit of space to sort everything out."

"Wow, that is elaborate. I never took you for such a skilled liar. I guess being a lawyer has its perks, huh?"

"Mock me all you like," she said. "Neither of us are exactly angels."

"Abby, let me clarify what is going to happen, so listen carefully. To stop all the damaging rumours, you will agree to this proposal."

"Proposal?"

He frowned. "Well, yeah, I expect you to agree to my marriage proposal and declining is not a possibility."

"Are you serious? I will never agree to marry you."

Joey folded his arms across his chest and reclined in his seat. "You're hurting my feelings," he said sarcastically. "I'm deadly serious, Abby!"

"And so am I. I am not accepting your proposal, Joey."

Maintaining a calm tone, he threatened her with a smile, boasting his own cleverness. "Abby, you have no other option but to comply. Shall I disclose the truth to my mother if that suits you better?"

Aware of Angela's penchant for gossip and rumourmongering, Abby recoiled at the thought of having her reputation tarnished. She knew all too well how damaging such revelations could be coming from someone like Joey's mother.

"You built a good name for yourself, Abby, do you really want my mother to your ruin your reputation?" He was enjoying exerting this power over her in retribution for what she had done.

"You're completely insane!" she said.

"Oh, spare me your hypocrisy!" he replied. "You, who have kept the existence of my own flesh and blood hidden from me for five years! Five years, Abby! And now you dare to act like the victim?" His voice rose as he continued. "For this deceitful act, there will be consequences you must face."

After a moment of tense silence, she leaned in closer and spoke in a calm yet firm tone. "Joey, please stop this madness. This is nothing but blackmail and manipulation. I thought you were better than this."

"I am merely a reflection of what you have made me."

"I want no part in this twisted game of yours, Joey. I do not love you, nor do I ever want to be with you. In fact, I despise you, you... you are pathetic!" Her raised voice garnered attention from the other patrons in the cafeteria.

"Love has nothing to do with it," he snapped back, his words betraying the hurt that lay beneath his tough exterior. "Either you submit willingly to my demands and come to my bed, or we enter into a marriage devoid of any true affection." What he truly wanted was to exert his dominance over her in the bedroom.

"You are delusional! You need professional help. I will never agree to such an arrangement. I refuse to surrender myself to you."

"We shall see about that."

Abby finally broke the prolonged silence with a question. "What do you expect from me, Joey?"

"This is how it shall unfold: My legal representative will draft our marriage papers, which you will sign willingly before we inform our families together. Starting tomorrow, you will come reside under my roof."

Abby shook her head vehemently. "I wouldn't even sign your birthday card, let alone the marriage certificate. Your anger blinds you if you think this could ever work out. Let's get one thing straight. My parents won't approve of this sham marriage, and neither can I."

He chuckled softly at her defiance. "Don't concern yourself with your parents; they will fall into line."

She gently rubbed her stomach, grimacing in the process.

"Are you alright?"

"Joey, I cannot accept your proposal. Please be reasonable."

He let out a sarcastic laugh. "Abby, are you kidding? Why didn't you inform me I was a father? Why did you hide the truth from me? How could you be so selfish and cruel?"

His words flowed effortlessly from his mouth, forgetting the fact he had abandoned her to pursue his own dreams.

When she climbed to her feet to leave, he said, "I would not do that if I were you."

With a sardonic grin on his face, he issued one final ultimatum: "This is your last opportunity Abby, otherwise members of the Italian community will learn about your scandalous secret."

She paused. "Okay, you win! When and where should we meet to sign these papers?" she asked, slowly sitting down.

"Meet me here later today at 2:30 pm," he said smugly. "And don't be late!"

Abby frowned. "Fine."

"Good," he responded, nodding in approval, and settling comfortably in his chair with an air of pride.

With smudged mascara punctuating her teary eyes, Abby stood and walked away, flicking her head back one last time to look at Joey. "Your parents will be so proud of this fake marriage!"

CHAPTER 42

Joey's heart was entirely captivated by Abby as she headed to the elevator. He had never imagined she would accept his proposal; he had braced himself for a dramatic refusal, maybe even a coffee cup flying his way. But watching Abby closely, he saw her main focus wasn't on societal expectations but on protecting her family's honour and reputation. This newfound understanding made Joey realise Abby was ready to put her family's needs above her own happiness.

To Joey, this seemed like a favourable twist. His parents frequently urged him to settle down, so this was a perfect way to meet their expectations, gaining both a wife and daughter at once. However, Joey was deeply troubled by the knowledge that he had pressured Abby into marriage for his own benefit. He was aware of his own flaws and less-than-honourable intentions, even admitting to himself that he didn't deserve her.

Yet, Joey saw this as an opportunity to change their story—a chance to begin again, take things slowly, and seek the happy ending they both truly deserved. Ignoring Abby's belief that their marriage would be a mere facade, Joey committed to becoming a better person for her.

Rising with newfound determination, he called his lawyer while heading to the underground parking lot, ready to start this new chapter with sincerity and hope.

* * *

Embarrassed despite her high intelligence, Abby took a moment to dry her tears. It seemed as though she had made a pact with the devil by rekindling a connection with the man who had previously shattered her heart. This bold and risky decision would undoubtedly have significant repercussions on her relationships with her loved ones. However, fate appeared to have different plans for Abby, constantly presenting unexpected opportunities that were difficult for her to resist.

She had always envisioned a life where she would meet a partner, fall in love, tie the knot, and build a joyful home for herself and Ruby. But achieving this dream required facing her vulnerabilities head-on and actively participating in the dating scene, something Abby had struggled with for years. Consequently, she turned down potential partners such as Adriano, the security clerk, Dr. Denver, and even Luciano Zappia from college. In her mind's eye, Abby pictured an intimate garden wedding with traditional decorations like crystal chandeliers, flowing drapes, white linens, rose centrepieces, and candlelight, all creating a soft and romantic ambiance. She envisioned herself wearing her mother's intricately designed wedding gown embellished with lace appliques that accentuated her slender waist. Walking down the aisle escorted by her father, Abby imagined feeling like a princess, relishing a fleeting moment of pure bliss that could never be replicated.

Instead of living out this fairy tale scenario only hours from now, Abby was in the hospital cafeteria alongside Joey and the registrar, preparing to sign away her future to the very man who had once broken her heart and caused immense pain. Though longing for a happy ending filled with romance and joy, Abby understood such aspirations were simply not meant for her.

Returning to Ruby's room, Abby spent the next couple of hours engrossed in reading and playing with her daughter. While visitors came by to offer support and engage in light-hearted conversations with her parents, Abby couldn't shake off an impending sense of unease. When she checked the time on her watch at 2:10 pm for the umpteenth time, it drew her mother's attention.

"Everything alright, love?"

"Yes, everything is fine. I just need to step out for a moment to make a few phone calls." She hoped her mother wouldn't press her further for information.

"Are you sure you're okay?"

Aware of her mother's tendency to worry, Abby said, "Yes, Mama, I'm fine." She kissed Ruby on the cheek and explained she would be back soon before excusing herself from the room. Putting on a brave face for those around her, Abby held uncertainties about the path she was about to embark on, one that would inevitably alter the course of her life forever.

As Abby slowly walked through the long hallway, she couldn't help but wonder if her complicated life was somehow connected to the mistakes of her ancestors. Yet, she hesitated to dwell too much on these vague ideas as she stepped into the elevator. She tried to reassure herself that there might be some bigger plan at work. Still, Abby couldn't shake the feeling that luck might not be on her side lately.

Acknowledging it might be one of the most foolish decisions she had ever made, she felt like there were no other alternatives and reminded herself it was purely transactional and lacked any emotional or sexual connection. It was simply a business arrangement without intimacy.

Joey's actions had instilled fear and turmoil within Abby, but she remained resolute in her determination not to succumb to further wrongdoing or allow him to dictate her fate. Her strategy involved entering a temporary marriage with Joey until Ruby regained her strength, at which point she planned to file for divorce. Their union would exist only on paper, with both parties residing in separate quarters. Seeing Joey again brought back all the suppressed feelings from years ago, but for now she had to pretend to be content playing the game with her enemy and nemesis.

Joey remained seated in his original position as Abby approached him, causing her heart to quicken its pace. A grin crept across his face as he admired her form from top to bottom. The two gentlemen flanking Joey rose from their seats. "Abby, allow me to introduce you to my legal counsel Jeffrey Reynolds and Paul McKnight, our ordained officiant."

Both men leaned forward to shake Abby's hand warmly. "It is truly a pleasure to make your acquaintance," they chimed in unison with cheerful expressions.

Joey's lawyer handed Abby the contract with a pen. "Please read the contract thoroughly and if you have any questions, let me know."

"Thank you," she responded, nodding.

Their unwavering gazes focused on her as she skimmed through the contract and read the following statement:

In Queens, New York City, on Saturday, December 29th, 2012, I, Jeffrey Reynolds, oversaw the formation of this marriage contract between Joseph Giovanni (referred to as Subject A) and Abagail Di Manos (referred to as Subject B).

Minor Children – Section 1

A. *Subject A & B are the biological and legal guardian / parent of Ruby Di Manos (age five years).*

B. *Subject A & B will have joint custody of any children they may have.*

Partnership Provisions – Section 2

A. *Subject A & B will reside at property 130 Georges Parade, Manhattan.*

B. *Subject A & B will occupy the same bed.*

C. *Subject A & B will need to acknowledge their marriage as a 'real marriage' and will commit to intimate arrangement and loving relationship in the best interest of this marriage.*

D. *For the benefit of Subject A & B, they will treat each other with respect and kindness.*

E. *There will be a clear understanding of the emotional, physical, and sexual needs of the spouse.*

F. *In order to establish and maintain a healthy, loving, caring relationship, Subject A & B will comply to these rules:*

1. Contribute to a satisfising marriage.
2. Develop the ability to forgive.
3. Show admiration and respect.
4. Subject A & B will be faithful at all times.
5. Infidelity is breach of this contract.
    i. Subject A & B will be faithful at all times.
6. NO SECRETS ALLOWED
7. Subject A & B will be open and honest with each other.
8. Good communication and listen clearly.
    i. Take the time to understand what Subject A & B wants and needs.
9. Openness and willingness to explore intimacy of sexual needs and desires.
10. A happy and lasting marriage is built on continual work and commitment.
    ii. Subject A & B will learn to comprise, negotiate conflict, and seek expert advice for relationship issues if needed to help overcome obstacles.
11. Subject A & B need to be accountable in the relationship, accepting responsibility.
12. Subject A & B to commit to regular date nights.
13. Subject A & B will make available their geolocation via cell phone application.

Term of Marriage – Section 3

G. This contract will take effect on the date the contract was signed and dated.

Intimate Disclosures – Section 4

H. Subject A & B will acknowledge that intimacy is an essential element of the relationship and must experiment with one another.

I. Intimacy is priority of this relationship.

J. Both parties will agree to engage in sexual activity multiple times a day unless partner's period impedes with such activities.

K. Anything of sexual nature includes:
    1. Sexual intercourse.
    2. Erotic practises.
    3. Full body touching and kissing.

Expenses – Section 5

L. All expenses inclusive to daily utilities, household maintenance, and food will be paid in full and handled by Subject A.

M. All material assets will be paid in full by Subject A.

N. Child school fees, uniform, tutoring, and other expenses will be paid in full by Subject A.

O. Holidays and recreational activities will be paid in full by Subject A.

Consent Policy – Section 6

P. This agreement is consensual by Subject A & B,
    i. Joseph Giovanni and Abagail Di Manos have agreed to the execution of this agreement.

Q. I declare this agreement is of my own free will, I was neither forced, harassed, or blackmailed into signing this marriage contract.

A. If Subject A & B decides to terminate this marriage or disobey the clauses within the marriage contract, Subject A & B will need to pay the other party $10,000,000.00.

B. This contract will not be altered, amended, revoked, or cancelled in writing.

Dated: ....
Signatures: Joseph Giovanni ....
Abagail Di Manos ....

Abby's face lost all expression. "Joey, this is unbelievable! It's completely ridiculous!" Her voice was tinged with exasperation. With deliberate intention, she raised the contract in her right hand. "You can't be serious! Are you really serious about this? The proposal doesn't feel right to me. As a lawyer, shouldn't I be questioning its ethics? I'm just not sure I can sign something like this." She dramatically tore the contract in two. A sense of satisfaction washed over her as she reclined in her chair, observing the knowing glances exchanged between Jeffrey and Joey.

Joey nodded and Jeffrey took out multiple copies of the contract from his briefcase, placing one on the table in front of her.

Jeffrey shrugged. "Joey warned us this might happen, so I came prepared." .

"Warned you that I would find this unrealistic contract a load of hogwash? Who wouldn't? Sorry, but I refuse to accept this."

She rose to leave when Joey interjected in a composed manner. "Abby, sit down!"

"Joey, I'm not accepting this contract; it's a joke!" Her emotions were fuelling her inability to control her words.

In a measured tone laced with authority, Joey reiterated his stance. "The choice ultimately lies with you, Abby. However, you must understand the consequences should you choose not to sign."

"Do you all hear what he just said?" She shifted her line of sight from Jeffrey to the wedding celebrant. "This veiled threat smacks of blackmail tactics, which blatantly contradicts clause S of Section 6 on consent within your ridiculous agreement."

She levelled a pointed accusation at the celebrant. "And you, how much were you compensated to turn a blind eye to this charade?"

Their lack of response or acknowledgement gave Abby amusement. She turned towards Jeffrey, her eyes filled with disappointment and disdain as she delivered her cutting remarks. "Truly, I had expected more integrity from you. It appears you are merely just another dishonest lawyer."

Joey snapped with annoyance. "Abby, sit down, will you? We're not done here!"

The hardening of his features and chilling intensity in his gaze only served to escalate the tension in the room.

"Are you absolutely certain about marrying her," asked Jeffrey. "I don't particularly like you either!"

"I refuse to mix with lawyers who engage in blackmail and corruption."

"That is enough, Abby!" Joey shouted angrily; his voice laced with fury. "You are free to leave, the deal is off!"

Undeterred by his threats, Abby retorted nonchalantly, "What are you going to do? Ruin me? Ruin my family? Go ahead!"

"No, Abby! That is not my intention. I am simply trying to protect you," said Joey.

But Abby remained sceptical. "Protect me from whom, Joey?"

"My mother, Abby."

She scoffed and said bluntly, "Well, I'm not her biggest fan, anyway."

Many people were looking at them now, their outbursts attracting undue attention.

"Please, sit down and let me explain!"

Abby reluctantly sat back down.

"You've always had a knack for captivating an audience," he said. "Some things never change."

Clearing her throat, she put her hands on the table and sighed. "I cannot accept these terms as laid out in the contract. It lacks flexibility and only serves your interests. We need to make adjustments that fit our current situation, which we must mutually agree upon before I sign anything."

Joey leaned back, folded his arms, and said, "Okay, then. Let's delve into it further."

Abby picked up a copy of the agreement and stretched out her hand for Jeffrey's pen when she felt a vibration in her coat pocket. Retrieving her phone, she glanced at the display and said, "Sorry, I need to take this call from Dr. Denver." She relocated to another table in the cafeteria near the frosted window ledge where Joey couldn't see her.

"The test results have been received, except for yours," said Dr. Denver. "We are still awaiting the delivery of your result. However, we have some great news. We have found a potential match for Ruby."

Happy tears welled up in her eyes, and she was so emotional she could hardly speak.

"Abby, are you there?" Dr. Denver asked.

"Sorry, yes, I am here." She then burst into laughter, followed by more smiles and tears of pure joy upon hearing the news. In that moment, all she wanted was to rush to Ruby's side, embrace her tightly, and shower her with kisses. She continued crying uncontrollably but in a positive way; an emotional wreck filled with immense happiness.

She picked herself up from the floor and asked Dr. Denver who the donor match was.

"Joey Giovanni, his body tissue is compatible with Ruby's."

Abby was neither surprised nor shocked. She knew there was a possibility Joey could be the perfect match; unsurprisingly, they had the same blood types.

Today, her heart was filled with warmth and tenderness as she resolved to make a sacrifice for her child's safety. Her love for Ruby was so profound that she was willing to do anything to see her grow into a lovely young woman. Abby comprehended the gravity of the situation but believed with all her heart that Ruby's chance at a joyous, healthier life made everything worthwhile. Even with some limitations, Ruby would have the opportunity to chase her dreams, find love, and leave her own gentle footprints on the world. Although hesitant about Joey being the donor, she recognized it as the only way to safeguard Ruby's future.

Shortly after, Abby returned to her seat at the table. She asked, "Where do I put my signature?"

Their faces registered utter shock and disbelief, their eyes growing wide in astonishment.

Abby noticed Jeffrey and wedding officiant Paul raise their eyebrows at her, while Joey leaned back in his chair, carefully observing her for a moment.

"Please put your initials here and there," Jeffrey instructed, pointing directly at the document.

Abby complied, signing the contract before handing it to Joey. A few moments later, Paul produced the marriage certificate and guided them on where to sign. Shortly after, he announced, "You are now officially husband and wife."

Abby glanced at Joey, who wore a satisfied grin, but suddenly she didn't feel like celebrating with him anymore.

As he got up from his seat and reached out his hand, Joey murmured, "Shall we, my beloved wife?"

Hoping to keep this marriage a secret until it was annulled, Abby rejected his offer and declared she was heading back to Ruby's room. Then she walked off.

CHAPTER 43

"What did Dr. Denver say?" asked Joey as he caught up with Abby and stepped into the elevator.

Clearing her throat, she said, "They've found a suitable donor for Ruby. It appears you are the compatible donor. Were you aware of this?"

"If you're insinuating that I bribed Dr. Denver, let me make it clear that I absolutely did not. I had no involvement, Abby. The test results speak for themselves; they are based on facts."

Abby was taken aback by the unexpected presence of the Giovanni family, pondering whether Joey orchestrated their appearance purposefully. Yet amidst these musings, there were more pressing matters at hand. Hurriedly making her way to Ruby's bedside, Abby eagerly shared the news of Joey's compatibility as a donor with those present. The room erupted into a jubilant celebration, filled with cheers and hugs as joy overflowed into the hallway where Micky and Tony enthusiastically embraced passersby.

"Abby and I also have some very exciting news to share with all of you," said Joey with an air of excitement, causing Abby's mouth to go dry with apprehension.

She hoped he wasn't about to reveal their marriage at that moment. "Shhh!" she whispered. "Not now, Joey."

Despite her desire to escape from the situation, she knew there was nowhere to hide. With sweat beading her forehead and tension mounting, she realised she was trapped.

Her mother turned to Angela. "Do you know what's happening here?"

"My guess is as good as yours," she replied with a shrug.

Abby whispered to Joey. "Please, not now. I will tell Mama and Papa later."

Joey winked and smiled grimly.

"Abagail, what's going on?" her father asked impatiently.

"Spit it out, Joey!" said Mickey, closely eyeing Abby.

"Let me introduce you all to my wife, Abby," Joey said calmly and casually as he pulled her close and wrapped his arms around her waist with a huge grin.

Abby felt extremely uncomfortable; why couldn't he keep these details to himself?

A brief moment of silence ensued as everyone processed the surprising news. Abby sensed it was all downhill from this point forward, fearing a backlash of epic proportions.

"This is madness!" said her father incredulously. "Abby? Is this true?"

With a heavy heart and downcast gaze, she nodded. "Yes, Papa... it is true. I'm sorry."

"Well, this is certainly unexpected," Angela muttered.

Frank raised his eyebrows and asked Adriano, "What's wrong? Why are you angry that the kids got married?"

Abby noticed her father didn't want to answer his question for obvious reasons.

"What the hell?" Tony's voice boomed.

Micky's gaze lingered upon Abby in a contemplative silence, his eyes searching for answers as her own nervously shifted away from his intense stare.

Frank, ever the voice of reason, interjected with a sombre tone. "The children must love each other; that's why they got married. Today's youth is different from ours; they rush into things. I suppose congratulations are in order then... although I'm disappointed none of us were invited or even told beforehand."

"Why and when did this happen, Abby?" asked Gabriella.

"Today, we got married today. It doesn't matter why. The most important thing right now is Ruby will receive the treatment she needs. Can we focus on that?"

Adriano stood up abruptly, his features twisted in anger as he addressed Abby directly. "After everything he has put you through, you agreed to marry him?"

"Whoa," said Frank, clearly taken aback by Adriano's outburst. "What's going on here? What did Joey do to Abby?"

Joey, sensing the tension rising around them, turned to his father and placed a comforting hand on his shoulder. "Dad, I can explain but not right now, not here anyways. Let's go to the cafeteria." He held their gazes before extending an invitation to Gabriella and Adriano. "Can you please join us?"

Micky and Tony exchanged knowing glances before turning back to Abby, overwhelmed by the scrutiny of those around her.

Sensing her daughter's unease, Abby turned to Ruby with a reassuring smile. "Baby, I need to leave for a little while. Uncle Micky will take good care of you until I come back."

Ruby nodded understandingly.

The two families gathered in the cafeteria, anxiously awaiting Joey's return with trays of coffee. The tension constricted Abby's throat as she braced herself for what was about to unfold.

She had pleaded with him to keep their marriage hidden, emphasising this was not agreed upon, and was neither the time nor place, but he had comforted her by promising everything would be alright.

Taking a deep breath, she lowered her head and nervously played with her fingers in her lap beneath the table when Joey returned with the coffee trays and sat down next to Abby. His relaxed posture showed how confident he was about the way this would play out.

"About five and a half years ago, Abby and I were secretly in a romantic relationship. We were young and naive, and one thing led to another. After some time, we discovered that Abby was pregnant. I made the huge mistake of abandoning her during the difficult period. All I wanted... I just wanted to avoid my responsibilities and leave town."

Joey's eyes teared up.

Angela reacted fiercely. "Oh my God, Joey!" she said, covering her mouth in shock. "How could you do that?"

Frank asked, "So Ruby is my grandchild?"

Joey nodded. "Yes, Dad, she is."

Angela's eyes filled with tears, and she made no effort to conceal them.

Joey's voice trembled as he continued to address his family and the Di Manos family. "Mother, Father, I must humbly confess that in a moment of sheer panic and overwhelming fear, I made a grave mistake by choosing to flee from my responsibilities rather than confront them head-on. The prospect of becoming a father at such a young age filled me with terror and conflicted with my career aspirations, leading me to pressure Abby that I now deeply regret. I was not prepared to take on the role of a father, and so I selfishly pushed for an abortion without considering the consequences of my actions. It was a cowardly decision. I then cut off all contact with her while I planned my future. I was selfish, arrogant, utterly thoughtless, and the weight of my guilt has burdened me for far too long. Every day that passes, I continue to punish myself for hurting Abby. The guilt has haunted me for as long as I can remember, and now is my chance to make amends."

Turning towards Abby and Mr. and Mrs. Giovanni Di Manos, Joey bowed his head. "Abby, Mr. and Mrs. Giovanni, I realise mere words cannot undo the pain and suffering I have caused you all. My attempts to offer excuses are feeble at best and will never fully make amends for the harm I have inflicted upon you. My actions were unforgivable, and I can only hope you may someday find it in your hearts to forgive me."

Frank's eyes blazed with anger. "Adriano, how could you keep this from me? We have been friends for so long! If only you had informed me sooner, perhaps we could have persuaded Joey to do right by Abby and Ruby! How much time have we lost with our granddaughter?"

Adriano hung his head in shame as he admitted his wrongdoing. "I deeply regret withholding this information from you out of fear for Abby's well-being. The scandal surrounding Ramona Giuseppe's daughter served as a stark warning, and I felt compelled to shield my daughter from similar judgment. Joey had no intention of marrying Abby; he abandoned her without a second thought. My actions were driven by a desire to protect my daughter through the toughest time of her life."

"Five years, Adriano. Five years! We could have handled things differently."

"You are right, but the marriage would not have survived because Joey would have left her to pursue his career or held resentment towards her forever. Your son was not ready to be a father, and there was no way I'd leave my daughter to fend for herself against nosy small-town gossip. Still, I am sorry."

The two men sat in silence for some time, avoiding eye contact and refraining from speaking further.

Angela placed her hand on top of Gabriella's. "I deeply apologise for Joey leaving Abby like that. As a mother myself, I understand why you would want to shield your daughter. If I had a daughter, I would also strive to protect her reputation. However, what truly pains me is that as Ruby's grandparents, we have missed out on the most precious years of her life, and we will never get that back. How could you do this to our family?"

Gabriella's voice trembled as tears streamed down her face. "Angela, I wanted to tell you... but we couldn't risk it. There was too much at stake." She reached out to comfort Angela, only to have her gesture rejected abruptly. The tension between them grew as accusations and regrets piled up.

Abby glanced at Joey with a mixture of disappointment and resignation, knowing he bore much responsibility for the fractured relationships around them. With trust shattered and friendships strained, Abby knew rebuilding those bonds would require time and effort, if they could even be salvaged at all. The aftermath of this revelation left wounds that ran deep, leaving uncertainty about whether these relationships could ever be repaired or if they were beyond repair altogether. Only time would reveal the true extent of the damage done.

"Mum... Dad... it is all my doing," Joey said solemnly. "The fault lies squarely on my shoulders—I messed up gravely and take full accountability now." He paused briefly before continuing. "Mr. and Mrs. Di Manos acted solely from parental instinct to protect their daughter; they bear no blame here, direct your anger towards me instead. I screwed up here. Don't ruin a perfectly good friendship. I understand I have caused you all a great deal of pain, but we can overcome this together. Let's not lose our friendship, we've been through a lot together."

Abby's phone trilled unexpectedly; Dr. Denver was calling.

"Hello," she answered.

"Abby, Ruby is booked in for the transplant over the next few days. In the meantime, can you drop by my office to sign some legal documents?"

"Yes, certainly, I will be up shortly."

"Is Joey with you?" he asked.

"Yes, he is," she replied.

"Okay, well, please inform him it is imperative for him to come upstairs to sign some legal documents."

"Okay, we will be there shortly."

"Is everything okay?" asked her mama, concern evident in her voice as she looked at Abby.

"Yes, Ruby is scheduled for the transplant in the next few days," Abby explained, trying to keep her emotions in check. "Joey and I need to sign some legal documents."

A collective sigh of relief and joy spread through the room as everyone processed the news. Abby then turned her to Joey, feeling a mix of emotions. "Dr. Denver wants to see us immediately in his office."

Abby and Joey stood up while everyone else remained seated. They made their way towards the elevator, Abby stealing a glance back at the two families who were engrossed in conversation, hoping perhaps they could work things out.

"They will be fine, they'll get over it soon enough and we will all be one happy family again," Joey said with a faint smile.

Abby just gave him a sideways glance and let out a weary sigh as she stepped back slightly, creating some distance between them. "You're enjoying this, aren't you."

Joey simply smiled but said nothing as they stepped into the elevator together. As the doors closed behind them, Abby felt a sense of relief; her secret was finally out in the open.

In Dr. Denver's office, they were met by the transplant team standing beside Dr. Denver himself. "Abby," he began solemnly. "We have followed all necessary criteria to find a suitable kidney for Ruby, and fortunately we have found a compatible donor. Now, Dr. Kitchener will explain what comes next."

"Miss Di Manos, our anaesthetist will be present to administer the anaesthesia that will put Ruby to sleep. Following that, I will begin the surgery. There are different methods of kidney transplantation, and an incision will be made in the lower abdomen area near the groin. The surgery typically takes around three to four hours but can vary depending on recovery time. If you have any questions, feel free to ask at any point."

Abby nodded. "Thank you."

Dr. Kitchener clasped her hands together, making a single fist. "During the surgery, Ruby's new kidney will be extracted from Joey and inserted into her body. The kidney will be connected to her blood vessels and bladder so urine can flow normally. A catheter will also be placed in her bladder for five days. The kidney should start functioning immediately, but it can take a few days or weeks for some individuals. Ruby will be closely monitored with daily tests to ensure the new kidney is working properly. She will need to stay in the hospital for a week to recover and will need to take immunosuppressant medication for the rest of her life. Do you have any questions, Miss Di Manos?"

"What potential side effects might ensue following this kidney transfer procedure?" asked Abby.

"Potential side effects may include urinary tract infection, blood clots that will be treated with medication, urine leakage, and organ rejection where the immune system attacks the transplanted organ. Before Ruby is discharged from the hospital, we will arrange for blood tests, scans, urine tests, and other examinations at the transplant centre. As time goes on, she may require fewer check-ups."

They left Dr. Denver's office after an hour with the surgery scheduled in two days. Abby remained quiet for some time before finally speaking up. "Joey," she said softly. "Thank you for covering the cost of the transplant and for saving my daughter. Our daughter Tears welled up in her eyes as she spoke, and an emotional sniffle slipped out unintentionally.

Joey took a calculated step forward towards Abby, his movements slow and deliberate as he extended his hand to gently grasp her arm. Abby's body instantly tensed up as she turned to face him, a multitude of emotions dancing across her features.

"In all honesty, Abby, there is no need for you to thank me for rescuing my daughter. I would have done the same for anyone in need. But let us not forget the deal we made. You must fulfill your end of the bargain. And one more thing: it is crucial you inform Ruby of my true identity as her father."

"I promise I will tell her after the transplant," Abby replied, the strain evident in her voice as she struggled to maintain her composure under Joey's intense gaze.

"No, Abby. It can't wait any longer. It must be done today, or I will take matters into my own hands." Joey let go of her arm.

Abby took a deep breath, shaking her head in protest. "Please, Joey, give me some time."

But Joey was resolute in his decision. "I will break the news to her myself if you do not act soon," he warned before turning away from her.

Abby could not bear the thought of Joey revealing such life-altering information to Ruby without proper preparation. With determination, she paced down the hallway.

Yet, Joey swiftly caught up to her and forcefully pulled her closer towards him, encircling his arms around her waist as they made their way towards the staircase on the west wing.

"What are you doing? Let me go!" Growing more determined, she tried to break free. "Please release me!"

"I'm afraid I can't do that!" His amusement vanished, replaced by a cold expression.

As they found themselves alone in the stairwell, Joey pressed Abby against the wall with force, leaning in close to whisper in her ear. His demeanour shifted from amusement to cold seriousness as he reminded her of the consequences should she fail to uphold their agreement.

"Sugar plum," he began but with an underlying edge to his tone. "Listen closely, there are repercussions if you go against our agreement." A sly smile appeared on Joey's face as he held Abby captive.

Abby, feeling a surge of frustration and exasperation, emitted an audible sigh before allowing her eyes to roll in a display of annoyance. "I am not insinuating I have any intention of violating the terms of our contract. All I require is a little more time."

Joey shook his head in disapproval and took a deliberate step closer towards Abby, causing her eyes to widen in surprise as she instinctively drew in a deep breath. The scent of his presence enveloped her senses as she contemplated how pleasing he smelled at that moment. His fingers delicately grasped her chin, drawing her even nearer until their faces were mere inches apart.

"My darling wife," Joey uttered softly, yet his voice retained its characteristic coldness. As his hand extended towards her neck to gently brush away a stray strand of hair, Abby found herself both taken aback and intrigued by his unexpected actions. While she derived pleasure from his touch, she hesitated to acknowledge the burgeoning desire within her. She pondered whether he detected the flicker of excitement reflected in her gaze but swiftly schooled herself to maintain composure.

Abruptly, Joey pressed his cool lips against her skin, alternately nibbling and sucking on the tender flesh. A rush of exhilaration surged through Abby's veins as she endeavoured to remain still, shutting her eyes and tilting her head back to fully immerse herself in the intimate exchange.

Abby involuntarily released a soft whimper of delight upon feeling Joey's touch intensify. He then cupped her face with intent to engage in a kiss but instead diverted attention by disclosing, "I have made arrangements for someone to collect your belongings as well as Ruby's from your residence."

Abby's eyes flew open in disbelief. "What?"

"I trust you heard me clearly."

"Without Ruby by my side, I'm not going anywhere."

"Hold on a moment, Abby, I do not expect you to return home with me tonight; however, commencing tomorrow, you can go to our home to freshen up rather than making the journey back to your parents."

Reluctantly, Abby agreed. "Very well... I suppose that arrangement will work, but I'll pack my own things."

"Move!" Abby commanded sternly while casting him an unyielding look before storming past him towards the stairway door.

"You are free to leave now, dear wife," Joey declared calmly as he relinquished his hold on her.

Silent and seething with anger beneath the surface, Abby pushed past him vehemently and proceeded towards the staircase exit with determined steps.

CHAPTER 44

The Di Manos and Giovanni's made their way back to the hospital ward, where they patiently waited for Abby and Joey to return.

As Abby entered the room, Gabriella paused from her rosaries and inquired about Dr. Denver's plans for Ruby. Before Abby could respond, Joey arrived on the scene.

"The surgery is scheduled within the coming days," he said, delving into the specifics of the procedure, potential risks, and recovery time. Abby was taken aback by Joey's assertiveness; she had not anticipated him taking charge in such a manner.

Abby then made her way over to Ruby's bed and sat beside her. A hush fell over the room as she discussed the upcoming surgery with her daughter.

"Mum, will I be okay?" Ruby asked.

"Absolutely, my love," Abby said, pulling Ruby into a tight embrace before continuing. "And when you wake up, we will all be here."

Abby looked around at their gathered loved ones, hoping for some words of comfort.

"Yes, darling," they collectively chimed in. "We'll be right here by your side."

But before Abby could say anything else, Joey came forward with a grin, his attention focused on Ruby.

Abby let out a breath she was holding.

"Sweetheart, I have an incredible surprise for you."

With eager anticipation, Joey settled beside Ruby, his eyes brimming with excitement.

Abby gazed deeply into Ruby's eyes, her heart filled with a mix of love and a touch of apprehension. "Ruby," she began gently, "do you remember when I mentioned that your dad couldn't be here because he was working far away?" Abby's voice softened as she prepared to unveil a significant truth. "Well, sweetheart, the truth is that... Joey is your father."

Ruby stared at Joey with wide eyes, trying to comprehend the enormous news despite feeling unwell. Abby noticed Ruby's confusion and emotional turmoil, so she softly caressed Ruby's arm and asked if she was alright. For a few quiet moments, Ruby seemed lost in thought. Suddenly, her green eyes twinkled with a wonder she had been yearning for. "Daddy?" she murmured, her voice barely above a whisper before she leaped into Joey's arms, her heart full.

Overcome with joyous tears streaming down his face, Joey ran his fingers through Ruby's hair as he held onto her fragile body. The room resonated with weeping and heartfelt sobs as everyone bore witness to this magical union between father and daughter. With tender kisses on her tiny fingers and cheeks, Joey wrapped Ruby in a warm, loving hug, as if trying to make up for lost time. Finally, he found the courage to speak, his voice thick with emotion. "I'm so sorry, darling," he said. "I regret being away for so long; I promise never to leave you again. You are my precious daughter."

Abby reflected on how foolish she had been to keep such a significant secret from Joey for so long. This heart-wrenching moment between father and daughter evoked tears of both joy and sadness from both families in the intimate hospital room.

Several moments later, after a brief pause filled, Joey tenderly drew back from Ruby's embrace. Gently cupping her delicate face in his hands, he gazed into her eyes with an expression of deep affection. "I love you, my princess," he whispered before placing a gentle kiss upon her soft cheeks. The room was suffused with a mixture of tears, hugs, and heartfelt emotions that soon transformed into radiant smiles and joyous laughter. It seemed as though Ruby's Christmas wish had been granted, bringing a sense of warmth and happiness to all those present.

With a radiant smile lighting up her face like the glowing embers of a hearth fire on a winter night, Ruby nestled close to her father on the hospital bed. His strong arms enveloped her slender frame in a protective embrace, creating a cocoon of safety and love around her fragile form. As they settled into their snug embrace, Abby observed the intimate bond between father and daughter with a mixture of admiration and longing in her heart.

Joey's tousled hair cascaded over his forehead in disarray as Ruby animatedly updated him on the latest news from school, friends, and activities. His attentive demeanour and playful interactions with Ruby revealed a side of him that Abby had never seen before—nurturing, loving, and overflowing with paternal care.

These heartwarming moments served as a balm for Abby's wounded soul, filling her family with comfort during these trying times.

Within an hour, Joey had seamlessly transitioned into the role of a devoted father figure, forging a deep connection with his daughter based on unwavering love and understanding. Enraptured by his child's presence, he hung onto every word she spoke and effortlessly stepped into the role of hero in her young eyes. Their bond was palpable; it radiated genuine warmth and strength that transcended mere blood ties.

As twilight descended upon the hospital ward, the Di Manos and Giovanni families bid farewell to Ruby as they prepared to depart for the evening. Much to everyone's surprise, Joey reappeared at the door not long after their departure. A mischievous grin appeared as he asked cheekily if he could join them for some quality time. Ruby's eyes sparkled with delight at the sight of her father's return.

"Daddy, you came back!" she said before launching into his waiting arms once more.

"Why did you come back?" Abby asked, genuinely happy to have him back with them.

"I wanted to spend the night with my new wife and daughter," he said, filling Abby's heart with immeasurable joy, though she tried to hide it, not quite ready to play happy families just yet.

Throughout the remainder of the evening, they bonded as a newly formed family unit, sharing laughter, hugs, and light-hearted banter that warmed even the coldest corners of their hearts. Their interaction was so seamless and natural that it impressed even the hospital staff.

As night fell like a velvet curtain over their shared space on the sofa bed while watching Disney Channel reruns together, Ruby eventually succumbed to sleepiness, nestled between her two parents. After tucking her in gently like a precious treasure safeguarded against harm or loss, Joey turned to Abby with concern on his handsome face. "How are you holding up?"

"I don't know... I feel scared," she said.

"She will be okay," he said, reaching out to clasp her trembling hand.

"I don't know what I would do without her."

With a gentle touch, he tenderly brushed her cheek with his thumb, conveying both care and concern. "Abby, I assure you that won't happen. I need you to remain strong for Ruby and for us. Can you please do that?"

She nodded, her voice quivering with emotion. He wrapped his arms around her waist, pulling her close as their rekindled love simmered between them, stirring deep within her core.

"I will always be here for you and Ruby. I can't change the past, but I want to make amends for my terrible mistakes: encouraging you to have an abortion, abandoning and disappointing you. I know you have doubts now, but if you can find it in your heart to forgive me and give me a chance to set things right, I promise I will never hurt you or our family again. Let me rectify my wrongs with love and restore the joy we once shared together. Please open your heart and allow me to be by your side forever. Let's start anew, rewrite our story together. Losing you once was unbearable; losing you again is something I cannot fathom. Baby, grant me this opportunity to bring back smiles, laughter, and love into your life once more. I am deeply regretful."

As she gazed into his eyes, she felt her heartbeat quicken. His sorrowful eyes reflected his acknowledgment of his mistakes and failures. Abby realised she was willing to forgive the man who had promised to save her daughter's life, understanding that he genuinely cared for Ruby and sincerely apologised for his past actions. She pulled away from Joey and sat up straight before turning to face him.

"I will start by giving you half a chance at redeeming yourself for saving Ruby's life but I'm uncertain whether I can fully open my heart to you Joey." Abby had endured so much pain that she couldn't simply ignore it and follow her emotions blindly. Though she yearned to hear these words for years, a voice inside warned her not to trust him completely and urged caution against falling in love once more.

"Are you being sincere?" He appeared bewildered as he spoke those words when Nurse Gretchen suddenly entered the room, interrupting their conversation about Ruby's condition.

"I apologise for the interruption but I must check on Ruby," Nurse Gretchen explained before leaving them alone once more.

Ten minutes passed before Abby returned to sit on the sofa while Joey stood over her. "You realise I won't give up."

Just then, her phone buzzed, causing her to jump up from the sofa and reaching over to answer it; it was a message from her legal assistant, Patricia, checking in on their well-being including well wishes for Ruby's recovery, which brought a smile to Abby's face.

Her smile quickly vanished as Joey loomed over her. "Who was that?"

"Oh... nobody." Her lack of conviction was evident and didn't go unnoticed.

"Abby... you're lying!" he said, causing dread to grip her heart. "This goes against our agreement, you know this."

"Are you kidding? Our marriage is strictly business, I don't love you remember?" Abby sighed heavily, feeling weighed down by uncertainty about what lay ahead with Joey insisting they avoid emotional entanglements.

His mouth tightened visibly as a growl escaped his throat. "We had an agreement, and you must uphold your end of the bargain."

Faced with this conflict between their obligations versus their true feelings, Abby decided it was time for honesty even if it meant risking what little stability they had left. "Our marriage may have started off as strictly business, but secrets have come out now so let's move towards an annulment."

Joey seemed taken aback by this sudden declaration. "So does this mean you no longer wish for us to remain married?" His tone shifted significantly, prompting Abby's head to tilt slightly.

"Joey... love cannot be forced."

The corners of his mouth curled into a devious grin. "I assure you, my dear, I have no intention of coercing you into anything contrary to your wishes. However, you do belong to me, and you will come to me willingly."

Abby rolled her eyes in exasperation at his audacity, turning away from him as a crimson blush spread across her cheeks. "Does that frighten you?" she asked with a gentle sigh, trying to sound casual even though a bit of anxiety lingered in her heart. Deep down, beneath her façade of indifference, she harboured a profound love and care for him that she struggled to conceal. The allure he held over her was something she dreaded acknowledging, fearing the vulnerability it exposed within her.

In an effort to shield her emotions from Joey's discerning gaze, Abby resolved not to betray her true feelings. "Your arrogance won't succeed in this game, and I will never give in to you."

"We'll see about that!" His response was swift and bold as he encircled her waist with his arm, drawing her closer towards him in an intimate embrace.

"Don't touch me!" she said, fighting against his grip.

"Do not resist me," he urged as he claimed her lips with fervour and intensity, his hold on her unwavering despite her protests.

Unable to deny the magnetic pull between them, Abby succumbed to the passion ignited by their kiss as he enveloped her in his arms, deepening their connection with each passing moment. His hands tangled in her hair as he guided their bodies together forcefully, overwhelming her resistance.

A soft whimper of desire escaped Abby's lips before she abruptly pulled away from him, breathless and conflicted. "This is not the time nor place," she said breathlessly as she glanced at Ruby sleeping peacefully in the bed.

As the reality of their moment together began to settle in, Abby felt a wave of guilt and shame. She couldn't shake the feeling of remorse for sharing a kiss with Joey while their daughter was so close by. With her head bowed, she glanced at him, her eyes showing both regret and an undeniable longing.

"You seemed to really enjoy that," Joey remarked softly, a playful sparkle in his eyes as he looked at her.

Something awakened within Abby, a deep yearning that surged through her. She found herself drawn to Joey, longing for him with a passion that seemed to blur the lines between tenderness and desire. As they leaned into one another, their closeness sparked a warmth that enveloped her, pulling her into a world where they existed only for each other.

The undeniable attraction between them did not stop Abby attempting to deflect his assumption with a forced laugh. "You are mistaken; I did not get any pleasure from that whatsoever."

"Believe what you will, my darling wife," Joey replied with a sly smirk.

CHAPTER 45

In the early hours, Abby awoke with a sense of fear and anxiety. After trying in vain to drift off once more, she reluctantly opened her eyes. Sitting up, she wrinkled her nose in contemplation as she observed Ruby peacefully sleeping nearby and Joey soundly asleep in a recliner chair by her side. A flicker of relief and a smile crossed Abby's face. Quietly rising from the sofa, she tiptoed towards the bathroom.

* * *

As the night softly lingered, Joey gently awoke and looked over at Ruby. A quick glance at his watch told him it was still the early hour of 4:00 am. He'd been nudged from his slumber earlier when a nurse had come in to check on Ruby, leaving him feeling a bit restless and unable to slip back into deep sleep. Noticing that Abby was no longer on the sofa, he saw the gentle movement of the bathroom door as it quietly swung open. In the soft lighting, he saw Abby quietly making her way to Ruby's bedside. With a loving touch, she gave Ruby's forehead a gentle kiss and lovingly smoothed her hair. Joey softly closed his eyes, deciding to let them have their tender moment, as if he were still fast asleep.

* * *

Abby glanced at Joey, still peacefully sleeping, and took a deep breath. She reflected on how an innocent kiss had blossomed unexpectedly into a passionate moment, awakening a longing for a deeper connection with him. Her heart fluttered with the thought of what their future might hold together, a journey filled with love and commitment. Despite past challenges, Abby felt a strong sense of destiny bringing them back together. With determination, she longed to claim every part of him – body, heart, soul, even his name – as hers alone. She was ready to forgive and rewrite their love story.

Summoning newfound courage she never knew existed within herself, Abby leaned in close to Joey and dared to press her lips against his. Uncertainty nagged at her thoughts – what if he woke up? What if he questioned her actions? Did she have an explanation prepared? Would apologies be necessary?

Abby found herself transported back to their youth when love was pure and reckless. Embracing the vulnerability of the moment in the dim light surrounding them, she nervously brushed a hand through her hair before leaning forward once more to gently capture his lips.

Suddenly startled by his eyes snapping open, Abby gasped for air and fumbled for words of apology before being silenced by

Joey's unexpected response. Pulling her onto his lap, he met her hesitancy with unwavering passion, surpassing all expectations. Though she attempted to break free from his grasp and voice her concerns, Joey held firm and urged silence with a finger pressed against her lips. In that brief and enchanted moment caught between the real world and a dreamy realm, they felt a warm and tender connection that went beyond words, holding onto the beautiful magic blossoming between them.

"This won't do!" Joey tutted, lifting her and placing her backside on the bathroom vanity.

In one smooth motion, he flicked on the light, locked the door, and was on her, lips pressing into hers and hands burrowed into her hair.

"What if Ruby wakes...?" she asked between kisses, her arms flung around his neck.

"We'd better hurry then. Get those clothes off."

Abby grinned. "Take me back to that day on the beach when you made me a woman."

Their clothes slid to the cold tiled floor. His eyes roamed every curve and detail before focusing on Abby's smooth vulva. His arousal grew.

"You are beautiful, Abby. Stunning. I've missed this view. I want you."

Abby licked her lips sensually.

"Long time, no see. Oh, it's smaller than I remember!" she teased.

"Way to knock a man's confidence. I think the big fella is just shy to see you after all these years."

Abby raised an eyebrow. "I think he needs a big, wet hug."

"Now we're talking."

Joey wrapped his arms around her waist, feeling the contours of her body against his chest, kissing and nibbling her neck while she dug her nails into his back. Caught up by the moment, eyes closed, she groaned as he tilted her head back. She intertwined her tongue with his. With one arm supporting her, he used his other hand to caress each breast, teasing and sucking on her hardened nipples. His hands travelled down her hips, along her smooth thighs, until he gently stroked and stimulated her dripping vulva. A surge of ecstatic desire coursed through her, and she cried out his name. Her muscles quivered beneath his touch, and she couldn't help but whimper. Carefully parting her hot, slippery folds, he inserted a finger inside and vigorously rubbed her clitoris with his thumb. Their mouths locked together, and he increased speed.

Abby's vulva begged for more stimulation; she yearned to ride him.

Encouraged by her moans, he rubbed her swollen lips even harder. Then he dropped to his knees, spreading her thighs, delving deep with his tongue flicking against her clit. She thrust her hips towards his mouth, spurring him on. His hands reached for her breasts as his tongue plunged deeper inside.

"Oooooh, Joey," she gasped. Her knees buckled, so he grabbed her arse cheeks for support, still pleasuring her with his mouth. Her hips traced circles, and her near-constant gasps and moans spurred him on.

She anticipated what would happen next—after teasing her to near-orgasm, he'd stand to his full height, lock eyes with her, and lift her with those powerful arms. Tensed shoulders, back ramrod straight, like she weighed nothing at all.

Abby breathed his masculine scent, wrapping her legs around his waist and rubbing her slick wet folds against the head of his member. She moaned with her nails carving his skin, he murmured her name. He entered her forcefully, encompassed by her heat and tightness. Their mouths met in a passionate kiss, and Abby closed her eyes as his pace intensified, their bodies becoming a single entity.

Rising to the challenge, Joey deepened their kiss, gripping handfuls of hair with each powerful thrust. The bathroom filled with their rapid breathing, urgent moans, and the lingering smell of sex. Ruby would wake soon, meaning they'd have to finish, but neither Abby nor Joey wanted this glorious moment to end.

Like a ticking bomb set to explode, they released themselves completely into one another's bodies. Joey's hot cum spurting powerful bursts into her, while she whimpered one last time.

When they finished, she could barely stand.

As first light broke over the horizon, Joey seemed entranced by the deep pools of Abby's eyes. In response to his unwavering stare, she bestowed upon him a brilliant smile that elicited a matching grin from him in return.

"Will you tell Ruby the good news, or shall I?" asked Joey.

Abby was well aware of the topic at hand. Following a night filled with passionate intimacy and heartfelt conversations, she had made the decision to move in with Joey and solidify their commitment to each other in marriage. She emphasised their union would be based on true love rather than a mere contractual obligation, sealing their bond with genuine emotion and devotion. It was clear her feelings for him ran deep once more, and she could no longer deny the depth of her emotions; she was ready to take a leap of faith alongside him as they embarked on this journey together. Their destinies were intertwined, bound together by an unbreakable connection.

In response to Joey's proposal, Abby chuckled softly. "You can tell her."

With Ruby by his side, Joey whispered tenderly, "Baby, you and Mummy will come and live with me once you have fully recovered."

Ruby looked a bit puzzled by the announcement, her expression shifting like a curious kitten trying to understand a new toy.

Both Joey and Abby shared a laugh at Ruby's reaction. Moving closer to Joey, Abby wrapped her arms around him as he reciprocated the gesture. Grasping his forearms tightly, she expressed her approval with a pleased smile. "Yes sweetie, it's true."

"Ruby, I love you and your mother very much, and I want us all to live together, just the three of us."

At this, Ruby let out a giggle and clapped joyfully with a sparkle in her eyes while they all laughed together.

After clearing his throat, Joey turned towards Abby. "Abby, my love for you knows no bounds. I eagerly anticipate spending eternity by your side along with Ruby."

His words resonated with such genuine emotion that Abby couldn't help but believe in their authenticity. Retrieving a velvet box from his pocket, he revealed a stunning, pear-shaped diamond ring inside. Abby gasped in astonishment before covering her mouth with her hand, tears glistening in her eyes as she looked upon him deeply. "Oh, Joey, I love you, too."

As he gently placed the ring on her finger, she gazed at its beauty with awe and whispered her love for it. In response, Joey softly praised her beauty, pulling her into a tender and heartfelt kiss.

Their warm moment was playfully interrupted when Ruby wrinkled her nose and blurted out with a grin, "Ew!"

CHAPTER 46

Abby stood in the doorway of the hospital room, surrounded by a multitude of family and friends from the Giovanni clan, her heart heavy with emotion as she watched Ruby and Joey being wheeled out. Tears streamed down Abby's cheeks as she enveloped Ruby in a tight embrace.

"Mummy, please come with me!" Ruby begged, her eyes filling with tears as she gazed up at her mother, full of desperation.

"Sweetheart, please try not to cry," Abby replied softly, her own voice trembling. "I can't go with you just now, but I promise I'll be there when you wake up. Daddy will be by your side every step of the way."

Joey reassured his daughter, promising to never leave her side. Ruby nodded in acknowledgment, her gaze shifting between her parents who exuded nothing but unconditional love for her.

"I love you so much, princess," Abby choked out through her tears, holding Ruby close and showering her with kisses before tucking Costa into her arms for comfort. Turning to Joey, she took his hand as a gesture of unity in their shared grief.

As Joey wrapped his arms around Abby, comforting her in her time of need, she buried her face in his chest and let out uncontrollable sobs.

"Babe, look at me!" he said.

She lifted her tear-streaked face, finding solace in his unwavering strength that provided a glimmer of hope.

"We will be okay, I promise," Joey said. "Please stop crying, baby. I love you."

Abby clung to him tightly, seeking refuge in his embrace as she struggled to contain her grief and fear.

With a trembling voice and tears still flowing freely, she managed to speak through her sobs. "I love you too, Joey. I'll be waiting for you."

With unwavering focus, she watched Ruby and Joey gradually disappeared from view, never once diverting her gaze.

Sitting nervously on the edge of the theatre room seats, she nestled close to her family, her heart echoing the tension that filled the air. She observed the room, where silence reigned and people seemed withdrawn into their own worlds; some stared blankly at the floor, while Angela and her mother murmured prayers with their rosaries. She tried to hold onto hope, willing herself to focus on the positives even as anxiety gnawed at her insides. Closing her eyes, she took deep, calming breaths.

Out of nowhere, a sudden wave of nausea surged through her, her hands instinctively resting on her uneasy stomach. Deep down, she believed that everything would turn out alright, yet a small seed of doubt persisted in the back of her mind, refusing to be silenced.

In those moments, she sent up a heartfelt prayer, imploring God to bring Ruby and Joey back safely and to surround their family with His gentle kindness.

When she opened her eyes, the soothing presence of her father was there; his arms wrapped around her in a comforting embrace, pulling her close. "They will be alright," he whispered, his words wrapping around her like a warm, protective blanket.

"I hope so, Papa," she murmured back, her voice tremulous with both hope and longing.

"Are you happy?" he asked gently, his eyes searching hers for reassurance.

Feeling the weight of her father's concern over her sudden marriage to Joey, Abby took a deep breath and gently reassured him. "Papa, I really am happy. Joey's a wonderful man and an incredible father to Ruby. We share a deep love for each other, something that's always been there."

Her father's eyes softened as he listened. "I can see how much he cares for you, Abby. It's evident in the way he looks at you, in every little thing he does to bring that beautiful smile to your face. Just a few days back, he came to talk to your mother and me. He was earnest in seeking forgiveness, pouring out his heart about how much he loves you, promising to always keep you safe, and hoping for our blessing."

Abby felt a warm glow envelop her heart. "And what did you say, Papa?"

"We gave him our blessing, my dear. We saw the sincerity in his eyes and welcomed him with open hearts."

Abby's heart swelled with gratitude and relief. Her father's acceptance was more than she could have hoped for, and she felt the past gently fading away, leaving room for a bright future. With tenderness, she leaned over and wrapped her arms around him. "Thank you, Papa. This means everything to me."

After enduring four agonising hours of anticipation, Dr. Kitchener emerged clad in surgical garb from the operating room. With bated breath and anxious hearts pounding as one united front, they rushed forward to greet the doctor standing before them at the sliding doors.

In a calm and composed voice, she said, "The surgery was a great success; both Ruby and Joey are fine and will soon be taken to the recovery room."

Abby threw her head back and released a loud breath. "Thank you so much, Dr. Kitchener!" Relief flooded through Abby, and she offered immense gratitude to God for the abundance of joy and happiness that filled their hearts on this day.

* * *

Joey awoke in the sterile, white room, his mind slowly clearing from the effects of anaesthesia. The realisation of where he was and why hit him like a ton of bricks as he gazed up at the ceiling, blinking rapidly to focus his vision. Attempting to sit up, a sharp pain throbbed through his head, causing him dizziness. Determined to push past the discomfort, he mustered all his strength to raise himself slightly before succumbing to the urge to close his eyes.

As he tried to relax after the surgery, thoughts of Ruby flooded his mind. Despite his overwhelming desire for sleep, Joey forced his eyes to stay open and survey the room. His face twisted with agony as he saw Ruby's fragile figure lying motionless in the adjacent bed. Anxious for her awakening, he called out her name in hopes of rousing her from her unconscious state.

"Ruby, sweetie, can you hear me?" His voice echoed into the silence of the room, but he received no response from Ruby. Desperation crept into his tone as he repeated her name with increasing urgency. A chilling fear gripped his heart as he contemplated the worst. In a sudden surge of panic, Joey tested his own physical abilities by wiggling his toes and legs beneath the blankets covering him. With great effort, he removed the cannula from his arm and struggled to swing his legs over the edge of the bed. Weakness and unsteadiness plagued him as he managed to stand upright, swaying precariously.

Seeking stability, Joey leaned heavily on a nearby brown recliner chair positioned between their beds for support. Slowly making his way towards Ruby's bedside, he clutched the edge of her mattress and leaned in close to check if she was breathing. Taking hold of her hand gently, he squeezed it while monitoring her vital signs on the heart monitor beside her.

When Ruby stirred and opened her eyes ever so slightly before drifting back into unconsciousness once more, Joey let out a loud sigh of relief. Exhaustion was crippling Joey, so he settled into a chair next to her bedside table, tenderly placing a kiss on her hand before surrendering to fatigue.

Despite his best efforts to remain awake and keep an eye on Ruby's condition, sleep finally claimed him as he rested with his head drooping over the edge of the bed in silent vigilance over his daughter's well-being.

Ruby awoke later that day to the dazzling sight of the sun's rays flooding her room, temporarily blinding her with its intense glare.

She cautiously shut her eyes before slowly reopening them to assess her surroundings. Squinting at the ceiling, she then scanned the room and noticed her father's head resting on the edge of the bed. Sitting up gradually, she peered down at her slumped father and gently shook his shoulder, "Daddy, wake up!"

When he didn't respond, she tried again. "Daddy, it's me, Ruby. Please wake up."

After a few tries, Joey stirred and opened his eyes, greeted by Ruby's bright smile. His heart swelled with joy as he pushed himself up and focused on her pretty face radiating happiness. Witnessing his daughter's renewed vitality brought him an overwhelming sense of contentment. Returning her smile, he took her hand in his and asked how she was feeling.

"I'm tired, Daddy," Ruby replied.

"I know, sweetheart. The medication will wear off soon." He wrapped his arms around her small shoulders.

With nothing else to do but enjoy each other's company, they engaged in a playful game of I-Spy, sharing laughter and teasing each other. They invented silly games, made funny faces, and discussed their lunch plans together. "Ruby, would you like to try eating bugs with me?" he asked.

"Eating bugs? Daddy, that's so gross," she replied, laughing even more. He jokingly tickled her and continued to make her laugh with his silliness, their voices filling the room.

As Joey held his precious daughter close, he felt blessed and proud to be her father. Her sweet innocence had captured his heart completely; he adored her beyond measure. In that moment, he realised the profound impact Abby had made on his life by giving him such a precious gift.

Joey's slightly off-key singing made Ruby laugh, "You're so silly, Daddy."

"Am I?"

"Yeah, but you are awesome."

Her compliment brought tears to Joey's eyes. "I love you, Ruby," he said, feeling grateful for this special alone time he had with his daughter. They talked about activities she wanted to do, favourite foods, and places she dreamed of visiting.

A strong desire welled up within Joey to actively participate in Ruby's education—helping with homework tasks, taking trips to the library together, reading her stories, and assisting with school drop-offs and pickups whenever needed. This newfound commitment filled him with a deep sense of purpose and fulfillment as he envisioned playing an integral role in his daughter's growth and development.

* * *

Abby's heart was overwhelmed with a myriad of emotions as she stood in front of the transparent barrier, peering through it to witness the unparalleled connection shared between her beloved husband and cherished daughter. Basking in the love and support emanating from Joey, Ruby's eyes sparkled with joy as she gazed at him with reverence, seeing him as the beacon of light that brought purpose and significance to her existence.

As Abby observed the profound impact Ruby had on Joey, moving him to tears, which he discreetly batted away, she knew this moment held something truly extraordinary. She clutched tightly onto the small golden cross hanging from her necklace, bringing it up to her lips as she whispered a heartfelt expression of gratitude to the Lord for blessing her with the reunion of her precious family.

"Abby," Dr. Denver called out.

Abby turned to face Dr. Denver and Dr. Kitchener. She expressed gratitude once more to Dr. Kitchener for her efforts and thanked Dr. Denver for his support.

"You're welcome," said Dr. Kitchener. "Ruby's test results were great; her kidney is functioning properly with a creatinine level of 0.6, as it should." She smiled and winked. "I guess that means I have done my job properly! She will need to take anti-rejection medication for the rest of her life, all provided upon discharge along with a prescription for refills."

Hearing this news brought tears to Abby's eyes. "I understand, thank you again."

"My pleasure," she replied. "Now, let's go and see the dynamic duo, shall we?"

Abby entered the room with Dr. Denver and Dr. Kitchener.

"Mummy!" Ruby shrieked.

Abby hurried over to her daughter, embracing her tightly.

Ruby attempted to lift herself up to fully embrace her mother.

Joey returned to his hospital bed and sat on the edge.

"How are you feeling, Joey?" asked Dr. Kitchener.

"Not bad, a little tired and my muscles hurt."

"It's normal to feel exhausted after surgery. You need to make sure you get plenty of bed rest. Nurse Gretchen will attach the cannula again to administer fluids to help you relax."

Joey nodded.

"Are you feeling drowsy?" she asked.

"Yeah, I was earlier, but it's passed now."

"Do you have any chest pain?"

"No, I don't."

"Okay, very good. Your blood test and observations are good, but I would like to keep you here for a few days."

"Yeah, that's fine," Joey responded.

"One more thing. No lifting anything heavy for about six weeks, okay? And if you have any questions, please let Dr. Denver know."

Joey thanked her with a smile, assuring her he would follow her instructions.

Abby focused on Joey while she attentively listened. His green eyes, surrounded by dark circles on his pale face, still captivated her when he gave a victorious smile.

Abby silently mouthed the words *thank you*, causing her smile to widen when he nodded.

Then Dr. Kitchener approached Ruby's bed and greeted her warmly. "Hello, missy."

Ruby shyly responded with a "Hello."

Dr. Kitchener observed the stuffed teddy bear that Ruby held close to her chest and asked who it was.

"His name is Costa."

"Hello, Costa."

Ruby smiled.

"Ruby, would it be okay if I check Costa's breathing with this long thingy here?" she asked, gesturing to her stethoscope. "This helps me to hear the sound of Costa's heart beating."

Ruby glanced up at her mother, and Abby smiled ruefully. "Costa is a toy, silly, not a real person."

When the laughter subsided, Dr. Kitchener slapped her forehead. "Oh, silly me."

Ruby smiled brightly when the doctor pretended to think, scratching her head. "I thought Costa was my patient."

Abby smiled and saw that Joey also had a smile.

"No, I am your patient," said Ruby.

"I didn't know, I'm sorry, Miss Ruby," Dr. Kitchener said in a goofy voice.

Ruby giggled again. She agreed when Dr. Kitchener asked if she could check Ruby's breathing, rewarding her with a red lollipop from her pocket when she had finished.

Ruby's eyes sparkled with excitement.

"You can have the lollipop after lunch," Dr. Kitchener told her.

After the doctors and nurse left the room, Abby's eyes fell upon Joey as he began to move across the room. Startled by his actions, she quickly called out to him, "Where do you think you are going? Get back into bed this instant!"

Joey paused in his tracks, turning back towards Abby with a mischievous grin on his face. "Okay," he said nonchalantly, slipping beneath the sheets. "But only if you come and lay next to me."

Abby hesitated for a moment, glancing over at Ruby, who was engrossed in watching the Disney Channel on the television. "Not right now."

"I missed you," Joey said.

Abby felt her heart swell with emotion. "I missed you, too."

Suddenly, Joey pulled her closer to him, leaning in for a kiss. Alarmed by his actions, Abby held up her hand as a barrier between their lips. "Joey, stop! You need to get some rest and go to sleep."

Reluctantly, Joey obeyed her instructions and covered himself with the blankets while Abby tucked him in. Just then, her phone began to vibrate on the bedside table near Ruby's bed. Glancing at the caller ID, which displayed Dr. Denver's name, Abby's anxiety spiked as she answered the call.

"Hi, Matty," she said tentatively.

The urgency in his voice sent shivers down her spine. "Abby, we need to talk. Where are you?"

"I am standing outside Ruby's room in the corridor," she replied. Sensing something was wrong, her face turned pale as her mind thought the worst.

Dr. Denver quickly arrived and stood before Abby, exuding both warmth and urgency. "I need you to stay calm, alright? Can you promise me that?"

Abby's heart pounded. "What's happening, Matty? You're frightening me."

After a pause, he said, "We've got the results from Ruby's blood test." He hesitated again, amplifying the seriousness of the situation. "Ruby... she's not your biological daughter!"

Abby's world tilted. "What do you mean?" she asked, her voice quivering with disbelief. The news seemed surreal, a puzzle that refused to be solved. "You must be mistaken, surely?"

Her words lingered in the air as Abby struggled to comprehend him, her mind racing to dismiss what seemed an impossible claim. "This must be a mistake!"

Dr. Denver's expression was filled with empathy. "I assure you, it's no mistake. There's no DNA connection between you and Ruby."

Abby's stomach churned as waves of anxiety crashed through her. Denial set in swiftly. "This can't be true! I gave birth to her. No, Matt, labs make mistakes, samples get mixed up. This sort of error happens all the time. Run the tests again, she's my daughter!"

Tears cascaded down her cheeks.

"Abby, please, there was no error. We ran the tests three times, independently. Each one confirmed that you are not her biological mother." His voice was steady yet filled with empathy.

"Then there must be a malfunction in your equipment," she yelled, glancing desperately at Ruby through the observation window.

"Abby, our equipment is fine. I even had tests done separately at St. Vincent's Clinic, using a favour from a colleague of mine."

"Run the test again, Matt!" she pleaded.

"Abby, trust me; the results are accurate."

Overwhelmed and feeling dizzy with shock, she shut her eyes, focusing on her breath.

"Okay, tell me this. If Ruby isn't biologically my daughter, how on earth does her DNA align so perfectly with Joey's?"

"Well, Ruby's blood test results showed an incredible match with Joey, which means their blood types and tissue compatibility align seamlessly; it's like pieces of a puzzle fitting perfectly together. In the intricate world of organ transplants, these factors are everything. Almost like destiny was at play, Joey turned out to be the perfect donor for Ruby's kidney transplant. It's as if the universe conspired to give us this chance, a rare stroke of good fortune that could dramatically change Ruby's life for the better."

Abby was on the verge of collapsing when Dr. Denver swooped in to catch her, gently guiding her away from the room before settling her into a chair.

"Matt, Ruby is my flesh and blood. I bore her for nine months; there is no doubt in my mind she is mine. I would know if she were not."

"If I were to venture a guess, it appears plausible that Ruby may have been inadvertently switched at birth. Instances of infant swapping have been documented over the years. Due to advancements in security measures like name tags, such occurrences remain exceedingly rare. Yet, scandals involving child exchanges can still transpire, particularly when a sickly infant is exchanged for a healthy one."

Anxiety gripped Abby's chest as she felt the onset of a panic attack. "Are you suggesting someone intentionally swapped my baby because Ruby was ill?"

His sombre response affirmed her fears. "Yes, Abby, it is within the realm of possibility and probability. We must report this matter to the authorities without delay and launch an official investigation. It is imperative we reach out to the monastery where you resided during your pregnancy and scrutinise their medical records."

Overcome by despair, Abby collapsed to her knees in uncontrollable sobs, struggling to breathe and clutching her throat.

Abby grappled with the prospect of disclosing this truth to Ruby and Joey—a disclosure that could shatter their world and jeopardise her marriage. Torn between revealing the secret buried deep inside her or shielding them from further pain, Abby found herself paralysed by indecision. Would Joey blame her parents for sending her away during pregnancy? Would he hold himself accountable for overlooking any signs of deception?

Dr. Denver wrapped his arms around Abby, holding her tightly as her body trembled with the weight of her grief. Her sobs were raw, each cry echoing the deep pain within her. He could feel the desperation in her shaking form. The weight of the secret pressed heavily upon her, a silent tension that seemed to make breathing harder. "Ruby and Joey can never find out about this," she confessed, voice trembling with the gravity of her words. Her heart ached at the thought, terrified of the chasm it could create between them. "I... I can't bear the thought of losing them."

Emotion flickered across her features, a mix of desperation and love. "I don't want anyone to treat Ruby differently. She's everything to me, and she deserves to feel that love unconditionally."

Then, a shadow of yearning crossed her face, deeper than fear or love. "But I need to know about my biological daughter," she murmured, her soul drenched in a longing that words could barely capture. "Is she safe? Is she even alive?" her voice lingered in the air, a haunting echo of uncertainty and hope, revealing depths of vulnerability few ever saw.

"I understand. Can you recall any details from your pregnancy?"

"During my pregnancy, there are pieces I struggle to hold onto. The head nurse mentioned my daughter's weight at birth—3 pounds, she said. But later, when we measured her ourselves at home, it was a mere 2.5 pounds. At that moment, I brushed it off as just another mistake. But looking back now, an unease stirs within me because very nurse took Ruby away for a bath. Now... now I question everything."

"Breathe Abby, breathe," said Dr. Denver.

Determination was etched across Abby's face as she clung to his coat. "Help me find my daughter; I need to find out what happened to my baby and who took her."

"I promise to help you find your lost child."

Dr. Denver assisted Abby to her feet. "Follow me, I have a plan, but it's important you refrain from crying. Can you manage that for me?"

Abby nodded and wiped away her tears.

"Come, the others will awaken soon, and our time is limited."

They rushed to his office. Abby was seated in a chair directly across from Dr. Denver, who sat behind his large, oak desk. With a sense of purpose and determination, he reached for the phone and proceeded to make several important calls. The first on his list was to an individual whom he referred to as an old friend from their university days, a former detective turned skilled investigator by the name of Jack Morrison.

Following this call, Dr. Denver then dialled the Convento de Santa María en Aracoeli in Italy.

As Abby observed with keen interest, Dr. Denver retrieved his trusty notepad and began jotting down various names that seemed to hold importance. Intrigued by this sudden development, Abby found herself leaning forward in her seat, drawn towards the desk as she attempted to catch a glimpse of the written words. Amongst the names listed were Father Michiel's, Sister Mary Rosetta Mancini, and Dr. Lucio, all of whom struck a chord of familiarity within Abby's mind, sending shivers down her spine at the implications they carried.

The realisation that Sister Mary Rosetta Mancini may have been involved in some capacity left a bitter taste in Abby's mouth, causing her stomach to churn with unease.

Dr. Denver concluded his final call and quickly jotted down some additional notes on the same sheet of paper before fixing Abby with a concerned gaze. "Are you alright?" he asked.

Abby remained silent, unsure of how to process the flood of emotions coursing through her at that moment. "What happens next?"

"We have to wait for Jack to call," he replied.

"How skilled a detective is he?" she asked.

Dr. Denver raised an eyebrow. "He is incredibly intelligent, and I'm not just saying that because he is my friend. He has an impressive track record with numerous arrests and solved cases. Put it this way, he makes Sherlock Holmes look like an amateur."

As time dragged on relentlessly, Abby's anxiety intensified while waiting for Jack's anticipated call. She strode back and forth across the room, every step imbued with a restless tension that gripped her being. Her heart pounded in her chest like a wild drum, each beat echoing the storm of emotion wreaking havoc within her. Her eyes darted around, searching for solace or an answer in the silent and indifferent surroundings.

An eternity seemed to pass before the moment arrived, stretching each second into a taut thread of anticipation. Finally, when the long-awaited echo reverberated through the dimly lit room, Abby's heart surged with a mix of hope and desperation. The sound was more than just a signal—it was the potential key to unlocking the mysteries that haunted their case. Her breath hitched, and her pulse thrummed fiercely beneath her skin, a testament to the gravity of the moment.

Observing intently as Dr. Denver engaged in conversation with Jack over the phone, Abby hung onto every word exchanged between them.

Dr. Denver diligently transcribed an address provided by Jack onto his notepad before turning towards her with a solemn expression.

"What's going on?" Abby pressed urgently when he thanked Jack and ended their call, her heart pounding erratically at the prospect of uncovering pivotal details surrounding their mysterious case.

"I'm finding it difficult to find the right way to break this to you," he said, his voice heavy with emotion, shaking his head slowly as if each word carried a tremendous weight. "There was another young girl, around the same age as you, living at the monastery during the same period you were there. Her labour was induced, leading to complications during surgery. Tragically, she passed away shortly after giving birth. The child, a delicate little girl weighing only 3 pounds, came into this world with fair hair, green eyes, and pale skin. Sadly, she was also born with a medical condition that had been identified early in her mother's pregnancy."

Abby sat perched anxiously on the edge of her seat, as though she were trying to balance on the thin line between disbelief and a harsh new reality. Her fingers clutched the armrests with a grip that seemed unbreakable, as if letting go might lead to an unwelcome plunge into uncertainty. Her entire frame quivered visibly, and her eyes, swollen from a sea of tears that had poured relentlessly, painted a picture of profound distress and emotional turmoil.

"Sister Mary Rosetta Mancini." Each word seemed to weigh the air around them, pressing down with the gravity of the sad reality. "The information we have reveals a truth both shocking and painful. The children were switched at birth." His voice, though soft, carried the weight of a thousand unspoken emotions. A silence followed, filled with the tension of a looming storm, as his eyes conveyed the depths of their predicament. "She left the monastery five years ago," he continued, as though unravelling a tale from a sinister fable, "to seek a life of normalcy. During these years, she's been raising your daughter as her own, at this address." He extended his hand, the piece of paper trembling ever so slightly, holding not just an address but the very heart of their tangled destinies.

"It is crucial that we inform the authorities immediately and let them handle the situation," he said, his tone underscoring the urgency and necessity of action.

The realisation hit Abby like a thunderbolt, an unrelenting force tearing through her heart. The woman she had trusted implicitly—a figure of warmth and wisdom akin to a grandmother, a mother, a beloved sister, and a loyal friend—had committed the ultimate betrayal. This woman, who had woven herself seamlessly into the fabric of Abby's life, had taken her precious daughter away, leaving behind a hollow void that threatened to consume Abby with its darkness.

Yet, amid the sea of grief and disbelief emerged a flicker of unyielding determination within Abby. It was a raw, fierce urge that propelled her forward through the seemingly insurmountable darkness. She refused to be paralysed by despair; instead, she chose to channel her pain into a resolute drive to reclaim what was rightfully hers: her precious daughter. As tears threatened to blur her vision, Abby brushed them aside with a newfound clarity of purpose. She steeled herself for the daunting journey ahead, vowing to confront every obstacle and challenge with relentless tenacity. Her heart, though battered and bruised, thumped with a solid rhythm of resolve, promising victory against all odds.

Abby swore to unravel every lie and face every deception to restore the one bond that was sacred and irreplaceable. She envisioned the reunion, her daughter safe and enveloped in the unwavering warmth of maternal love, and this vision fuelled her undeterred spirit. She knew the path would be fraught with trials, yet she was undaunted, driven by a mother's unbreakable strength and resolve.

In this harrowing saga of betrayal and determination, Abby emerged as more than just a mother seeking her child. She became the living proof that love, in its purest form, knows no boundaries. Standing on the edge of despair, she was prepared to conquer any obstacle in her quest to reclaim her daughter. The path before her was shrouded in uncertainty, fraught with danger, but one certainty remained: Abby's unwavering determination would light her way through the darkness. Her sole mission was to return to where they both truly belonged, enveloped in the infinite warmth and protection of a mother's eternal love.

THE END

Bermingham BOOKS — Where Best Sellers are Made